2021 Inlandia Creative Writing Workshop Leaders

Alaina Bixon

Wil Clarke

Carlos Cortés

James Ducat

Andrea Fingerson

Renee Gurley

Stephanie Barbé Hammer

Tim Hatch

Allyson Jeffredo

Mae Wagner Marinello

Richard Allen May III

Rose Y. Monge

Jo Scott-Coe

Lydia Theon Ware i

Frances J. Vásquez

Victoria Waddle

Romaine Washington

This event is supported in part by an award from the National Endowment for the Arts. To find out more about how National Endowment for the Arts grants impact individuals and communities, visit www.arts.gov.

Matching funds generously provided by Dr. Paulette Brown-Hinds through her directorship with the James Irvine Foundation and Inland Empire Community Foundation's Mapping Black California Fund.

This activity is also supported in part by the California Arts Council, a state agency. Learn more at www.arts.ca.gov.

In Memory of
Roberto "Tex" Murillo

BY FRANCES J. VÁSQUEZ

Esteemed community leader and Inlandia supporter, Roberto "Tex" Murillo passed away on May 29, 2022 in Riverside. Roberto distinguished himself for his commitment and advocacy for social justice and educational equity, particularly on behalf of his beloved Casa Blanca Barrio. He served on the Casa Blanca Community Action Group (CAG) and was a founding member of CAG's Education Advisory Committee. He participated in Tesoros de Cuentos Creative Writing Workshop at the Salvador J. Lara Casa Blanca Library.

As a cultural warrior for social justice, he was motivated by the injustices committed against Chicanos. He channeled much of his anger in his writings and by community activism and getting into good trouble. Many referred to him as Casa Blanca's historian who documented the storied history of Casa Blanca and its residents.

He was a regular in the Local History section of the Riverside Main Library where he conducted research. The trajectory of his work changed the day a librarian gave him a copy of a July 12, 1911 local newspaper report on the school board proceedings held the evening before when two unnamed women from Casa Blanca presented a petition to request a school be built in their neighborhood. It became his quest to identify the two women activists from Casa Blanca.

Roberto's research findings inspired him to write, "Casa Blanca en Huelga" to encourage unity in the community and motivate residents to vote. The true story of triumph and hope describes how voters got rid of an ineffectual City Councilmember in 1946. His mantra: by working together in unity, the community can tip the balance of power. The story was published in the 2018 Writings From Inlandia. He subsequently self-published "Huelga" and included pictures and illustrations. He wrote poetry, primarily in Spanish — his language of the heart. Two poems, "En la Sombra del Aguila" and "Pastor" were published in the 2020 Writings From Inlandia.

Rest in power and peace, Roberto Murillo — tesoro de Casa Blanca.

Contents

Janet Lako Alexander

Charlie Elish / Drill Ye Tarriers 15

Riverside Transit: Route 14 18

Juniper Berries from Mom 21

Don Bennett

Change of Heart 22

Chasing Sleep 25

Mary Briggs

Taco, my darling six lb chihuahua 28

My Microwave Memoir 29

Tortillas for Lunch 30

Think Before You Leap 31

Georgette Geppert Buckley

Destination 34

Craig's Folly 35

Respite 36

#5 37

Rosé Croquet 38

Alben J. Chamberlain

A Thousand No's to Reach a Yes 40

The Gifts of Big Trees 43

Post-Pandemic America 47

Natalie Champion

Remember Me 50

Rick Champion

Flying High 51

José Chávez

Summer Girl 54

Just Quiet 56

Aliens Have Landed in Moreno Valley 59

Deenaz Coachbuilder

from the ashes 61

The Last Farewell 63

Partners of the land 66

empty spaces of our heart 68

Letters my mother wrote me 69

Sylvia Clarke

How I See It Now...71

Treasured Object/Special Date 73

Epitaph 76

Wil Clarke

Africa and God 77

Budget Inn Hobbs NM 80

Encounter in North Las Vegas 82

James Coats

After the Story Has Come to an End................................84

Our Seeds 85

Smile of Life 86

Elinor Cohen

A Very Short Story About Drinking Coffee.....................87

Carlos Cruz

The Story of Mary Hernandez: As It Was Told To Me ...90

Brian DeCoud

My Barbecue Journey..95

Chuck Doolittle

"If Only I Could Remember...If Only I Could Forget..."...............100

My Happiest Moment...102

A Memory I Don't Want Dying With Me 105

Jerry Ellingson

Getting Started 107

Ellen Estilai

Miss Dickinson Regrets..111

(De)Composition..112

Bryan Franco

Why I Keep A Midwife on Speed Dial 113

because you have nothing to be jealous about 115

Forgiven 116

The Least Sweet Fruit on Planet Earth...........................118

Nan Friedley

File Box..119

Tidy Pantoum 120

Between Salon Visits in a Pandemic 121

AARP Member Since 2012...122

catastrophe 123

Camille Gaon

Gonna be Baking Brownies for the Beatles 124

Richard Gonzalez

Uncle Juan Invents a Burrito 129

Mark Grinyer

Refreshing the Light 132

Lies 133

The First Winter Storm 135

My Mother's Wake 136

My Grandpa's Hatchet 138

Milan Hamilton

Change of Heart 140

A Chair at the Table 141

Intimacy 142

Babies and Bathwater 143

Mercy 144

God Save the Queen 145

St. Valentine was No Romantic 147

Nikki Harlin

The Dead and Restless 148

Doralba "Dora" Harmon

El abuso del hombre hacia la mujer 149

Edna Heled

Astraphobia 155

Forked Lightning 156

The Little Old Man 157

Richard Hess

The Terrible Winter of '75 158

Saving The Galaxy – Again! 160

Adversity is Good for You! 162

Connie Jameson

A Barnyard Transformation: Celena's Magic 164

Marlene Jones

Fourth of July 2021 166

Surreal 168

Retirement 170

Jessica Lea

Wabi-Sabi Writing Desk 172

Stealth Gardening...173

Fantasy Careers 174

Ghost Rider 175

Merrill Lyew

Excavation..176

Jacqueline Mantz

Nano and the Shiny Coins..177

Joan Didion Died...178

Bites of Life 179

Save Me 181

Suspended in Wing 182

Bring the Breath 183

Mae Wagner Marinello

I Wanted To Write About..184

Ruthie Marlenée

Children of the Chaos of Change...................................190

Terry Lee Marzell

A Sewing Machine 194

My Introduction to French Cuisine................................198

KaShawna McKay

Calling Out 201

Mary McLoughlin

Dyslexia 203

The Ceili 204

Carmen Melendez-Gutierrez

My Life in 6 Pages...205

Barbara Meyer

Barbara Meyer 211

A Pot in Our Bathroom..212

Marvin Meyer

My Trip of Childhood & Youth Nostalgia.......................213

Perseverance..216

My Very Happy Memory with Daughter Janetta 218

Rose Y. Monge
Nopales: La Planta de Vida 220
Summer 1986 in Mexico City. 224

Barbara Mortensen
Job Hunting with Chopsticks 227
What's for Dinner 229

Cindi Neisinger
La Reina De Beaumont 231

S. J. Perry
Dear Ground Squirrel 235
I dwell in a House—taken over 236

Christine Petzar
Dad's Greatest Hits: A Father's Legacy 237

Janine Pourroy
Work 239

Cindi Pringle
Sturdy Legs 240

Edgar Rider
Pesticide Facials 243

Robin Woodruff-Longfield
Nobody 245
Hillsides (after H.D.) 246
Another Yellow Brick Road 248
What Remains 251

Marilyn Sequoia
Dance, My Life 252
Make-Up 257

Kristine Ann Shell
This Little Piggy 259

Ben Simmons
Oracle on Madison 261
It's An Easy Life 262

Lynne Stewart
Albatross 267
Another Blank Sheet of Paper to Author 269
Discovering Boys 271

Scharlett Stowers Vai

Edward Kay Villegas Stowers: 274

Heather Takenaga

Correspondence 279

To Whom It May Concern: In The Event of A Death.........280

Mirrors..282

Pandemic Blinks 284

Elizabeth Uter

The Amazon 286

All Ruined 288

In Ruins 2 291

When Darkness Rushes...293

Gudelia Vaden

Bird Watching...295

My First Inlandia Workshop 296

Frances J. Vásquez

Tesoros de Cuentos...298

Sister Celine Vásquez: Stellar Guiding Spirit Full of Grace 302

Irma Gabriella Vazquez-Garfield

Diplomas on the Wall: A Story of Perseverance 310

José Luis Vizcarra

Experience and Passion...312

Financial Education 314

La Chancla (The Sandal) 315

Oh Lord Why Did You Make Me Poor?............................316

The Difference Between a Transaction and a Transformation..........318

Contributor Bios...320

About Inlandia Institute 332

Inlandia Books 333

Hillary Gravendyk Prize poetry series 334

Charlie Elish / Drill Ye Tarriers

BY JANET LAKO ALEXANDER

My mother likes to tell a story: my sister was playing with the neighborhood kids in Blythe. One said, "I'm Mexican, and I'm proud." Another said, "I'm Armenian, and I'm proud." Judy ran home to ask her mother what she was, so she could be proud too.

"You're *American*," said Mom.

I used to think this was the saddest story I'd ever heard.

> *Drill, ye tarriers drill.*
> *And drill ye tarriers, drill!*
> *Oh, it's work all day for the sugar in your tay*
> *Down beyond the railway.*
> *So, drill, ye tarriers, drill.*
> (Spoken) *And blast! And fire!*

I never knew Charlie Elish, my dad's father. But my mother, who should know, tells me he was Irish, really Irish, not from a book like I am.

> *Every morning at seven o'clock*
> *There's twenty tarriers a-working at the rock.*
> *And the boss comes along, and he says, "Keep still!*
> *And come down heavy on the cast iron drill."*

So many things I never knew: how did this dapper little gent come to live among the flat lands and twanging voices of East Texas, an Irishman in Big Sandy? How was it that this ladies' man with a flower in his lapel came to marry my grandmother from Georgia?

Why does my father never speak of him?

So, drill, ye tarriers, drill . . .

Sure, he liked a drop or two. He enlisted Cousin Shorty to warm the barstools with him, Shorty with his bride at home looking at the clock and fuming. Sure, he rolled one dime after another into the jukebox, and slow danced with women in ruffled blouses to Hank Williams' lonesome wail. A charming smile, a touch of his fingers to her palm . . . He would deftly pluck a phrase from the air and offer it to her like a yellow rose. Did the sparkle of his eyes, pale blue stars, blind her to the dust and crickets down by the river where they lay?

> *Now our foreman is Dan McCann,*
> *I'll tell you sure, he's a blame mean man.*
> *Last week a premature blast went off*
> *And a mile in the air went Big Jim Goff.*

It is tempting, Charlie, to draw your portrait as an artist. You conjured words, urged them through hoops, carved your children up with them. But you were no James Joyce, no ethereal man of letters. You sweated in the railroad yards of California and died there before I was born. The questions that wear your face haunt me. What job was so important that it couldn't wait another day for the blaster? What possesses an untrained man to try his hand at explosives? Why didn't your boss stop you? You blew yourself to smithereens, a fine Irish word.

> *Next time payday comes around*
> *Jim Goff was short one buck, he found.*
> *When he asked why, came this reply:*
> *"You're docked for the time you were up in the sky."*

I gather the pieces and fit them into a picture, a culture, an identity. Some of them are missing, so I fill in with the Spanish I learned at school and from friends, with the corridos and hip-hop

I hear on the radio, with the books by Angelou and Kawabata and yes, James Joyce. Sometimes I look into the brown eyes of a friend, and forget that unlike her, I do not have the lovely dark skin of a Native American. And sometimes I dream new endings to your story, endings where you, like Jim Goff, fall harmlessly from the sky. Where you, like a prodigal Tim Finnegan, awake.

And blast! And fire!

Riverside Transit: Route 14

BY JANET LAKO ALEXANDER

Tuesday morning, 7:13.
I run the last block past the Fox Theatre
To the waiting bus.
The door sighs closed and shuts out Weasel,
Still arguing with himself.

Darnell, the driver, looks
Like Little Richard in uniform.
His sly smile reminds me my hair
Is wet, my makeup slapped on.

I sit halfway back
Behind a Chicana wearing
A jungle print. Her boyfriend's
Shirt says "Pit Bulls Only."
Across from me, a woman
Reads a book in Hebrew.
My dress is crisp
But my heels frayed with walking.

"My Cherie Amour,
Pretty little one that I adore…"
Darnell sings with slow jazz
Phrasing. On University we pass
Antique stores and pawn shops.

Orange Street: the bell rings.
A man in a suit steps down

At a bail bond office.
Outside the new jail
Is a blue-and-white sculpture
Of shapes forming parents and a child.

There's First American Title,
Snapped together from LEGO Bricks
And white plastic trim.
An old man climbs on the bus
With a cane; a grimy CAT hat
Shades his eyes.

Darnell is telling us how
Bus drivers get dates.
"When I see an attractive lady
Putting her lipstick on,
I jam on the brakes. Then I
Stop the bus, apologize,
And help wipe her face."

Olivewood Street: Frame houses
With blind, boarded windows.
Jacarandas. The arroyo green
With pines and palms.
Pit Bulls Only is telling his girl,
"If a dude hits my car,
I have to kill him. If a chick
Hits my car, it's all right."

The windows rattle

As we pick up speed, curving
Past Pachappa Hill.
"But when we get behind
Closed doors, and she lets her hair
Hang down—Ah ha ha!"
Darnell's laughter sounds like barking.

Empty parking lots at the Plaza Mall.
I ring the bell and sway, pole by pole
To the front door.
"Goodbye, young lady."

I thank Darnell, and hop
Down the three steps.
The Blanket Lady, vast and regal,
Climbs aboard. All day she will travel
The bus lines, swathed in her smelly blanket.

Tomorrow we will re-create this world.
But for now, I cross Central Avenue
To my cubicle and files.

Juniper Berries from Mom

BY JANET LAKO ALEXANDER

This juniper berry necklace –
193 wizened, reddish-brown didzé
mingled with minute sky blue beads –
has strands that separate like rivulets
and rejoin, falling in four tassels.

That hot afternoon in the Navajo Nation
a Diné artisan sold you the necklace.
You asked permission
to photograph her,
sitting under an umbrella
  in her blue velvet blouse.

You always loved taking us traveling with you.

Now I wear your necklace as a talisman
as if to put on your artistry and stubbornness.
I glide my fingers over the
smooth,
 hard berries,
  as self-evident as a river rock,
 as fluent as the water that shapes it.

Change of Heart

by Don Bennett

My heart problems began in the mid-1980s, and by 1988 I'd had a heart attack and triple bypass surgery. By September of 2011, I had been diagnosed with congestive heart failure and was told that there wasn't anything more medically that they could do. My cardiologist in Northern California was going to pack up my records and send me to Stanford University Medical Center to see what they could do for me.

In November of that year, we came down to Loma Linda to be with family for Thanksgiving. While we were here, my pacemaker, which also had a defibrillator, threw me into a wall. After a visit to the Emergency Department at LLUMC, I was admitted to the hospital.

A month later, while we were visiting again after Christmas, the same thing happened and I was admitted to the hospital again. But this time, we didn't go back home afterwards. This was the beginning of several more months of numerous hospitalizations. It became clear that I was too sick to be able to travel back home, and our kids urged us to consider relocating here.

We began a search for a cardiologist down here. Donna contacted a physician friend of hers and asked him if he could recommend a cardiologist. He did, and before we knew it, we received a phone call from the cardiologist. As it turned out, Donna's friend was in the middle of a cruise, but he nevertheless called his cardiologist friend. During their conversation, he learned that Donna's dad had been his mentor while he was doing his cardiology fellowship here at Loma Linda. Thus, the reason why the cardiologist called us.

My first visit to Dr. Gary's office was rather eventful. I hadn't been feeling very well that morning, but by the time I was in an examination room at the doctor's office it was almost lunch time and the office nurses had gone to lunch. When the doctor came in, he immediately saw that I wasn't doing well. He laid me on the exam table, started an IV himself, and then called an ambulance and told them to take me straight to Loma Linda Medical Center.

That was the beginning of his dogged pursuit of getting me on the heart transplant list at Loma Linda. It wasn't easy to convince them, because I would be the oldest diabetic to get a transplant if I actually got on the list. It turns out that the immunosuppressant drugs needed to prevent rejection often cause diabetes in transplant patients, and if patients are already diabetic, it complicates matters even more. I didn't find out until later that Dr. Gary didn't think I would survive more than two months without a heart transplant.

On the evening of June 21, we attended a performance of Wizard of Oz, which was the culminating event after a children's theater camp which our granddaughter had attended. After the performance, I was sitting in the car waiting to see our granddaughter before we went home. I recognized the heart surgeon as he walked past our car. His daughter had been one of the children in the play with Maddy. That night, we received a call from the heart transplant coordinator, saying that there might be a heart for me the next day. I had been on the transplant list for just 11 days. There were three others ahead of me on the list who had been eliminated for various reasons.

About ten o'clock in the morning on June 22, we got the call asking us to come to the hospital as soon as we could. By five o'clock that evening, the long surgery began, and Donna received updates every so often on her cell phone as the surgery progressed.

At my first visit to Dr. Gary's office after the transplant, he called the nurses over to see me in the exam room. He exclaimed, pointing to me, "Do you remember dead man walking?" I then added, "It's the greatest comeback since Lazarus!"

In the years since all of these events took place, I have often thought about Ezekiel 36:26, which says: "And I will give you a new heart, and I will put a new spirit in you. I will take out your stony, stubborn heart and give you a tender, responsive heart." It's been nine years, and I am ever grateful for my new heart, as well as what I'd like to think is a softer spirit.

Chasing Sleep

BY DON BENNETT

Night has fallen
It's getting on to dark
Test my bloods, take a shot
Start to wander towards
Going to bed
I don my armor
My big boy pants, scrubs,
Cotton socks and gloves
Sink beneath the covers
Sort of
Close my eyes
Begin to drift
Loud knocking at my consciousness
"You forgot to take your pills!"
Oops
Down the pills with a shot of water
Start all over again
Seems I'm on the road to nowhere
But moving right along
Change course
Start again
Getting tired and out of breath
Gotta keep moving and
Begin to focus on the mountain I see
Shrouded in fog in the distance
Lost track of time

Unsure

I remember the bigger rocks

I stumble a few times and

Have to stop

Lay down and wait a bit to

Catch my breath

Trudge on

Keep climbing

Ready to go again

Reach a plateau

I notice the fields below

I see Mom's legendary 32 fruit trees

Scattered beehives throughout

The mother holstein grazing in the pasture

A pair of calves

Running about

Udder chaos

Mama cow checks the salt lick

Casually walks towards the barn

Seeking a little solitude

My mother tells Tommy and me

Put on your honey masks

Go to the hives

Get some honey

Grumbling, off we went

At the first hive

Gently lifted the top

Angry, irritated bees

Bees inside our masks
Flying in circles
Tommy and I run
Dive headfirst into water trough
No honey collected
No thanks from Mom
The fog begins to lift
I see angelic faces
Underneath blurry lights
I hear voices
"If he can stand, he goes home
If he can't, we admit him"
I get to go home
A voice whispers to me
"You're out of the ER
What will you do now?"
My answer is what I always say
"I'm going to IHOP!"
At home I drop into bed
And dream of blissful sleep
Next morning I wake
Check the obits
See if I'm still alive
Fill my day
Nighttime comes
Start all over again

Taco, my darling six lb chihuahua

BY MARY BRIGGS

Taco, my darling six lb chihuahua, short light beige coat, big wide eyes, big long pointed ears. Long legs, for a pint sized little one, that is. He was 10-years-old according to the vet, when I adopted him. His foster mother, from whom I got him, my friend, who called herself the crazy cat lady, called him Curly. Probably because his tail curled like a piglet's tail.

My Microwave Memoir

by Mary Briggs

Oh, my precious microwave
If you were lost and gone forever
How would I function another day
Breakfast, lunch and supper
You are always there
You beacon me for breakfast
With hot oatmeal or cream of wheat
No freezing cold cereal for me
You lovingly provide me, on special days
Scrambled eggs, omelets to my taste
Side orders I desire
Potatoes, cornbeef hash, ham, whatever I wish
Without you, lunch would be a cold sandwich
Dinner, endless trips to McDonalds, Taco Bell, Del Taco
Carl's Jr, Jack in the Box, fast food forevermore
Or lonely, costly Bistro meals
Midnight cup of tea, warm nighttime snacks, morning hot coffee
What more could one desire
I have you on a pedestal. I bow to you daily
True! It's hard to read the menu numbers without bending over
But it's a curtsy, any way you see it
My precious microwave
Don't ever leave me. I love you.

Tortillas for Lunch

BY MARY BRIGGS

I had attended Kindergarten in Stockton, Ca., however, this was my first day in school in a strange new city and a scary new school in East Los Angeles. As we got ready for school, I watched my Mama begin to make mine and my sister's lunch. I cringed as I saw her unwrap the dish towel and take out the handmade flour tortillas. near tears, I whined, I want bread, not tortillas. There was no bread in our small shack home, only handmade flour tortillas, which was our daily bread. To pacify me, Mama said she would make the tortillas look like bread. She cut the round edges off, cut the tortillas to the size of bread slices, spread the mayonnaise, added the bologna, wrapped up the tortilla sandwiches in wax paper, and stuffed them in a brown paper sack.

That didn't fool me, I don't know about my sister, but I was still very upset about the tortilla sandwiches. Off we went to our first day of school, I pouting and unhappy, both of us scared. At the dreaded lunch time, I was too embarrassed about our Mexican lunch to sit with the other children. So I grabbed our lunch bag and my sister and lead us around the school yard, searching for a secluded place to hide with our lunch. We found a lonely spot, far from where I imagined the glaring eyes of others would be. There we ate our tortilla sandwiches by ourselves.

As soon as Mama learned about the free lunch program, she enrolled us in it. We no longer had to hide to eat our tortilla sandwiches. Attempting to analyze my feelings of embarrassment, I believe, I just wanted to be like the other children. I didn't want to be different. Today, I wish I had some of my Mama's handmade flour tortillas, right now.

Think Before You Leap

BY MARY BRIGGS

In my senior year in high school, the last semester, I signed up for Senior English. As I walked in, I saw many in the class are the top students, the ones who have scholarships to universities, the ones who are straight A students, who will be going to prestigious colleges. I'm petrified. I was already scared, thinking about when I would be required to read in class. In this last year, this final semester, I've come to realize that I'm not fluent in either English or Spanish. I speak Spanglish. When speaking English, if an English word escapes me, I throw in an appropriate Spanish word. In speaking Spanish and cannot find the right Spanish word, I use an English word. In the Hispanic community in East Los Angeles, I am a Pocha, American born of Mexican parents. There are many English words I cannot pronounce. I am in dread of having to read in English classes. I'm terrified, afraid I'll be humiliated, sneered, laughed at, or worse, thought stupid.

To add to my dread and fear of humiliation, the teacher assigns us an essay on our religious beliefs. The following day, mine is the only one she reads aloud in front of the class, praising it as the only essay of individual thought, criticizing the class for their consensus of group beliefs almost insinuating the class is a flock of sheep, stating only one person differed. I thought everyone believed in the Origin of Species, in evolution. It was taught in school, that's where I learned it. The silence was ominous. Now I was terrified. I felt like a Salem witch, in fear of a witch hunt. Thankfully, she did not name the writer.

But I lived in fear of exposure.

For three or four days, I sat in class, dreading assignments and class participation, observing the bright students and the lone Japanese genius in class. One morning, towards the end of the week, the Drama class teacher walked in, asked for volunteers to the Drama class. He had a shortage, needed students. I saw my salvation. Before I realized what I was doing, I raised my hand, and left the classroom with the Drama teacher. Rationalizing my decision, thinking I would learn something useful that I needed, how to better express myself, perhaps learn useful facial expressions, voice modulation, improve my posture, acting, all I imagined an acting class had to offer.

There was none of this, immediately the teacher informed us, the class was required to provide a short program, consisting of a short play for the student body in the school auditorium. Immediately, he picked the four or five students for the play. Then announced, the rest of the class had to come up with a short skit of our own design and perform it in class. That was our assignment and our grade. We were on our own. Bewildered, disappointed and lost, desperately, I searched my mind, my minute knowledge, my lack of experience. After exhausting all my possibilities, I could only come up with karaoke. I would dress up as best I could, with modesty, as a Rock Star, pretend to sing a hot Top Tune, as I'd seen on TV. I didn't even know what a Top Tune was, since I did not listen to any music. After school I only had time to help with dinner and with washing dishes, then finish the night with homework.

After listening to the music I picked and bought, my stepfather lent me one of his records. This is a better record, he told me. It was Rock and Roll, definitely more appropriate. On the appointed day I did my pitiful amateur performance. To my horror, at the end of all the class skits, the teacher announces he will add my skit to the end of the auditorium school play. What could I do? Nothing but accept my doom and comply.

On that dreadful day, I dress in my most modest, respectable, body hugging dress. Determined and brave as I can manage, I step up on stage and do my number. Mouthing into the mic, gripping it tightly, wiggling and stomping as modestly as I can manage and still look sexy. Trying desperately to keep a smile on my face between lyrics and even more desperately trying not to look at the sea of students. At the end, the students clapped, of course. I have always believed the audience was just being polite. I was heartfully grateful for their polite generosity.

In retrospect, at the end, instead of having to read in a class of 30 students, I ended up having to perform in an auditorium for the whole school, about 400 students. Did I learn my lesson, to think, consider before you leap. Of course not!

Destination

BY GEORGETTE GEPPERT BUCKLEY

Begin Slowly
From Riverside 91 W.

Greened Hills
Blurred blue blossoms
80+ m.p.h. fast track

Bottleneck to
605 N.
Rt. Lane (remain calm)

105 W. carpool lane
Triggers Childhood Memoir
Joyful sidewalk parade

66mi.,1 ½ hrs. El Segundo
Parental's reminiscent
Main street, IL

4 Generations distant together
2 Adorable grandkids
Cherishing new memories

Craig's Folly

BY GEORGETTE GEPPERT BUCKLEY

Gonzo's brouhaha
became cattywampus and donnybrook
escalated to sharp snickersnee
as a mugwump wabbit
canoodled his niece.

After all this malarky
the goombah absquatulated.
The indolent freely
passed Campari widdershins
gossiped then pandiculated.

Respite

BY GEORGETTE GEPPERT BUCKLEY

Crash into glass door
Tiny neon olive belly
white and black wing stripes

I croon to
quivering black beak
And darting beady eyes

Presenting water on doormat
I photograph its luminous
it shoots out of patio

A raven darts in
barely missing the window
turns and departs

Terrified
Tiny tanager
Are my efforts in vain?

#5

by Georgette Geppert Buckley

Chanel
Fabricates
Fame

Floral
Musk
Civet

Minimal
Linear
Decanter

Stopper
Mimics
Steeple

Black and white
Elegance or
Nun's habit

Potion
Tempts
Fate

Rosé Croquet

BY GEORGETTE GEPPERT BUCKLEY

Cinnamon fragrance of my husband's 'famous' oatmeal with raisins awoke me. I quickly put the kettle on. Sipping my intoxicating hot peppermint chai coconut latte, yet not packed, I felt unprepared for our trip west. Thank God we weren't due in El Segundo until three. I relaxed, glancing at my tulip tree painting and savored the last sip.

After donning a red and white floral dress completed with a red, white, and blue vest, I noticed the blue bird sky beckoning, and wound around the curved pathways of our senior apartments. Lingering to observe the dance of the yellow and black zebra butterfly around the lush magenta blossoms of the crepe myrtle, I found myself inhaling the sweet minty scent of the eucalyptus and woody scent of rosemary nearby.

Almond milk washed down my sticky sunflower seed and sliced ripe banana on gluten free multigrain and a tart dark chocolate quenched my appetite. I loaded the dishwasher and set it on hot prewash. I packed lightly as it was only an overnight trip. We loaded the Escape complete with nut and fruit snacks and water bottles.

My older sister and husband graciously hosted a BBQ at their red tiled roof home. It was nice to unwind and catch up while enjoying sweet apple sausage, long hotdogs, baked beans, potato and fresh fruit salads at their red and white gingham covered dining room table.

At my mom's French windowed home atop the hill, we took a nap. When the rest of the local clan arrived later there were hugs all around. We partnered up and played Rosé Croquet, a popular new tradition. We laughingly break all rules taking turns with our cohorts, interspersed with sipping a sweet and light rosé. Our matriarch's ball struck the last pole first and won!

Amidst patriotic decorations in the enclosed porch, we partook of my sister's traditional trifle with raspberries and blueberries. As my husband had picked apples from our balcony, we contributed an apple crumple adorned with Bing cherries and blueberries. The grands enjoyed the brownies they concocted.

Four generations sat in three rows of striped, cushioned folding chairs facing downhill wearing jackets and some warmed with throw blankets. The booming, popping, and crackling colorful fireworks seemed more spectacular maybe because of last year's hiatus.

Upstairs later that evening, my husband and I viewed El Segundo's water tower tricolored light show. After my shower, I slipped into bed happy with a loving sense of family closeness that we had missed. How lovely to hug each other this year! Fourth of July has been bittersweet the past six years as it was my parents' anniversary.

A Thousand No's to Reach a Yes

by Alben J. Chamberlain

My teacher always told us,
"It takes a thousand no's to get to yes."
Perhaps, that's why so many
talented artists put their dreams to rest.

After so many rejections, its easy for
an artist to give up and concede defeat.
It's worse if there's a family
that needs shelter and food to eat.

In America, we say we appreciate the arts,
yet it takes a thousand no's to reach a yes.
How many talented people we'll never
see or appreciate, I can only guess.

A thousand no's is often enough to bury talents.
We'll never know how much creativity it kills.
Countless impoverished artists are forced to
throw in the towel and find a job to pay the bills.

Laura went to Nashville after the folks
back home said her voice was heaven sent.
For a decade she sang at countless gigs
but barely covered her food and rent.

She wrote and sang a dozen songs,
but none of them the bills did pay.
Then, she wrote a single hit song

and her career was on its way.

Daniel wrote five novels over eight years,
yet made no professional or financial progress.
Then, a reviewer praised the sixth one he released
and soon folks said he was an overnight success.

This influential reviewer said this
novel was contemporary and bold.
To Daniel, though, it seemed no
different than the ones that never sold.

Everyone marveled at Jennie's paintings.
Fortune and fame were at hand, she was told.
Still, when she put them up for view in
the gallery, the majority were never sold.

Then, she started painting 'Modern Art'-
just random objects you use each day.
Rich folks with too much money began competing
with each other on how much they would pay.

Jerry was a theatrical fool who got
a starring role in every student play.
After college, he moved to the hills
of Hollywood, CA to work and stay.

He joined the Screen Actor's Guild
and found bit parts on many shows.
How he survives in that expensive city,
no living soul in his family knows.

Tina was a lead singer in a country band
that played at gigs all over the land.
They entertained countless people, but when the
show was over, she slept in the back of her van.

Fortunately she didn't give up and eventually
fame and record contracts were found.
Now, she travels in the band's spacious
tour bus as they sell out shows all around.

A thousand no's to reach a yes, a thousand
poems that will never see the light of day.
There's always a battle between writing
for fun and the desire to make it pay.

A thousand no's to reach a yes, the odds
might be better on a foreign battlefield.
Still, all the years of toil and rejection can
often, some unexpected masterpiece, yield.

Facing a thousand no's to reach a yes, a wise
writer would throw his hands up in the air.
This writer, though, is just too old and stupid
to heed the daunting odds or even care

The Gifts of Big Trees

A Natural Poem

BY ALBEN J. CHAMBERLAIN

Looking over an old-growth forest
my oldest son seemed to be perplexed.
Finally, he asked me a question that,
for many seasons, had him vexed.

"Dad," he asked, "What's the purpose of preserving
all these trees standing here so numerous and tall?
It seems to me that, if you've seen
one tall tree, you've seen them all."

"Isn't this forest expanse less important
than our ability to meet human needs?"
I could see right off where this reasoning
came from and exactly where it leads.

I replied, "Son, those trees aren't mere objects
taking up space in the forest down there.
They are daily removing methane, dust particles,
and excess carbon dioxide from our polluted air.

If humans want to keep breathing then,
about tall trees, they need to care.
Mature forests, by far, put the
most vital oxygen into our air.

They temper our climate and atmosphere
through their living cycles every day.

These are services that we humans
can never hope to replace or repay.

Mature trees are living pumps, efficiently
drawing out vital water from the earth.
Their leaves transpire water vapor creating
a beneficial cycle, thus proving their worth.

Their roots and root fibers are able to
penetrate and open up the hard soil.
The falling rain and living organisms can
move downward without trouble and toil.

Their branches and leaves slow down the rain
so it won't wash away the fertile ground.
Without all the mature forests, there wouldn't
be many productive ecosystems to be found.

Trees, bushes, and vines are the foundation of
the food chain, through which living energy flows.
Countless insects, birds, and other animals
consume leaves, flowers, and fruits as they grow.

Only the life-giving chlorophyll of green leaves
can create food from the energy of the sun.
Without this daily food production, every
food chain and ecosystem would be undone.

Mature forests provide a habitat for life
from microbes to the largest of mammals.
Birds, reptiles, amphibians, and insects are among

the countless species of benefiting animals.

Big trees build up soil fertility through all
the leaves, bark, and seeds that rain down.
Without mature forests, very few fertile
places on earth's surface could be found.

In any ecosystem, trees are the greatest
contributors to the landscapes' biodiversity.
Without the presence of tall trees most plant
and animal species would face a harsh reality.

Big trees lock away carbon in
their trunks, branches, and stems.
If all this carbon was released to the atmosphere
there would be no way to make amends.

Mature forests provide food and medicines
to countless forms of animals and to men.
So, you see, son, the decision to cut
them all would be more than a sin.

For centuries, forests have provided us with beauty
and places to contemplate, explore, or rest.
They're a place for inspiration to our kind
as countless artists and holy men can attest.

Who can fail to gain perspective or sense wonder
in the presence of mature forests of tall trees?
The human spirit would soon wither
without such natural marvels as these.

The greatest human need is for more forests
for our planets' ecosystems to thrive.
If we only focus on our immediate needs
for resources, our species won't survive.

So, you can see, son, that being down to
one tall tree would be more than a disgrace.
In such a world, we'd quickly see
the end of our human society and race."

Post-Pandemic America

My Hopes and Prayers

BY ALBEN J. CHAMBERLAIN

America the beautiful

America the ugly

  America the wonderful

  America the terrible

    America the wise

    America the foolish

When this global pandemic is finally over, which of these labels
will you choose?

I hope and pray that you will choose.....

A greater appreciation of and more unified
family over divorce and family dissolution.

More care for and cultivation of friends over our
culture of narcissism and self-aggrandizement.

A greater sense of charity and sharing over
our gospel of wealth and personal prosperity.

A greater respect for health and well-being over
our fast-food culture of excess food and drink.

A greater appreciation of hospitals and our medicines
over our continual fighting over how to pay for them.

A greater respect for teachers and classroom learning
over taking instructors and their wisdom for granted.

Taking time to develop our own talents and fun over
our obsession over televised sports and entertainment.

A greater appreciation for the ability to work over
our constant desire to work less and for greater pay.

A greater gratitude for coworkers and loyal friends over
our constant sniping and complaining on social media.

Gratitude for the great bounty of food we enjoy over
taking our food for granted and wasting so much of it.

A thankfulness for the gift of travel and association over
grumbling over crowded airports, aircraft, and small seats.

A greater appreciation for our technology and communications
over taking it for granted and using it for frivolous pursuits.

Greater respect for our dedicated healthcare workers over
complaining about how much they get paid and their benefits.

A greater desire to help and serve others in our community
over "They don't deserve it" or "That's not my problem."

A greater knowledge that as a nation "We're all in this together"
over apathy, careless disrespect for neighbors and self-service.

Gratitude for the simple grace to meet with old
and new friends to eat, talk, and to learn together.

over

Always finding excuses to stay home, and take
care of our own business before thinking of others.

A greater appreciation of church, meditation,
song, and prayer to soothe our souls.

over

Our constant fighting and division over political,
social, and economic issues of the moment.

A greater sense of our need to act as one world
and voice to solve our common problems,

over

our constant feuds and fights over our cultural,
economic, religious, or trade differences.

Remember Me

by Natalie Champion

Loving wife, mom, sister, auntie, and soon to be grandma to
  Kieran Zachary

Cat momma to Princess Tabitha and Milo Morris

Caring and inspirational teacher

Poet, dancer, walker

Voracious reader

Flying High

by Rick Champion

Youngest brother was anxious. I observed, "There's an olive orchard outside of town." As we started down the street, No Vacancy Lady caught up and beckoned us up the stairs. She kept saying "Nice young men." Our room had beds for us on one side, and two more buried under female stuff.

Little brother and I went in search of souvlaki and retsina. We returned to a dark room. When the door opened, a female voice announced, "Our roommates are here."

Little brother insisted, "I can't sleep in a room with women that I don't know."

I advised, "Calm down and go to sleep."

A second female voice emphasized, "Great idea. Everyone stop talking and go to sleep."

When morning came, I wanted to hang out together, but the women were on their way to the boat.

Gene and I took a table and waited for yogurt with fruit and honey, bread, and coffee. I explained that Odysseus had passed by this island on his way home from Troy.

"Ten years?" Gene asked, "What took him so long?

Homer had explained: Distractions, including lotus fruit, monsters, and women – a sorceress, a seductive nymph, mortal women, and female deities.

Our guides had arrived - Nordics with Viking flags sewn on their backpacks engaged in democratic discussion of which way to go. Following them would take us to the beach.

Gene was pleased that the beach was clothing optional. Mother-daughter drama was in progress. Daughter was decently covered, but mama was scolding. Did daughter have virgin eyes? My thought was, "Not anymore." Momma was determined to drag daughter off the beach. Daughter was resisting.

The ice cream boat pulled up to the shore. Captain Ice Cream had priced his wares just below market. Word spread quickly. Nordics swarmed the boat and picked it clean.

Gene wondered why the Greeks had a thing about being naked. I answered, "Not just the Greeks, but the Nordics. Their countries are dark and foggy much of the year. They flock to islands of blue sky to soak up sun while it shines. The Ancient Greeks found the human body beautiful, which goes a long way towards explaining why Aphrodite and Calypso so often went baby bare or chose clothing sure to malfunction. If I was ever reincarnated, I would be a sculptor specializing in erotic female deities – but only if I was buff enough to cut stone. Otherwise, I would follow Botticelli painting goddesses arising from the sea and teasing with pretended modesty."

Gene called out, "Up in the sky!" Against the blue, someone was hanggliding. King Minos of Crete had problems with a half-human, half-bull creature who required human sacrifice. Daedalus corralled the Minotaur in the Labyrinth. But Minos was not as pleased as he should have been. Daedalus and his son Icarus were imprisoned with no good to be foreseen. Daedalus was inventive. He fashioned two sets of wings with feathers stuck on with wax. Being buff, they would flap their wings to fly away from Crete to Santorini. Daedalus safely landed, but Icarus did not. He had ignored his father's warning to stay away from the sun. The wax melted. Icarus crashed into the sea.

Gene was skeptical. No matter how buff, humans can't flap strongly enough to rise into the sky. Wax and feathers are poor design. The NASA guys would recommend a better design so that Daedalus and Icarus would have a better chance. Gene had worked on the Space Shuttle. I respected his opinion.

I translated a business deal and then returned to my spot to daydream about Penelope. Would I finally make my way across the last few miles of open sea to be with her? Would she recognize me? Would she scold me for leaving her home to do double duty? What about the nymphs and goddesses? No point in lying. She would know.

Soon Gene was flying over the turquoise sea and hanging naked from the blue sky. A cable pulled him in a loop, letting him land in shallow water where he made his way to dry land. With great excitement, "There's nothing like the sun and wind. You should try."

"No thanks. If I want to take off my clothes, I can do that on land. It's time for us to be on our way to Ithaca."

Gene was skeptical. "Are there nude beaches in Ithaca? Cheap food? Places to stay?"

"Yes, to all," I answered.

Gene countered, "We have all that here, so why move?"

I understood how Odysseus felt when his men insisted on staying on the Island of the Lotus Eaters. But no problem. I'd try again next year. I studied Greek and planned a route. But then COVID hit. I'll try again when it is safe to do so.

Note: Gene was on target in suggesting that NASA had constructed a human powered craft, although powered by foot pedals rather than arms.

For history and techie details see: MIT Daedalus https://en.wikipedia.org/wiki/MIT_Daedalus

Summer Girl

by José Chávez

Next to a convenience store
that sells cheap gas for commuters,
I see her again at her shop.

Tie-dyed summer blouse,
a splash of crimson,
yellow, and sparkling orange.

Just after dawn,
there's a fragrance
of lilacs in the air.

Rustic freesias
swoon in clay pots
when she strolls by.

Daisies stare behind
dark eyes, carnations
beg, "Come to me."

From a crate of tulips,
she looks up
olive skin and green eyes.

Should I stop,
ask about calla lilies,
When do I plant red roses?

Maybe we'll talk weather—

heat and drought
that lasts too long.

An early fog
lingers while the sun
waits to break through.

I hesitate
and look toward
the busy freeway onramp.

On a clear morning
I'll meet her.
I'll whisper her name,

My Flower Girl.

Just Quiet

BY JOSÉ CHÁVEZ

I
Time sneaks up on you they say
You don't have enough time
Or too much time on your hands

It may catch you when you awaken
Overshadow your life gradually
Like a dark vaulted ceiling dripping sweat

Caught us off-guard a week before Christmas
Shopping's done flashing lights shimmer
On our artificial holiday tree

No time to pour morning cup yet
My brother called early with the news
Said Phillip was alone when it happened that night

And together they watched Batman
That sunny afternoon & Phillip felt good
He later worked out at the gym

Remembered by friends at the service
Fished together laughed at his stories
Drank imported French Vodka

A newly married couple spoke about
Friendship & how he helped them
Move into their new apartment

Everyone admired his sense of humor
Great under pressure they said
Girls remembered big dancing eyes

Privately family thought it could have been
Something he saw in the Gulf War
He also told some family he did things as a Marine

II
No more long commutes through snow
In the narrow canyon to work in the big city
No worries about the new house payment

Or if he could afford a plasma screen TV
Had enough to pay off his student loans
Or had saved enough for a Mexican vacation

Broken pieces left behind—3 children to raise
One from a previous marriage
Prepare them for college and new jobs
Ready them for responsibilities and babies of their own

We have a story about a car accident
that broke his leg when he was ten
At age three he said that his aunt's hair
Looked like broccoli
How do you forget that

Time changes everything they say
but time really changes nothing
We change but not always for the best

A large halo surrounded the full moon
Before the memorial service that evening
To help us forget that smoke and mirrors
Can hide nightmares and menacing voices

Dreams crashed against canyon walls
and quickly floated down the Rio Grande
No fog no haze no goodbyes to share
Forgiveness was never asked for ... Just quiet

Aliens Have Landed in Moreno Valley

*Press Release: Tele-Chavez Inland News Service,
Feb 3, 2022*

BY JOSÉ CHÁVEZ

Starships or UFOs have appeared in Mexico City, London, Paris, and even San Bernardino for many years. Millions have been amazed, if not frightened by these sightings, wondering if humans are under attack or if advanced civilizations are spying on us. A recent alien conference in Roswell, New Mexico, though well-attended, could not shed any new light on the subject.

One of our freelance reporters has discovered the real reason. Travelers from a distant galaxy have displayed interest in Earthly cuisine for many years. Curious inter-galactic chefs have nearly completed an extensive tour of restaurants in Mexico and France. They were delighted with sumptuous dishes of fish ceviche, carne asada tacos, and coctél de camarón in México City and Guadalajara. In Paris and Bordeaux they dined on filet mignon, chicken cordon bleu, and escargot.

Recently, they landed in Moreno Valley excited about a unique gastronomic experience awaiting them in Southern California. To their dismay, they discovered a strip mall mecca of franchises, an assembly line—selling burgers, fries, pizza, and deep-fried tacos in a box. At one hamburger chain, they ate something resembling a croissant for breakfast, and another served a type of nugget with chicken, but no one could explain what part of the chicken it came from.

The following day, they ordered tacos at another eatery with a sweet orange chipotle mango salsa and french fries mothered in a sauce called chile cheese—nothing like that in México! They noticed people always seemed to be in a hurry and paid for, speed, efficiency and familiarity for frozen food, fried, paper-wrapped, and super-sized. Nevertheless, a few of them turned a lime-green color of frustration if they had to wait in a long line of cars.

Hungry aliens didn't have to leave their spacecraft at all, and some swallowed their meal before exiting the busy drive thru. They experienced hot and juicy sensations, pulsations, palpitations, heartthrobs, and salivations during the daily bustle. **Hurry, hurry, faster, faster, move that line,** they shouted.

Noting their dour expressions and hands rubbing stomachs, a kind citizen explained the benefits of antacid tablets to the weary diners. Unsatisfied and slightly green, they agreed to stimulate their palates on other shores—perhaps they'd sample Sashimi in Tokyo or Tikka Masala in Mumbai.

One last cruise down Pigeon Pass Blvd., to Bountiful St., the sign read: In-N-Out, next to the tire store. Ay Dios Mío, they're selling nostalgia with patties not frozen, fresh-cut french fries, and milkshakes. There are white paper hats on wait staff and colorful T-shirts for the little crawlers back home. They all smiled literally from one large ear to another after sampling the freshness, flavors, and ambiance. Not one alien complained about the long wait in line, nor turned green. Before they left, the head chef of the visiting group excitedly asked the manager if they delivered their food since they had just secured a Door Dash account. Now, they were just like humans!

The following day they sent a communiqué to a distant planet. **We're departing for home and returning to Earth ASAP with our families and appetites.** We send a hearty shout-out to our future California compadres. There's room for a few more migrants in our Golden State. Have a safe intergalactic journey, Buen Provecho, and Bon appetit!

from the ashes

BY DEENAZ COACHBUILDER

yesterday, when she hurried along
hers was a welcoming home
the reassuring voices of children
as she busied herself with the evening meal
the quiet bedroom waited impatiently
for her nightly sojourn
a book lying enticingly open
lit by a glowing lamp
her beloved's warm body to cuddle against

all, all scattered fragments swirling blindly
as dried wildflowers in the wind

soon her lips forget laughter's curve
droplets of misery fill each unsought dawn
the parched hours drag

she stumbles onto the backyard garden
granite piercing her startled bare feet

numb fragments of faded hopes,
    beg to be recognized
cherished relationships stretched across the years
    the places she lived and loved in,
wrap around her a quilt
    embroidered in long lived grace
inviting her
        to go
looking for her life

within her bones
  stirs a cosmic struggle

warmth begins to scrape against her skin
the soft lament of the mourning dove
knocks gently upon the chamber of her bruised heart
sweet smelling currents drawn into her shuttered breath

double delight roses shiver desperately to seek her attention
yellowhite butterflies flutter invitingly around border lantanas
the startled new sun mingles with her unkempt curls

First published in *Open Door Magazine* The "Alternatives Issue."
  January 15th, 2022.

The Last Farewell.

BY DEENAZ COACHBUILDER

Farewell Again is a book of poems written by my father, Barjor Behramji Paymaster. The title refers to a poem he wrote for his mother, Tehmina on her demise in January 1950.

Farewell! Upon thy grave the sunlight gleams.
O would my riven heart could share thy bliss!
Farewell! And may thy sleep be free from dreams
If dreams still linger after Death's dark kiss.

It was September 2006. I was in Mumbai, India, having spent about a month with my father. I had retired early, so that I could visit with him more often, as he was elderly, now ninety-four, and living by himself. This had been a difficult stay. He was eating very little, bedridden, and not responding to his environment as he had done before. A close, trusted family friend, Dadi Daruwalla visited him every day. He had a competent night nurse, and a ward boy (trained to work in hospital settings) who met his physical needs during the day. But it was much more. It was his spirit that was subdued.

My presence seemed to make a difference over time. His food intake increased, he was alert, enjoyed listening to music, even reading for a while. He had been hospitalized after my arrival and was happy to be back in the comfort of his own home, on his familiar bed, knowing that he was surrounded by the artifacts of metal and ceramics that he had collected over the years, and his very beloved books, which at last count were over 9,000.

I spent as much time with him as I possibly could. After my morning breakfast and household duties, I would sit beside his bed, and read aloud parts of the three daily newspapers that arrived every morning. Then, the favorite classical tapes of his choice, or just listening to him reminisce.

The time for me to return to the U.S. was approaching. This time, I would be flying back within two months, as my son Sarvin had chosen to get married with his grandfather present in Mumbai in December. I was to be finalizing the arrangements, by returning to Mumbai soon from the U.S.

That day, I had shared segments of the daily news with him, as I relaxed in an easy chair close by. His eyelids were closed, covered with a dark folded handkerchief to shade his sensitive eyes. His breathing was even, but I knew he was not asleep. The following incident occurred, described in my poem:

Parting at ninety-four

I'm so sorry you're going
he said.
I'll be back soon
I spoke.
His words and mine
curled up into the air
and embraced.

I gazed at my father's closed eyes
and read the pages
of his soul.

Silently his soul breathed
I'll miss you.

Hurriedly his heart beat
I love you.
His lips lay silent.

I used to phone my dad from the U.S. twice or thrice during the week. On my last phone call, as usual I ended with "I love you Dad". His last words to me were "I love you darling". He said his "last farewell" to this world the next day, Sunday. It was that November in 2006.

Partners of the land

by Deenaz Coachbuilder

We fell asleep with clogged streets yellowed air
the polar bear, snow leopard, monarch butterfly,
 the green sea turtles
their habitat depleted
  the waters of the mighty oceans warming.

The earth became a quieter place.
Great cities fell silent.
Across the country forest birds were sighted in backyards
wild animals sauntered comfortably down urban streets.
Brash crows were ever bolder.

Can we not give them space to live?
Can we not strive for fresh air
clean streams,
where nature regains its rights
in harmony with humankind
each living
 generously.

We awoke to discover
       broken barricades
that death and disease strike
 the mighty,
    the neglected.

In an ideal world
let every tree become a poem
the earthworm reclaim its kingdom

the sky inherit the luminous stars
the rain and the rainbow
dance a duet
and at the end of our living,
partners of this land,
brush away
      our footprints,
leaving behind our words.

Published in *The Weekly Avocet*, December 4th, 2021.

opaque
    vacant houses

morning's
        uncreased side of the bed

hat
        swinging   on a hook

kitchen
with the smell of her
        presence

the fourth bridge player missing

flowers
  sent to make amends

the holes in communities
    dense cities
    rural counties

empty spaces of our heart
BY DEENAZ COACHBUILDER

Letters my mother wrote me

BY DEENAZ COACHBUILDER

On an ordinary sun-drenched morning
Dvorak's euphonious
  "Songs my mother taught me"
saturates awakening pores
the melody
clings to summer's flimsy garments
arousing memories…
  grandfather Behramji singing
                    to a fidgety child
his eyes pools of his mother's images.

My mother's epistles arrived once a week
slid into the metal mailbox
at a home I roomed in.
A student, far from family for the first time
in a continent
        half a world away
longed for, fretfully awaited,
these aerograms
folded carefully into several sections
were crammed with news of home and friends.
Nothing   too trivial
to be poured over, countlessly.
I would carry them into my room
careful not to fold or damage their
fine blue paper

artfully pry them open along predesigned folds
then savor each sentence.

Thirty years later, bedridden,
mother's external world framed
through tree shadowed windows,
her aerograms arrived once a month
to a home filled with my own family,
      half a world away
images   anecdotes   scents
so dear.

The melody ends   silence
sunlight fills the empty spaces.

How I See It Now

by Sylvia Clarke

During a Writers Workshop I attended the summer of 1985, I wrote about a traumatic incident I remembered from childhood. Just two months past my fourth birthday, Daddy and I were heading from our Montana home, a small sanitarium in Melrose, to the hospital in Butte to bring Mamma and baby sister Elvina home. The road was clear, but snow lay on the fields and in the ditches. I must have tired of looking out the window at the snow and sage brush because I decided to lie down in the front seat next to Daddy.

Daddy's lap looked like a good place to put my head. As I slipped my head under his arms and the steering wheel, the car jerked, and we landed in the snowy ditch. I don't remember what Daddy said, but I got the distinct impression that something I did made us go into the ditch. While he tramped through the snow looking for a way to get back on the road, I sat looking at my weeping face in the chrome knobs on the dashboard and thinking, "My fault! My fault!" Much of the joy of going to see Mamma and our new baby fled.

A few years ago, I shared this incident with a friend who was practicing counseling for her degree. She helped me reshape the story by asking, "How would you have felt if your father had asked you to help him get branches to put under the tires so you could get out of the ditch?"

Imagining that scenario changed it for me. I now have a different perspective and no longer feel the pain of that memory. Besides, I'm learning to be kinder to myself—to laugh at myself in place of crying or feeling guilty.

When I think of that incident now, I realize that my father was probably startled by my putting my head in his lap. After all, I didn't ask permission first. I just moved by impulse. He may also have been very sensitive in that area of his body and overreacted, jerking the steering wheel. That was the move that put the car in the ditch.

In my mid-forties, I came to the realization that I have many of the symptoms of ADHD: distractibility, forgetfulness, impulsiveness, inability to sit still, etc. When I turned 60, someone said, "I remember you were always a busy little girl." And Mother once told me that trying to teach me to sew was "like trying to harness a wild deer."

My college roommate, I remember, once said, "I'll go to church with you, Sylvia, if you will sit still!" I must usually have fidgeted. Perhaps it was my hyperactivity that distracted my father that December day and put us in the ditch. Time and maturity can change perspective.

Treasured Object/Special Date

BY SYLVIA CLARKE

While we lived in Iowa City, Iowa, where Wilton, my devoted husband, attended U of I getting his PhD, he gave me what is now a prized possession: a leather-bound gilt-edged Bible. It is special to me for several reasons. First is the love this special gift Bible represents. We were not flush with cash during those years.

Our two young daughters, Esther and Julia, crowded around me as I unwrapped the gift and oohed and exclaimed over this beautiful Bible. When I opened its pages and wrote the date, February 19, 1974, on the "Presented to" page, I thought of another February 19–one more than a decade earlier.

J. F. Kennedy is President, and I'm attending college in South-eastern Michigan. Besides studying and working part-time, I have a social life. I have dated a few different guys but am not ready to stick with just one or get serious in a relationship. One young man calls me out for avoiding him after just two dates. Dating more times than that almost amounts to "going steady", as others call it, which I think unnecessary. Develop a strong friendship, and loyalty automatically follows, doesn't it?

It's my second year at Andrews University, and I'm working for Mr. Davis in the custodial office. As the semester begins, a group of fellows who have been promised work gather in the hall outside the open office window. Mr. Davis goes to speak with them and tell them they are assigned to pick gourds on the farm today. As I stand back watching, I notice a redhead at the back of the crowd who speaks with an accent and wonder, "Hmm…Where does he come from?"

It's not very long before I find out his last name is Clarke. He works for our Custodial Department: I check the time cards. When I attended the October Alumni Weekend at my high school, I meet his parents and brother, missionaries on furlough from Africa. So, when Wilton—yes, I know his first name—exits the girls' dorm just as I am returning from the weekend, I say, "Hi, Wilton. I bring you greetings from your parents." He looks nonplussed.

A few days later I see him wearing a lavender Andrews U. sweatshirt. "You shouldn't be wearing that color with your red hair!" I remonstrated. I guess he noticed me then because when he comes past my desk after gathering his equipment, he starts trying to get my attention by touching my head with the broom handle, asking some inane question, or slipping something cold down my neck. Wilton even begins to ask me to do things with him—invitations I refuse because I'm not prepared. At this point in life, I'm not very flexible. I like to plan ahead.

The first weekend of December, Wilton invited me to go with him to hear the Vienna Boys' Choir concert at the college. I accept, and we have a lovely evening. In January, he invited me to Dr. Wood's home where his parents are visiting to celebrate his 21st birthday. While there, I overhear him discussing how to get his trunk to the ship for the trip back to South Africa. Guess he won't be around much longer. I don't know how I feel—Sad? Relieved?

A week later I learn Wilton has decided to stay at Andrews! What now? It's not up to me entirely, I see, because he makes opportunity to see me, even asking if I'll share my Western Civilization textbook with him, which I do. On Valentine's Day, Wilton approaches me with the question, "Will you go steady with me?" Now what?

"I need to think about it," I tell him, knowing I must deliberate and pray about it, too. He agrees to let me have a few days to process his request and come up with an answer.

Looking at the relationship from all angles, I agonize over the choice I need to make and pray often. "Please, God, is this the right thing to do?" I tell God I don't want to get serious now. I need to finish my education, but I admit I do enjoy his company. On the plus side, he's a good, reliable person—son of missionaries, hard worker, and shows confidence in the way he walks and talks. He's kind—and much more. On the negative side, "Do I want to give all this up just because I thought I wouldn't ever 'go steady' with anyone?" I ask myself. That answer seems fairly obvious.

A little later I consider this question: If I refuse, will I regret having passed up this opportunity? That's a hard one. "Okay, Lord," I decide, "I probably would!"

Consequently, on February 19, 1963, I tell Wilton I accept him as my boyfriend and will go steady with him. I know he has reason to want a commitment of some sort. Look how I treated the other fellows I had dated.

Eleven years later, I looked up from my lovely Bible and thanked my wonderful husband for such a thoughtful gift. I began using it in personal and family devotions, gaining strength for my day-to-day duties, finding texts that support my faith in God, and claiming comforting promises of His presence and help. At the time, little did I know that another important February 19 loomed in the future. Our son Fredrick was born on that date two years later—in 1976!

Today this treasure that came into my life on February 19 back then is held together by a cloth book cover. The leather binding is tattered, some pieces missing. Pages fall out; others I have marked with notes and passages underlined in different colors. So, this old Bible holds not only reminders of important dates in my life but also has life-giving news about who I am and where I come from. Its stories and promises show me how God deals with people like me and what lies ahead. That gives me reason enough to treasure it.

Epitaph

BY SYLVIA CLARKE

Her warm smile and caring heart
Mean she'll be remembered
As encouraging—her art
Of brighter hope engendered
In those she met or knew.

A youngster's struggle sleeping
Inspired bedtime angel songs
God's gift within her keeping
Released--sent where it belongs—
Blessing him, others, too.

Captivating stories heard
In her early years
Cultivated love for word
That brought laugh or tears.
Mental pictures they drew.

Reading, hearing, or writing
Story, experience, or song
These things were exciting:
For heaven made her long,
Hope, joy ahead in view.

Africa and God

by Wil Clarke

In December 1978, we had been missionaries to South Africa for 3 full years. These were the Carter years, and the whole world was experiencing fierce double-digit inflation. I had had no cost-of-living adjustment to my salary. What had been a very livable wage three years earlier, now was not covering our basic expenses. My savings were gone. We could not afford to run the old Peugeot we owned, more than the weekly grocery run of about 6 miles. We had bought no new clothes, because we couldn't afford them. We had an extra child in our family. Inflation had docked our money's buying power by over 50%.

We were due a three-month furlough home to the States in February 1979. We had requested that our furlough start in the middle of the year because that way we wouldn't have to buy heavy winter clothing that we would need in Michigan, but would not need in Africa. That request had been denied—if we delayed that long, policy required that they give us four-month furlough, and the mission board was not about to do that for us!

I said to Sylvia, "We have two choices available; we can take our furlough and come back and be unable to survive, or we can take permanent return to the States."

She replied, "We have given our lives as missionaries to Africa. I do not want to return permanently to the States. I don't want to raise our children there."

"They're holding a board meeting for our college this month. Let's pray the Lord to have them give us a significant increase in salary for 1979, as a sign that God wants us to return to Africa." So we prayed, and like Gideon in the Bible, we put out a "fleece". If God wanted us to return to Africa, He would give us at least a 10% increase in salary. That is a far cry from 50%, but it would be the sign we would look for.

After the board meetings, the president of the college called a special staff meeting and said, "You will be happy to know that the board has voted you a 10% increase in salary!"

My heart sang for joy! God had answered our fleece exactly the way we had proposed it.

Then the president continued, "Of course, you realize that the expenses for the college have been going up too. So we are going to raise your rent by…" And he went on outlining all the extra things that they were going to deduct from our salary. When he got done with his talk, we had actually gotten only 1.5% increase in our salary, before taxes.

I went home depressed. "God wants us to return to the States permanently." I told Sylvia. She was not moved. She still didn't want to leave the mission field.

That was all on Monday. On Friday, I got a call from a friend, Jerry, in Massachusetts offering us a job at a college there. Clearly God was indicating his plan for us, and showing us that He had our welfare in mind.

For over three months we lived in denial of God's express will. We vainly sought various ways to get around the fleece we had put out. I felt growing stress pressing down on me as I resisted doing what I knew God wanted me to do.

Finally, on a Friday afternoon in April, three-and-a-half months later, I got another call from Jerry, "I need to know now whether you're going to come here, or whether I should look for someone else."

"Give me until Sunday," I told him.

After we had eaten supper and had worship and put the kids to bed, I walked outside under the brilliant African sky. I looked up at the constellation of Orion—my favorite stars. Stress was pressing down on me like an unbearable weight. I breathed a prayer of desperation to God, "What shall I do?" I felt the presence of God very close to me.

"I already told you!" came a voice. Whether it was an internal voice in my mind or an actual voice through my ears, I don't know. But it had a sense of exasperation in it. My mind instantly returned to the 1.5%, back in December, 4 months ago. I had been resisting God for all that time.

"Okay, God! We're going back to the States permanently," I said out loud. Instantly I felt as though a great weight had rolled off of my shoulders. I breathed freely and joy flooded my whole being. I walked lightly back inside and said, "We're going back to the States!" Sylvia was dumbfounded.

We went to bed and I slept the sleep of the just. Sylvia couldn't sleep.

Finally, she woke me about 4:00 a.m. "I've decided I'm going with you!" she informed me. We flew out from Cape Town in July, after finishing the term I was teaching. It was definitely the best move for us.

Budget Inn Hobbs NM

by Wil Clarke

On our trip east, last summer, we decided to stay the night at Budget Inn in Hobbs, New Mexico. It was pretty run down. I think the poor proprietors are having a really uphill battle trying to stay alive. The couple are quite old and probably trying to make ends meet on an inadequate Social Security. Covid certainly has not helped them.

There was an immaculate Lincoln pickup with a huge engine in the parking lot. I didn't know Lincoln made pickups—I'm just uneducated. A young woman wearing short-shorts sat on the tail gate. A rather unkempt man stood in front of her. It was obvious that he was chatting with her just so he could stand there and feast his eyes on her. I chatted with them while I fetched something from our pickup, and they both responded with a lot of good humor. Meanwhile the man was running the back of his hand back and forth on the inside of the naked skin of her inner thighs. They both seemed to be enjoying the stimulation. They seemed to especially enjoy having a strange man watching their caresses. I left them together to delight in what meager pleasures they had been pursuing for the last couple of hours.

I asked Sylvia, "Would you like a hot meal for a change?"

She jumped at the opportunity: "On our way into Hobbs, I noticed a Mexican restaurant. There were lots of cars around it so it must be good. Would you like Mexican?"

We drove over there and asked to see their menu. They waved us into a seat. A cheerful waitress brought us a menu and some chips and salsa. I spotted the "chiles rellenos" (chilies stuffed with cheese) immediately. They are usually a favorite of mine. Sylvia read down the menu several times. She considered several dishes while our waitress brought us some water and long straws. Finally, Sylvia settled on "huevos rancheros" (ranch style eggs) without the meat.

"We can share the chilis and eggs," she suggested.

The waitress brought my chilis first, served on a large oblong plate with lots of rice, refried beans, and some chopped lettuce and tomatoes. Then she brought the huevos drowned in salsa, also with beans and rice. It makes my saliva flow just writing about it.

We said grace and then Sylvia took a big bite of eggs. She gasped. They were way too hot. Our waitress had lingered near us. She stepped over to our table, "Are they too hot?" she asked sympathetically.

"¡Son demasiado picante!" I commented.

"I think I can finish them if I eat them slowly." Sylvia volunteered valiantly. She always hates to inconvenience anyone.

The girl picked up the plate, "I'm sorry, I'll be right back." She disappeared and reappeared within 5 minutes with a clean plate and salsa on the side rather than smothering the eggs. This time Sylvia used the salsa that came with the chips and was somewhat milder than that on the side. I ate most of her salsa side and enjoyed it.

When we got back to the inn, the man and woman at the Lincoln were still enjoying their conversation.

Encounter in North Las Vegas

BY WIL CLARKE

The first day of our trip to Michigan we stopped at the Sunrise Inn in North Las Vegas. When I went in, the desk clerk was in a protracted phone conversation with a prospective guest who spoke loudly with an east-Asian accent. In the next 20 minutes, while I stood on one foot and then the other waiting, the clerk explained the cost of the motel and what all it included at least 20 times. I could see that she was at wit's end. She maintained her professional cool only by sheer force of will, and it was really costing her emotionally.

Finally, she said, "May I put you on hold while I wait on two sets of customers?" She sat back just shaking with stress and exertion. I congratulated her for not losing her cool. She relaxed visibly and smiled her appreciation. She had been telling the person on the phone that the room would cost her $99. I showed her Google's advertisement for $44. I was told this price was if I had booked it a week in advance through one of the online marketers and didn't include taxes, etc. In the end she let me have the room for $58. After settling in we went to the truck stop next door to get some supper.

Before going to the inn, we had filled the car up at a Pilot station in NLV. A very filthy woman in a tattered and dirty dress came to the car window and told Sylvia how she had 3 children, no food, and she was hungry. She certainly played strongly on Sylvia's heart strings. Finally, Sylvia pulled out a $20 bill and handed it to her. She blessed Sylvia profusely and then asked her if she could spare another $20. Sylvia couldn't.

Now as we walked into the truck stop for supper, this brazen woman walked jauntily into the bar in the truck stop with a man in tow. Of course, she showed no sign of recognition when she saw us. I assume that those three poor children went to bed hungry that night again (if indeed they existed!) Ms. Frump may also have gone a long way toward increasing that number to four.

There was also a Subway and a Don Taco next to the bar. The woman at the order desk of Don Taco spoke no English, so I ordered in my broken Spanish. She pointed to a notice board that offered chicken tacos for 99¢ on Tuesdays. I ordered two of them and a chile relleno, which I am partial to; Sylvia had 2 cheese enchiladas with a combination—salad, beans, and rice.

Back at our room we fell into bed exhausted, hardly considering this most recent affirmation of the recommendation that we not support panhandlers.

After the Story Has Come to an End

BY JAMES COATS

When the last bit of money goes
and your small business must close
Begin again

When the future's unclear
or your love disappears
Begin again

When your feelings are hurt
and the key doesn't work
Begin again

When you get in some mess
or fail your big test
Begin again

When your precise plans get ruined
and you don't know what you're doin'
Begin again

When the storm runs long
or the timing's all wrong
Begin again

When your big break runs late
and they ghost you on the date
Begin again

When you're not feeling the best,
take a moment to rest
Then begin again

Our Seeds

BY JAMES COATS

Deferred hope left waiting in the want, and for what
dream should I sacrifice? So much witnessing happens,
a day turns into an escape, a hiding place no longer safe to -
to survive a year, life becomes the opposite of grade A.
Happens again, all the time, seeds laid in the ground a dream.
What if our buried dreams do not have their growth deferred?

Smile of Life

BY JAMES COATS

Life it waits for me to love it like a newborn
swaddled so close to my chest, our heartbeats sync and
become a wound cuckoo clock, full of potential energy
trapped in bones, holding on to flakes of youthful health.

Health is precious these days, for nights are capricious
and mornings may forget to wake you from slumber.
I do not wish to mistake a full belly for living well
there is a deeper hunger inside, an appetite for freedom.

Freedom is needed in order to feel alive;
the space to stretch; to reach above and below;
to test the limits of imagination; and the depths of feeling.
This is why we search for anything resembling joy.

Joy in ourselves, in others' reflection, in this world.
I want this year to be one of abundance.
That may take surrendering every old idea we hold.
Let joy be the face of health, and freedom the smile of life.

A Very Short Story About Drinking Coffee

BY ELINOR COHEN

Most weekday mornings, I arrived to work at the Record Label/Mail Order Catalog/Secret Aboveground Spy Lair before Claire did, and was faced with my first crucial work-related decision of the day: whip up a cup of instant coffee in the break room which was really my desk, or wait for Claire and walk the extra long two-and-a-half blocks to the bakery for the fresh brewed real thing? Admittedly, most mornings I did both. I'd suck down a quickie Nescafé before Claire (dressed in all black) flung open the office door and announced she was ready for a caffeine injection. Then she'd punch her secret spy code into the box on the wall and roll her eyes about how absurd it was for mid-level spies to have to bother with such things. She'd stash her bag under my swivel chair, I'd swallow the last few sips from my non-biodegradable styrofoam cup (which I would rinse and reuse a couple of times over until it would start to lose its integrity, ouch), and we'd be off.

Down six flights of stairs, or the death-trap elevators if they happened to be working, and out the heavy glass and bronze double doors into the fresh air and Metro bus exhaust. We'd head north, past the windowless concrete dungeon that housed a coven of SBC telephone operators, the many chained-off parking lots with eroding asphalt and disgruntled valets, past colorful piles of discarded single-use plastic bags and broken glass. We'd stroll past the chic ramen spot famous for their sushi (do NOT call it the sushi spot famous for their ramen, and ESPECIALLY don't mention their cold pressed juices), and continue past the discount alcoholic beverage warehouse that used to be a combination wedding chapel/divorce lawyer firm (no kidding!). Occasionally (too often) the greaseball taxi driver with expired tags smoking an already half-smoked cigarette would try to attract our attention like a screechy feral cat, but we'd keep walking, having learned it was best not to interact. Then finally we'd reach the overgrown sidewalk rosemary bushes (we'd smell the rosemary before we could see it) and voila we'd arrived. Claire would pull open the screen door and we'd take our place at the back of the line. That's when things got stressful.

You see, Claire knew she wanted a large coffee with room for milk, but was she going to splurge on a pastry? Would it be a parmesan cheese stick, slightly warmed? A slice of sour cherry chocolate bread? An entire half loaf? Award-winning dulce de leche custard cup? Heavenly buttery flaky almond-filled croissant? Powdered sugar and raspberry jelly thumbprint cookie sandwich? Savory onion tart artisan rustic baguette brioche ciabatta focaccia buzzy buzzword? Something with <gulp> oh dear god, meat in it? Her options were practically infinite. This was a world-class establishment after all. I was going to want a cheese stick, but unpredictable Tropical Storm Claire had a major-league decision to make.

She'd make this decision with a thoughtful sassy style. She'd rub her lips together (no lipstick but a glossy shine most days), squint her eyes and tousle her short hair by running a few fingers through. Then she'd shift her weight from one foot to the other, and maybe back again. I imagine this helped her concentrate. At some point, the dozen other coffee-deprived bakery patrons squeezed haphazardly in the not-so-single-file line behind us would introduce a sense of urgency for her and she'd blurt out her choice, "Oh I'll have a cheese stick too." Success! Into the paper bag it would go, and we'd head out in a flash, anxious to see what other goodies the familiar counterpeople might have slipped in for us. (Once a madeleine cookie! Once a funky misshapen cheese stick! Sometimes extra napkins!)

We'd always walk back to the spy lair more slowly, less enthusiastically, a shared sense of dread as we imagined ourselves enjoying our delicious spoils under the watchful eye of the Head Spy Guy and Beelzebub, his dead grizzly bear rug. No lovely breeze (save for the drafty puffs of air blowing in through a cracked office window, only partially covered with plywood and therefore partially uncovered), no warm sun shining down upon our shoulders. Just the shrill sounds of ringing phones and police sirens and screaming car alarms from six stories down. Aaargh, Claire would say. And I would wholeheartedly agree. Aaargh.

The end. For now. Can somebody help? I'm desperate for a Starbucks.

The Story of Mary Hernandez: As It Was Told To Me

by Carlos Cruz

In 1946 when my grandmother was only15 years old she migrated from Mexico to the United States. Her name was Mary Cortez, but back then she most likely went by Maria. From the stories that have been passed on to me, I know that she grew up extremely poor in Guadalajara, Jalisco. There were times when food was scarce, and articles of clothing such as shoes were a luxury her family could not afford. I remember her retelling stories of how she would watch boys and girls her age walk to school. She would peek into the window of their classroom to see what was going on, and imagine being inside the class with them. From my understanding, school was not accessible to everyone in Mexico unless you had money. It was always her dream to be able to go to school. Even at such a young age my grandmother knew the value of education.

At the age of 15 my grandmother had an opportunity to leave Guadalajara and travel to the United States. Her older sister Socorro had somehow obtained papers to travel legally to the U.S. The details are unknown to me, but I do know that her sister was too scared to travel alone. In 1942, the U.S. and Mexican governments worked together to create the Bracero Program. I can only speculate, but this may have been the reason why she was able to obtain paperwork to travel to the US. At 15 years, she made the decision to use those papers, along with her sister's birth certificate, in order to travel all alone to the U.S. I can only imagine the courage it must have taken for her to get on that bus, with no idea what life would be like once she reached her destination. I think back to when my own daughter was 15 years old, and I couldn't imagine letting her walk to school alone.

It must have been both an exciting and frightening experience for her — traveling all alone to a foreign country, and not speaking a word of English. Once she crossed the border and departed the bus she sat down on a bench next to a woman with a baby. She sat there relieved that she had made it to the U.S. but also unsure of how she would get to her uncle's house who lived somewhere in Los Angeles. She had no money and no form of transportation. The woman with the baby was so preoccupied with everything, that when her bus arrived she grabbed her baby and rushed off to board the bus. My grandmother sat there wondering what to do next when she noticed that the woman had left something behind. It was a small coin purse with quite a bit of money inside. She quickly ran after the woman to give her the coin purse but she was too late because the bus had already driven off.

Every time my grandmother retold that story, she always made sure to mention that it was God's way of looking out for her as the reason the woman left the money behind. Relieved that she would now be able to buy herself some food she began to feel better about her situation. While purchasing food she met a young couple who spoke Spanish. They had just arrived in the U.S. as well and were headed to Corona to stay with some relatives. My grandmother remembered them as good Christian people, and felt safe enough to travel with them. She ended up living in Corona for some time, and worked in the citrus fields. She even agreed to be baptized as a Christian even though she had grown up her entire life as a Catholic — and was most likely baptized as a baby. She always spoke fondly of the time she spent with that family. Those people may not have been blood relatives but they treated her with kindness.

It was not long before she was in communication with her family back in Mexico. She wrote letters to her father explaining her situation and where she was living. Her father wrote back very concerned for her safety. He firmly explained that she needed to be with family, and gave her the address of his brother who lived in Los Angeles. My grandmother could not understand why her father was insisting that she go live with her uncle. She was happy living in Corona, but she did as she was told and headed to L.A.

Once she had moved in with her uncle and his family she quickly came to understand that it was a mistake to leave Corona. Her uncle's wife was not a very good person, and her cousins treated her like a servant instead of family. She had to wake up before everyone else in order to make tortillas. She was responsible for doing everyone's laundry as well as cleaning the house, and being expected to find a job and contribute to the rent. Even though she was in a bad situation she never let it discourage her. She was determined to learn English so she could gain some independence. She would listen to the radio or television whenever the opportunity arose and like that she taught herself English. She found work at a factory in Downtown L.A. and began making some money, but her uncle expected her to use most of her earnings to help pay the rent. After some time had passed, her uncle informed her that they were moving. My grandmother refused to go with them. She had decided that she would stay, and try to survive on her own. She figured she was already paying most of the rent, and would find some way to come up with the rest.

While working at the factory in downtown Los Angeles she had befriended an Italian woman named Rosa. They quickly became good friends. When my grandmother's family moved out, she asked Rosa to move in. They lived together for some time just working and enjoying each other's company. Eventually, Rosa met a nice Italian man named Armando. They began to date and were soon married. Although my grandmother was happy for her friend Rosa, she was also a little bit sad about losing the best roommate she had ever known. To her surprise, Rosa and Armando asked her to come live with them once they were married. She immediately said yes, and was so happy that she would not be living on her own. They always treated my grandmother like a daughter. I grew up thinking this nice old couple were my great-grandparents, and knew them only as Honi and Noni, a nickname my uncle had given them when he was a little boy. We used to go to City Terrace and visit them on weekends when I was a kid. The three of them would sit in the living room and talk for hours in Spanish. I always thought they were Mexican, and didn't learn the truth about their ethnicity until I was much older.

Eventually, Mary Cortez met a man named Arthur Hernandez. This man pursued her until she finally gave in and agreed to marry him. According to my grandmother, she only did this so "He would stop bugging her." They eventually purchased a house and began creating a family together in El Sereno, which is a predominantly Mexican neighborhood in Los Angeles. Although my grandmother had no formal education, she was a very smart woman. She understood the value of property and saved enough money to put a down payment on a second house. When she first proposed this idea to my grandfather, he refused to help her out. My grandmother, being the independent type of person, did not let that stop her. She explained to my grandfather that she would go out and find a business partner that would be willing to help her. Upon hearing this, he quickly gave in to my grandmother's request. She continued to be a self-made entrepreneur. She would babysit neighborhood children and started her own flower arranging business, and continued to invest in property.

A young Mexican girl who came to the United States all alone slowly built a modest empire for her family. She did not do this in order to get rich; she did it because in her mind she believed that if she bought a house for everyone, her family would never be homeless. At one point she even saved enough money to have a house built in Mexico for the family she had left behind. Family was everything to my grandmother, and everything she did in her life was to benefit her children and grandchildren. She lived a very modest lifestyle, and any profits she made went into helping her children and grandchildren.

I remember my grandmother as a short, chubby little woman with short dark curly hair but, I have seen pictures of her as a young woman. To my surprise she looked, and dressed like a Pachuca. All of my fondest childhood memories are from the time I spent living with my grandmother. She could be stubborn at times, and she demanded respect, but her love was unconditional. There were several times during my teenage years that I would have been homeless if it were not for my grandmother's willingness to take me in, no matter what type of trouble I had been involved with. Even as an adult, if I was struggling to find work, my grandmother would hire me to do odd jobs on one of her properties, and proceed to over-pay me for the work I had completed. She continued to value education even though she had none.

My cousin Paul was the first one in our family to graduate from college. I always knew she was very proud to have a college graduate in our family, so when I began to pursue higher education in my thirties, my grandmother was excited for me. I would call her on the phone and the first thing she would ask is "Are you still in school, mijo?" And we would end our conversation with her telling me, "Don't give up, you gotta make sure you finish school."

My Grandma Mary passed away before I obtained my Bachelor's Degree, but I know she would have been proud to know there was another college graduate in the family. Right now, I am in the process of obtaining my Masters Degree, and will go on to complete the PhD. When things are tough and I feel as if I'm not cut out for the life of a scholar, I hear my grandmother's voice telling me not to give up. So, there is no doubt in my mind that I will complete this program, not only for myself, but to honor my grandmother and the sacrifices she made for not only me, but her entire family.

My Barbecue Journey

by Brian DeCoud

I enjoy whiskey and whisky, watching basketball, and being in the world of barbecue. At this stage of the game they make for good hobbies, good conversation and meeting good, if not interesting, people.

The brown spirits can be smooth or biting, young or aged, light or dark, blended or not…just like people. Yes, having a toast has brought me to meet some very interesting people. Basketball is fast-paced, strategic. It can be one-on-one or a team sport, and sometimes, smooth or biting. Being a season seat holder has also brought me to meet some very interesting people. Barbecue encompasses all of these descriptors, and more.

I started my barbecue journey while couch-surfing one evening. Like so many others, I came across a television program called "BBQ Pitmasters." There were Cooks and Judges. It immediately had my attention. I was only so-so on the backyard pit, but I could sure eat good barbecue. I was hooked faster than a hungry fish.

After the first episode, I bee-lined to the computer and did a deep dive into becoming a barbecue Judge. Here was my first lesson: "Wait. This isn't an actual job? I don't get paid for this? I can't get paid to eat barbecue?!" Well, here's another time in life where I had to adjust my attitude. There it was, barbecue and eating, in one package. So how was I going to get it?

I convinced myself that if I got involved with this, I might not get paid, but I'd eat well. I didn't have any real hobbies at the time, so what the heck?

My search took me to an organization called KCBS, the Kansas City Barbecue Society. It turned out that they have competitions and classes that teach you how to be a Judge. (Just like basketball is a competition, SOMEBODY has to win.) OKAY then. I can do this.

My brother and I don't live near each other or see each other very often. I talked him into a road trip and a judging class in Lake Havasu, AZ. Of course, I got permission from the Bosslady first, and my world changed.

I have to mention the Bosslady here because she has been very lenient with me in this hobby. She tells her friends that if I could somehow make barbecue a paying job, I would. There came a point where she suggested to me point blank, "This IS just a HOBBY. RIGHT?"

That conversation actually helped me. This hobby isn't her hobby. It's mine. Therefore, I know that I have to get my chores done before I can go out and play in the barbecue field on a Saturday. If I'm really good, I get to go on a sleepover in another city. Barbecue has given me my Hall Pass.

It's done something else for me. I used to be just a so-so griller in the backyard. Yes, there is a difference between grilling and barbecue. My own backyard game has come sooo far. When I say that I used to burn, there really were days when I used to burn anything on the grill. Now, the Bosslady and several friends say that my barbecue is the best they've ever had. Of course, the best barbecue in the world costs 'Free.99'.

I am proud that I have learned more than enough to do volunteer barbecues for Veterans. My Dad was a Veteran. There are a number of widows and widowers in my neighborhood, so I do an annual barbecue and deliver meals to them. Before, it would have been burgers at a Block Party.

When you get involved in any organization, whether it's at work, volunteering, your neighborhood, or anywhere else, you're going to meet some tremendous people…and some 'unique individuals', which can be, as stated earlier, interesting. I try not to be too much of an oddball, and the tremendous folks are too humble to recognize that they are tremendous. I made a decision when I started judging competitions that, if I am different from these folks, it's really just too bad. They're going to have to get used to me being here. After all, there was barbecue to be had.

That being said, it's good to influence from the middle. Some of those tremendous folks have given me knowledge of the nuts and bolts and inner mechanics of the barbecue world, as well as friendship. That has given me confidence and led me to sharing insights with other Judges.

<u>But Wait. There's More</u>

There has always been a bit of a divide between barbecue Cooks and Judges. After all, they have poured their time, energy and money into trying to win a trophy, a check and applause from their colleagues. Many Judges chit-chat, eat, judge, do it again, and go home. Some Judges stay to talk with Cooks, some of whom are their friends. I have tried to bridge that gap with my own outreach. From the very beginning, I have visited Cooks, shown my face and asked about their equipment and techniques, in essence, taking a real and personal interest in their craft. Hey, I ALSO drove a long way here. I didn't want to do an eat and run! I, too, wanted value for my time! I wanted to learn. If they let me, I tried to help break down and pack their equipment for the drive home. Really, some of these folks were operating on zero to three hours of sleep in the last 24 hours. Lending a helping hand is an easy thing to do. Thanks, Mom and Dad.

Mingling with the Cooks at a Friday night Potluck and after competitions gave me the opportunity to cook with five teams, four of whom have walked in front of their friends to win trophies and checks. Wow! That one minute of glory, even as a teammate, was exciting! Imagine how high the winners feel!

There is a significant highlight here. In 2018, I made a trip to the American Royal Barbecue Competition, the biggest barbecue competition in the world. I partied a bit on Friday night, saw fireworks, and judged on Saturday. I had pre-arranged to cook with a Team from Palm Desert, CA on Sunday. After judging Saturday, we met and started prepping our meats for the Sunday competition. There were 467 Teams from across the country competing in pork ribs. That's a LOT of competition. When the Seventh-Place winner was announced, it was the Team I joined! Man, you just can't imagine the excitement and jubilation we felt. I have goosebumps while writing this.

In the meantime, I created a monthly BBQ joint get-together with Los Angeles-based Judges. The purpose was to find the best barbecue in Los Angeles. We found some really good barbecue and some not so good. Hence, the search continues.

Let's not forget the most beautiful benefit of food, though. Food brings people together. Breaking bread, or brisket, helps to leave the negative behind and focus on the good, even for a half hour. I'll never forget the night the group met at a joint in Pasadena, CA. This was a small, yet significantly diverse group of Judges/Friends. We had a Latin guy, a Black guy, a Jewish guy, an Asian lady and as my Dad used to say, a Heinz 57 (A little bit of this, a little bit of that). I'm confident that, if it were not for barbecue, there was no reason for any of us to be in each other's world. We didn't talk about politics, religion, or our differences. We talked about barbecue. (Actually, we also talked about the traffic we had to deal with to get to this dinner.)

When COVID came around, the camaraderie we built was threatened by not having any more outings. Lo and behold, along came Zoom. The outings switched to an online gathering. Through some fine-tuning, the call has grown to include Judges from all parts of California and some other states, talking about one subject…yup, the world of barbecue. We now have monthly Special Guests that share their experience, expertise and unique perspectives in barbecue. We've chatted with Cook Teams, CEO's, Vendors, Board Members, and many more. KCBS even acknowledged the Zoom calls by bestowing a Certificate of Achievement at the 2021 KCBS Annual Banquet. Creating this Zoom call and sharing the camaraderie with KCBS Judges has been very satisfying.

I used to say that being involved in the world of barbecue isn't going to change the world, but it makes me happy. A fellow barbecue Judge is involved on many levels in the world of motor racing. Every year he takes his RV to the infield of the Speedway in Fontana, CA. I told him that my Mom is a NASCAR fan. He invited the two of us to join him in the infield. When I say that we were 'right there', we were 'right there'! The Racers zoomed right by us with the sound of their 200+ MPH. It was a happy day for my Mother that I will never forget. I shared this story with another Judge. He corrected me by saying, "You say that being a barbecue Judge won't change the world, but it changed your Mother's world." I hadn't thought of it that way. He was right. It was a highlight that I would not have been able to share with her, had it not been for the world of barbecue.

If you are interested in becoming a member of KCBS, the Kansas City Barbecue Society, visit KCBS.US.

"If Only I Could Remember…If Only I Could Forget…"

BY CHUCK DOOLITTLE

There should have been more time with her. One minute we were enjoying ourselves at our new vacation home, the next came the diagnosis. Or, mis-diagnosis. What should have been a time to celebrate and anticipate making memories, spiraled into something no one expected. The maternal pillar of our family, my mother-in-law, Donna Pence, received devastating news.

In June of 2016, my wife and I were contemplating purchasing a second home in southern Oregon. Her parents had owned one in a little town called Alsea for the previous 20 years. Family vacations were centered around that twenty-acre, serene piece of heaven for roughly the same number of years. But as "Mom and Dad" as I affectionately called them, aged, caring for it became a bit too much. So, they sold, which created a void not only for them but the entire family. That's where we came in. We hoped that buying a home up there would allow them to still enjoy the area where they grew up, with less of the responsibility. Little did we know.

Mom, Dad, my wife and I had only begun our summer in the new place when Mom started having some issues with her dentures. At least that is what we thought was the problem. Several dentist visits, diagnoses and mis-diagnoses later, with increased pain and reduced eating, we realized the severity of Mom's discomfort. Unfortunately, we also realized dentists were not the answer. Her and Dad made the hard decision to pack up and head home to southern California and see her doctor. That was a blow to everyone. What had all started as a lovely summer, enjoying the new house and all that accompanies that, quickly turned to worry. And that was just the beginning.

The doctor was quick to dismiss what dentists had called thrush.

He said he wanted to order an MRI immediately and that he suspected cancer. His suspicion was confirmed and radiation and chemotherapy ordered.

Thinking back to that summer, I often ask myself "if only I could remember all the little things the four of us said to each other and enjoyed together." The conversations with Mom, the many board games we played, picking berries, restaurants we visited, family we visited; work we did around the new place. I wish I could remember every detail of every moment we spent together.

As much as I'd like to remember, I'd also like to forget. Forget Mom's many trips to doctors. Wipe away all the atrocities she was dealt while battling this behemoth of a disease. Ignore the thoughts of all the indignities she endured. Most of all, I'd like to forget January 31, 2017, the last day I saw her in this life.

But it's no easier to forget than it is to remember. Both seem very elusive. So, remembering the person she was is all I can do. And that is enough. Her warm smile and embrace, her laugh, her fun, competitive nature with me, the love for her family. All things beautiful. That is how I will choose to remember my "Mom" for the beautiful person she was.

My Happiest Moment

BY CHUCK DOOLITTLE

They say a watched pot never boils. Likewise, staring at a phone expecting it to ring appears equally futile. But that's exactly what my wife and I found ourselves doing in the last week of November, 1999.

From the moment we saw our daughter, Julia, on a video tape in early May of the same year, she was all we could think about. Seven months old, beautiful in every way, tiny sounds escaping her tiny mouth, muffled background voices repeating her name in Russian, "Yulia, Yulia" they would say. You could tell she had at least a bad cold, as she was coughing and sniffling as she curiously gazed into the camera. All the more reason we were in a hurry to get her home to California. Unknown to us at the time, it would be an agonizingly long 7 months before we would hold her.

The adoption agency, Life Adoption in Tustin, California, had warned us that the most difficult part of the international adoption was waiting after you'd chosen your child. That was an understatement. The months drug by as we waited for THE call – the one that would give us two precious weeks to get our affairs in order and fly to Moscow.

As the days drug by, we kept ourselves busy working as elementary school teachers and accumulating all the items we had been instructed to bring on the trip. There were boxes of diapers, wads of crisp, new single dollar bills, and a variety of other gifts to purchase. Evidently, we learned later, that gift giving was an embedded custom in the Russian culture. It allowed for preferential treatment on the part of the benefactor. So, the shopping spree proceeded as time continued to crawl.

The day the call came was both thrilling and manic. Instead of the two weeks' notice we had been promised, our plane was leaving in two days. That might not appear so daunting, but we were still without Visas. Two days to receive Visas was a tall task. If we hadn't learned by now, we were quickly discovering that the process we were immersed in was uncompromising. We were at the mercy of the adoption gods.

To make matters worse, the threat of Y2K was ever present. Worries of crumbling, "worldwide infrastructures for industries ranging from banking to air travel" loomed large. In many ways, we truly felt like we were carrying the weight of the world.

The day of our Lufthansa flight to Berlin arrived. There'd be a short layover in Berlin before continuing on to Moscow. Three more hours after the already 13 hours from LAX. My wife and I were filled with one part fatigue and one part adrenalin. Up to this point, nothing had seemed all that unfamiliar. The terminal in Germany, though not a carbon copy of America's airports, was somewhat similar. What jolted our systems into know we were out of our elements was the walk through the airport in Moscow.

Signs all in Russian. Russian language being spoken all around us. Security with some of the sternest demeanors we'd ever seen. We had a tremendous amount of luggage and needed a cart, but they cost money and again, everything was in Russian. So, we drug our luggage through a winding corridor which led to the security check. That's when things proceeded to get really scary. Personnel were carrying weapons and dead serious. We followed other people hoping they were leading us in the right direction. We eventually came to a manned booth, and moved toward it. We were shouted at and realized they only wanted us to approach one at a time. Good start. Now if we could just keep from getting shot.

Making it past the security checkpoint, rows of people appeared, many holding signs with names. We frantically looked for Doolittle, and it wasn't long before we saw it. We exhaled a collective sigh of relief. It felt as if we'd been holding our breaths for the last 10 minutes.

Our driver/interpreter was extremely friendly and helpful. He immediately grabbed a large portion and led us to his car. It was a small compact, as we later found out was quite common. We barely had enough room for the three of us and the luggage. He proceeded through downtown Moscow, leading us to our hotel. The first thing we noticed was a great deal of traffic and the intense smell of carbon monoxide. Emission control was either lacking or nonexistent altogether.

The remaining story was even more dramatic, tense, and stress-filled than the waiting. But that will have to wait for another day. Suffice it to say that through it all, nothing compared to the moment we held our 14-month-old baby girl in our arms for the first time. We had arrived in more ways than one at the start of a new adventure. We embraced with open arms the happiest moment of our lives.

A Memory I Don't Want Dying With Me

BY CHUCK DOOLITTLE

My Dad taught me tennis and golf. They became two of my favorite sports. I'm sure my love of them was due to him, as well as my love of the Los Angeles Dodgers. I don't always think back kindly when it comes to my dad. But I do when it comes to his love of sports and how that influenced my life. Especially tennis. I went on to play three years of varsity tennis at Corona High School. I never reached number one on the team, but I was number two for three years. I felt accomplished. There were many wonderful memories of playing on that team. But as great as those memories were, none were as fulfilling as one time when I was playing my dad.

My dad, mom, brother, sister, and I spent many hours over the years at the old Corona Civic Center tennis courts. Countless evenings of fun were spent learning the requisite skills to hit a tennis ball over a net more times than your opponent. As the youngest, and presumably the least skilled, I often was paired with my mom, who was a little less athletic than the others. However, we would also mix things up and rotate partners so, eventually, I'd play my dad. At this point in his life, he was the best of all of us. When you played dad, you wanted to be on your game. Partly, to show him how good you were becoming, and partly, so he wouldn't seem bored or unchallenged. Easier said.

From the get-go, I felt like I had something to prove. I was five years younger than my brother and seven years younger than my sister. I often wished I could be as good as them, not to mention my dad. But I was competitive and a pretty natural athlete. So, I just had to be patient, which wasn't my strong suit. Little by little the months passed and I noticed I wasn't being paired up with my mom as often. In fact, my mom was starting to suggest she sit while the rest of us played. My confidence was growing. As much as I wanted to beat my siblings, my main goal was to beat my dad. It seemed lofty, but I was determined. Since there were five of us, I didn't get to play him one-on-one as much as I wanted, but when I did, I loved it. I could gauge just how far I had come and how far I had to go to beat him - which would prove no small task.

Witnessing my siblings' improvement, I realized we were a gifted tennis family. My sister would go on to play tennis in college and my brother was good in his own right. As competitive as I was with my siblings, my main focus remained my dad. I could see that I was finally coming into my own as a solid player. And then the night arrived.

I couldn't have predicted this night. I just knew that I was going to be playing dad and would be giving my all to beat him. And that's what happened. First it was a game, and then it became a set. After losing that first game, dad wanted to go for a set and try to regain his dominance. But it wasn't meant to be. It was my night. From then on, the tide had turned. Though he would occasionally take a game here or there, that long time dominance was gone. The strange thing is, my feelings that day were not what I expected. Instead of jubilance for finally beating him, the paternal pinnacle of tennis in our family, my emotions seemed more sadness than elation. The passing of the baton came with a strong realization that time had caught up with my dad. As skilled as he still was, even he couldn't hold off the inevitability of his teenage son becoming the stronger athlete. And yet, he did win that night. He won my respect for handling with class an experience he surely saw coming, difficult as it must have been.

Yes, my dad contributed greatly to my love of sports. He most certainly instilled in me an appreciation for competition and the will to win. But he also showed me grace in defeat. And that was the true lesson from those family tennis nights that I would take with me for the rest of my life.

Getting Started

BY JERRY ELLINGSON

When she walked into the Drop-In Center that morning, I thought she looked familiar, but I couldn't quite place her. I walked over to her and said, "Hello." She asked if I had some time to talk for a few minutes.

"If you have time for a cup of tea or coffee and a muffin, we'll have this whole place to ourselves in ten minutes. Everyone's getting ready to go up the hill to the Salvation Army for lunch. I have someone new in town that I'm just getting some information together for and I want to get him with some people he can walk up with so he doesn't get lost. Does that work for you?"

She said that would be fine and headed to the coffee urn while I got back to the other guests as they prepared to leave. When everyone had left, I went back to her. She explained to me that she had some problems she needed to solve and she was so overwhelmed she didn't know how to start. She had heard that I could possibly help her with some of the things bothering her.

I invited her into the office, got out two pads of paper and pens and told her we could make a list of things she would like help with, and not to worry about putting them in order. We would just write them all down and sort them out later.

Her first item was obviously, her most pressing. It was her landlord. Jeannie was living on Quadra Island. It was just a short ferry ride from Campbell River. She had found a reasonably priced place to rent and had been there a couple of years, but her landlord was becoming more aggressive. He had even come to the point of suggesting that she might want to exchange sexual favors for part of her rent. When she declined, trying to be as diplomatic as possible, he began hanging around and waiting for her to come home from work at night. She was afraid, because, as a landlord, he had a key to her apartment and he reminded her often. She needed to find another apartment, but it wasn't easy in her price range. She was hoping I could refer her to some agencies that might help her find another place to live. That was her number one item on her list. I told her I could certainly help her with that, but number two on her list was her rights as a renter, and I could help her with the laws. We sat together and made our identical lists of about fifteen or sixteen items. Finally, she said, "I think that's it. There's just so much, I don't know where to begin and I feel so overwhelmed, I can't even think."

"OK," I said, "let's get started at the top, because that's the most important. We need to get you away from that landlord."

I pulled out a binder that held information on renters' rights. I had a lot of binders on a lot of subjects now. My husband and I had moved to Vancouver Island, British Columbia, Canada in September of 2003. My husband was Canadian, so I just came along with him. As soon as we crossed the border, he smiled at me and said, "Now you're the alien." We were so happy in our new home. Then, in February, he died of a heart attack and I was alone in a different country. In April, I saw a newspaper article about a drop-in center that needed volunteers. I went to the Volunteer Center, signed up and by May I was working there. It was a shoestring endeavor. They didn't have any funding – just raised what they could from the community. It needed help and I needed to throw myself into something so hard I could forget. I worked hard through the years to make Helpsync the best I could. I joined other groups and gathered as much information as I could to help locals in need, as well as those moving up and down the Island. I was proud of the fact that as an American, I knew how to help a Canadian living in poverty, get a divorce for free – and even found out how to have the filing fee waived. My notebooks held everything anyone might need.

I pulled a spare copy of the Renters' Rules out of my binder, highlighted some sections that pertained to Jeannie and gave them to her. Then I got some numbers out of my card file that could get her some leads on rentals that were reasonable. "This is your priority." I said. We talked about some things she could do to keep herself safe, without aggravating her landlord, until she found another place. Then we began walking through the list. She had a problem that needed law advice. I told her about the local lawyer that offered free help on Thursday mornings and offered to go with her. She thought a minute and then said, "No, I think I'm okay."

"Call me if you change your mind." I said.

"I will, but I think I can do all of this," she said as she looked at her list. "It doesn't seem like so much now that the hard stuff is out of the way."

She sat back in her chair with a relaxed "Thank you." "You know, I still have that lamp."

Then I knew why she looked familiar. When I first started at Helpsync, we had a monthly parking lot sale of donated items from the community to raise money for the rent. She and her boyfriend came to the very first sale I worked. They had just found an apartment together. There was a table lamp she fell in love with. It had a peach ceramic base. She asked how much it was. I told her $2.50. She looked in her purse and found some coins. She asked her boyfriend if he had any money. He checked his pockets and gave her everything he had. They counted their coins out and had 47 cents. I held my hand out to take the money and gave them the lamp. "But it's not enough." She said.

"It's okay," I said. "It will look beautiful in your new place." She was ecstatic when they left.

"Are you two still together?" I asked.

"No. We had just finished Rehab that day. He didn't make it. I couldn't stay with him and survive, so I broke it off." She thanked me again and promised to come back if she needed anything else.

"Or just to chat, anytime." I said.

Everyone would be coming back from lunch soon. But I enjoyed those few, blissful moments alone after she left. I remembered back through the years to the day Jeannie bought the lamp. As she walked away with her boyfriend, carrying the lamp, Kelvin, one of the Helpsync founders, walked up to me and said, "You sold the lamp." I told him the whole story and he smiled knowingly at me.

"Oh, Jerry," he said, "they will probably go around the corner and sell it for drug money."

Now, I had the knowing smile. I couldn't wait to see him. I wouldn't gloat too much when I told him about my day. Maybe just a little.

Miss Dickinson Regrets

BY ELLEN ESTILAI

Miss Dickinson regrets that she is unable to accept the kind invitation of Ms. Estilai to attend her imaginary dinner party.

Because I cannot stop for Fame
I dine alone—complete.
My table spare, the dinner fare
Not showy—but replete.

Not just because He will be there,
With Songs of Self and grass—
And organs pulsing, sinew, bone—
Forgive—I think I'll pass.

Instead, it's singing of Myself
That hampers me the most—
The queries of my fellow Guests,
The proddings of my Host.

Doubtless He'll sing of multitudes—
Of Space 'tween Suns and Worlds.
I'd just hum the pulses of
The Space between the Words.

(De)Composition

BY ELLEN ESTILAI

Purple irises—spent,
splayed atop pomegranate branches,
hide layers of abundance and regret,
an archaeology of excess, a diary of surfeit:
Tuesday's scallions melt into
Thursday's ignored avocados fade into
last year's squandered mulberries.

Pitchfork tines spear shriveled kumquats,
upend clots of shrunken cucumber,
surrender fists of spotted cauliflower.
But drunken fruit flies have no regrets.
Microbes toil without judgment,
make way for next year's abundance.
Our transgressions dissolve into absolution.

Why I Keep A Midwife on Speed Dial

by Bryan Franco

Anger does not always happen
as screaming,
yelling,
stomping of feet,
fists clenching,
teeth gritting,
furrowed brows,
tattered nerves.

Anger is not always
born of aggression.
It can be born
of hurt and confusion
from a womb unaware
of the existence of its pregnancy
conceived via an act
of deception or betrayal
from a night of passion
that materialized
into a morning after
that transformed
into an insidious,
compartmentalized ghost.

Anger is not always loud.
Anger can exist in silence and stagnation.
Anger may not have hard edges
that cut and bruise

all who come in contact with it.
It can be soft.
It can be amorphous,
made of quicksand,
encompassing its host
in suspended animation
causing phantom paralysis
till whoever owns it
realizes the phantom
is a phantom,
a figment
of an emotion
or a feeling
or a reaction
to a life event (or events)
that happened
in the past
that is exactly what it is: the past
which can't exist
in the present or future
due to the fact
that the past
can only exist
in the past
then the anger
starts to shed its skin
to reveal a hollow inside
that is a breath long held
now exhaled
and let go.

because you have nothing to be jealous about

BY BRYAN FRANCO

Allow me to introduce myself.
They say my skin is green,
but I ain't no Kermit the Frog;
I am Miss Piggy incarnate!

Honestly, my skin has no color.
Not even black or white.

I will be your best friend if you let me.

Of course, you will:
because the enticing aroma of my pheromones
is akin to carbon monoxide.
Except there ain't no little box
you can put in your basement
or wire to your heart or soul to detect me.

When we show up at a social event,
I promise to make you
the life of the party.

If we don't get invited back,
It is their loss.

We got each other's backs and all that.

Our you-know-what don't stink.

Our farts are made of carbon monoxide.

My toxicity has never killed anyone.

The more of me you breathe,
the more I will be your persona.

Forgiven

BY BRYAN FRANCO

I want to write a poem about forgiveness.

But

I am not sure

it will qualify

as a poem.

Maybe it will

just

be a list of regrets

of how I have chosen

to live my life.

I am unsure if I am capable of forgiveness.

I am unsure if I understand what this word is.

Besides powerful and confusing.

Is forgiveness

an idea,

a construct,

an act of contrition?

When I forgive someone else,

do I also

need to forgive myself

for finding myself

in a situation

that might have been

beyond my control?

Must I feel guilty

for not giving closure

to someone
who has wronged me?
Am I allowed
to forgive
and not forget?
Or will that
just
be lip service
to a word
that is so arbitrary
in its parameters
it needs
to be seen
as
an idea or construct?
Is forgiveness an all or nothing deal?
Is total forgiveness achievable?
Can there be levels of forgiveness?
Does it exist on a spectrum?
Does it exist on a spectrum?
Does it exist on a spectrum?

Forgiveness:
you exist in my vocabulary,
but I have yet to define you.
I shall try to write a poem about you
so you can exist in totality.

The Least Sweet Fruit on Planet Earth

BY BRYAN FRANCO

I am a connoisseur of sour grapes.
To be palatable, sour grapes must always be
sweetened and/or spiced up exponentially.
Making sour grape jelly takes an inordinate amount of sugar.
To ferment sour grapes, one must soak them in at least
1 ½ times the volume of raw honey for at least a month.
Sour grapes are most often used for vinegar,
but the vinegar can only be used in small amounts.
No matter how sour grapes are consumed,
no matter how sour grapes taste in their altered state,
sour grapes are still sour grapes.
Sour grapes will always cause heartburn
in one way or another.

File Box

BY NAN FRIEDLEY

Recently, I became
keeper of the dog-eared
flour-coated, butter-stained
recipe cards from her
kitchen and generations of kitchens
before hers

She was the one I'd
call if my white sauce was lumpy
I'm still following her
recipes hoping she's looking over
my shoulder reminding me
to keep stirring

Tidy Pantoum

BY NAN FRIEDLEY

my washer died today
had to find a laundromat
darks and lights loaded in baskets
quarters ready to feed hungry slots

had to find a laundromat
tiny box of Tide from a vending machine
quarters ready to feed hungry slots
sudsy clothes dance in the washer

tiny box of Tide from a vending machine
bathroom is locked, no key in sight
sudsy clothes dance in the washer
single sock searches for its mate

bathroom is locked, no key in sight
darks and lights loaded in baskets
single sock searches for its mate
my washer died today

Between Salon Visits in a Pandemic

BY NAN FRIEDLEY

I clipped my own bangs with dull silver scissors
leaned over the bathroom sink

referenced a step by step YouTube guide, eyeballed
my cellphone and the bathroom mirror as

dry hair was parted on the left, sliced at an angle
across my wrinkled, worried brow

randomly snipped stray strands hanging
annoyingly in my eyes

quick assessment in the mirror and I continued
the process until I was a twin

of my second grade school picture with stubby
bangs held back by butterfly barrettes

AARP Member Since 2012

by Nan Friedley

I remember things from long ago
avocado rotary phone on the kitchen wall

coily cord stretched to say "hello"
tv screens, black and white glow
three channels sign off, test pattern says, "that's all"
still remember things from long ago

cars were heavy and slow, no AC, just an AM radio
bench seat in the front, no seat belts, none at all
hand crank to close and open the window

typewriters were better than a written memo
tiny type, inky ribbon, return lever on the Royal
now replaced by a system known as Windows

Seems I forget names of people I used to know
common words I don't recall
memory is still here, just slow
it will come to me — maybe tomorrow

catastrophe

by Nan Friedley

look at ME
sprawled in the hall
waving my paw
under your door
meowing on behalf
of my little sister
Buttercup and ME
just letting you know
WE're hungry
you haven't fed US
for weeks
or days
or since this morning
or an hour ago
OUR bowls are empty
and so are WE

Gonna be Baking Brownies for the Beatles

BY CAMILLE GAON

Many moons ago in one of my nine thousand lives, I worked part-time as a private chef. I came under the radar of a head-hunter who contacted me about a live-out job for a young writer whose claim to fame was an almost decade-long hit of a multi-Emmy-ed TV series.

The client just moved into a newly built from scratch house in Beverly Hills. I was living in Malibu and only worked for clients in the Malibu area, but this was a very high-profile writer and I thought it would spice up my resume so I accepted the meeting. It also paid a lot, which was reason #1.

The house was pathetically nouveau-riche ostentation at its best. To my chagrin, the house manager had already outfitted the kitchen with what she thought a true chef's kitchen should be equipped with. Think Sears marries JC Penny and has a 99 Cent Store child.

The initial meeting went very well and I was informed by the prospective employer that one of the former Beatles had a house next door and would be coming over practically nightly when he's in town to hang out in "the playroom" which was sort of a cross between a studio for creative endeavors and an opium den. They liked to get high on marijuana and would require some really exceptionally sweet tooth focused munchies. "Oh, they will really love my rich double chocolate chip brownies with a mountain of freshly whipped cream," I thought to myself.

I assured him that I had lots of decadent desserts in the treasure trove of my sweets repertoire and also agreed that I would of course be extremely discreet about these "Enquirer-worthy" goings on.

He liked that I was unfazed by the celebrity of his neighbor and I credited my casual aplomb with which I took the news to the fact that I grew up in a neighborhood of celebrities as a child and currently lived in star-laden Malibu. As a child, I used to return Efrem Zimbalist Jr's escaped peacocks to him and trick or treat at Dick Van Dyke's house. So, I was pretty nonplussed when he mentioned the former Beatles' name.

Since I "passed" this part of his interview I was then invited to cook a demo-meal for him and three neighbors, all of whom were not Beatles, Stones, musicians or even anyone of any notoriety. "Good," I thought with assuaged relief, "I don't want the pressure of baking brownies for a Beatle on my maiden voyage in this ill-equipped kitchen."

I was to cook a simple Sunday dinner. They liked Mexican food so I decided I'd pull out all the stops and make my self-invented "Mexican Lasagna." It was always a crowd pleaser but it was not simple. I'd accompany it with a colorful Santa Fe style-salad and my non-traditional ceviche-style guacamole.

For dessert he wanted an apple pie with ice cream. My daughter excelled at baking pies and I paired it with a crème brûlée gelato from my favorite gelato joint in Beverly Hills.

It was all so promising. After this demo dinner, I'd be baking brownies for the Beatle who was my favorite when I was ten years old. I'd first laid eyes on him in person when I attended his California concert at Dodger Stadium back in the 60's. What a kick it would be cooking for someone of such iconic status who created music that was woven into my childhood and teen years that defined so much of those special times. With any luck maybe at least one of the other Beatles would join in as well.

I armed myself with everything I'd need for the dinner and even found a small miniature hot pepper plant to put on the buffet table where everything was to be self-serve. I brought my own lasagna pan and started to unpack the groceries.

The employer-to-be came in and said he had been gifted with this new fancy expensive German ceramic chef's knife and gave it to me to use. I'd never used ceramic before and looked forward to trying it, especially since his house manager had selected knives that were of questionable pedigree.

He mentioned that he was told it was very sharp and to be very careful. Inwardly, I laughed to myself, thinking I'd wielded much more dangerous looking knives and never had so much as a nick, but I smiled graciously and thanked him, chuckling to myself that telling a chef that a knife is sharp is like telling a surfer to expect sand at the beach. He said he was leaving for several hours and would be back for dinner at 7 and that one of his assistants would be upstairs if I needed anything.

I took the knife out of its "designed to be precocious" box, and while cleaning it before use, somehow managed to slice the shit out of my ring finger. Suddenly, my cocky attitude from earlier dissolved into thin air embarrassment and I had not even begun the labor-intensive prep work on this multi-course meal that had to be as presentation-worthy as a Queen at her Coronation.

Wildly searching for a First-Aid kit was to no avail. I didn't want to ask the assistant where it was and admit that I had klutzily cut myself with the knife! And a knife that came with a verbal warning to boot. So, I quadruple-wrapped a thick paper towel around my finger and kept replacing it because it continuously kept turning bright red. My next fear was that I'd run out of home-made paper towel bandages.

To touch on legalities at this juncture, I want to offer assurance that not a single drop of blood went into the making of the food. The sink was another matter.

Racing against the clock and floored over the Red Sea in the kitchen sink, I managed to stay calm. I always do well in a crisis, so I knew I'd somehow pull this off. I did however, pray that I'd make it through this without having the host and his guests arrive to find me passed out on the kitchen floor due to the extensive loss of blood.

This was way worse than the Julia Child cooking show segment where she cut her finger whilst deboning a chicken. I comforted myself with the fact that at least I was in good company.

If it could happen to Julia then it must be some sort of a rite of passage for a chef to endure this type of a frat boy hazing ritual.

Interrupting this moment of self-consolation, the assistant suddenly appeared on the upstairs landing which unfortunately overlooked the kitchen. He sprung up so abruptly that it was like a joker popping out of a Jack-in the box. "Oh no. How long has he been watching this performance from his nosebleed seat?" I dejectedly mused to myself.

He said he was going to take off and asked if I needed anything. I ate some crow and humbly asked for a Band-Aid.

I finished the prep and the dinner with haste and patted myself on the back with the non-bloodied hand for always allowing for last minute detours or unanticipated segues, commonly known as disasters. Ironically, the meal presentation looked like Martha Stewart put it together with no hint whatsoever as to the Jackson Pollock-esque shenanigans that took place on the kitchen counter battlefield a few hours earlier.

My daughter's home-made apple pie was also a big hit, so much so that the employer-to-be told me he ate an entire half the next day after smoking a joint.

But in spite of that, I did not get the job. At that news my first thought was that the Jack-in-the box ratted me out. The headhunter told me that the prospective employer decided to go with a chef that his writing partner recommended. This being the writing partner who recommended the builder, construction crew, house manager, landscape designer and untold, others whom he insisted were a must for a newly arrived big shot in the biz. It was just as well.

The commute on PCH everyday would have driven me to drink if not beaten out by the fumes in the "play room" where the former Beatle marijuana smoking and jamming marathons were to take place.

And last but not least, a further confirmation of the dodged bullet came when it was time to get paid after submitting my invoice to the business manager, yet another pick by the writing partner, for the "Demo Meal". It took over two months to get paid!

Well, the hell with marmalade skies from Lucy in the Sky with Diamonds!

Uncle Juan Invents a Burrito

BY RICHARD GONZALEZ

My aunt, Ruth Lopez de Franco (Cuca), arrived one day at our home in San Bernardino, circa 1950, and invited my mom to join her on a trip to Anaheim to look for and visit a long-lost member of the Franco family, a certain uncle (tio) Juan Romero. A member of the Romero family had lived next door to the Francos in Ontario where Cuca and Mom had grown up.

Their one-day trip was successful. During the dinner hour that night, Mom was delighted to tell us about the trip and laughed as she described Tio Juan's Mexican tortilla factory (tortilleria) and takeout food dispensary. Uncle Juan had used a Coca Cola sign to list the menu of items available such as tacos (made with corn shells), enchiladas, tamales, chile rellenos, or a dozen corn tortillas – each priced at 25 cents. At the bottom of the offerings was a hand-drawn listing for "burritos" also for 25 cents.

Mom and Cuca scolded him for coming up with a dumb idea for describing a flour tortilla taco as a burrito.

Tio Juan explained that there is a major ditch construction project on Pioneer Blvd and many of the gringos who work on it have learned to like the Romeros' foodstuffs. He often has to explain what Mexican food is all about. One day a new customer ordered some tacos and as he was leaving, he spotted Juan's kid who was standing by the deli case munching on a homemade (flour) taco.

The man asked, "what's he eating?" He told him, "A taco." The man looked at his order and asked, "Well what are these?" Juan said, "Oh, those are tacos also." Clearly, the man was annoyed and probably thought he wasn't getting the authentic stuff.

As soon as he left, Juan reminded his wife that she should make sure that little Pepe doesn't stray into the customer waiting area.

(Editor's note: the kid was eating a homemade flour tortilla taco. It was customary for Mexican families to make a morning batch of flour tortillas for the daily personal consumption and to offer any visitor a taco to go that was filled with whatever was brewing on the stove. For reasons unknown, flour tortillas were not readily available for commercial sale.)

A few days later a newcomer came in – a very tall gringo. As he was leaving, he spotted Juan's kid – again munching on a flour taco. "What's he eating?"

"Ay Dios mio, oh my God," Uncle Juan panicked. This man was huge. He blurted out, "Oh he's eating a burrito."

"How much are they?"

"Well, uh, 25 cents."

"Let me try one, he ordered."

Well, as he asked his wife to make one to sell, she started to argue with him, "One doesn't sell flour tortilla tacos because... "Shh, callate, shh, quiet," he told her. "Don't you see how big that man is? And didn't I ask that you keep little Pepe behind the partition?"

The same man came again the next day with his buddies and ordered burritos.

So that's how uncle Juan stumbled on to a new clientele of construction workers who suddenly preferred burritos instead of sandwiches.

We laughed at mom's story about Tio's escapade. But why did he name it a burrito?

Well, Juan explained that ever since he came to the United States, he thought it was funny that Americanos would name a wiener on a bun a "hot dog." So that's how he came up with a name befitting a Mexican snack.

A few days later, Mom came up with a plan to sell flour tortillas at our store. This time it was dad who was upset and scolded mom for coming up with a dumb idea. "Everybody makes them at home so why would anybody buy them," he demanded to know?

Oh yea, I wondered, who?

Refreshing the Light

BY MARK GRINYER

What do I know of this bright noise
crisp in the gray day's dawn? The voice
of breezes in summer leaves, lifting
the chatter of songbirds bickering
scattered seeds, sunlight flickering
like a nature show on TV screens
refreshing the light again and again
with sounds that bend like dreams
through crystal prisms of doubt,
grown amid some desolate scene
where greed transcends the night
made bright by the flush of dawn
the recent too-dark hours gone
into which I try once more to shout
against the noise, ignorant louts.

Lies

by Mark Grinyer

Death is the mother of beauty
Wallace Stevens

I love these lies, our lies, the promises we haven't kept
to diet and lose some weight, to leave the house
more often now that Covid wanes again.
The vaccine is in our arms. We'd like to think
we'll be safe away from home again—out.
We've stayed inside instead.

So I tell myself, "safety's not everything,".
and I tell you, "we'll be safe enough, I guess,"
when, as they asked, we visit our son and his wife,
and their ailing new dog, Mac. He has beautiful
brindled fur, but hip dysplasia may end his life.
This trip is nothing to fear, an afternoon's excursion
into the wilds of LA.

Mac'll be happy to see us, I think, as will the kids,
in their beautiful, renovated house, our old house.
We left it years ago, for a newer, more modern place,
and we've stayed away, for years. I went back, once,
but you've not visited it yet. It now has a yellow door,
colorful walls, and gray-toned wooden floors.
They've added a second bath, and a lovely, larger,
more modern kitchen. It's no longer the small,
50's tract house box we bought when you were pregnant
with our only son. But these may also be lies,

Beautiful lies, typical of love today.
I know that you don't trust this trip—
an hour or more on crowded freeways,
poking along from the suburbs into the city,
with me driving, my fists clenched
on the steering wheel of our old car.
We'll follow my one-time route to work.
It was easier then, when we were younger
and so much less afraid.

Near death from age, are we more beautiful now?
Will we visit again next week? Probably not.
We lie about trying to escape the prisons in which we live.
Behind locked gates and doors, away from bumbling,
weak-hipped dogs, the bustle of young beginnings,
we are locked in these old lies.

The First Winter Storm

BY MARK GRINYER

After years of drought
the first winter storm this year
is a cyclone bomb. It dumps
seventeen feet of water into
Northern California lakes.

It drowns a million acres
of wildfires burning the state;
good news, you'd think, but it
slides mountains into the ocean
and buries roads in debris.

Are we thankful for this bounty?
I don't know. But birds still search
the soaking earth for seeds to eat,
goldfinches seek their thistle feasts
and find them not where they should be.

They were lost in the summer's burning,
or buried by earth's collapse
flooding the slippery slopes
that cut off our retreat
into some less glorious place.

My Mother's Wake

by Mark Grinyer

Remembering Lt. Helen Lynch Grinyer, RN.

The day we buried my mother,
after the funeral services
    and after our trip to the veteran's cemetery,
    the twenty-one gun salute,
and a short drive to my brother's home,
the whole family was there.
    My brother pulled from their storage place
    two bottles of quality port.
My mom had hidden them away.
"For my wake," she said,
    "a proper Irish wake," where drinks are drunk
    stories told, memories are unlocked,
and laughter fills the room—or the patio, in our case.
Two bottles to loosen the tongues of all,
    the seven of us, her children,
    and her few remaining friends.
We sat in a ring on that crowded porch
and drank our fill that night. Most were drunk
    as they wanted to be when we opened that old port.
    Tiny glasses in hand, we toasted her long life.
It was a fine party, full of memories, tears and laughter;
full of stories told—stories of growing up:
    of those ringworm weeks in Maryland, when she treated
    our shaved heads with ether, as cold as winter ice;

the time, after an argument, when she threw her shoe at dad,

on the driveway in front of our house;

    or the time she saved a neighbor's child

    suffocating in a bed sheeted with plastic wrap.

He turned blue when his breathing stopped, but she revived him.

Her skills as a nurse were apparent then, to all,

    as was the love and care

    with which she lived and stood for life.

We laughed at the stories of ringworm and thrown shoes,

and cried for the child who lived,

    but was crippled the rest of his life. He still

    died young but was saved that afternoon.

Her wake stretched into darkness

past moonrise as we reminisced. We laughed. We cried.

    We took those memories home with us, and the heritage

    she graced us with, of love passed on with hangovers that night.

My Grandpa's Hatchet

BY MARK GRINYER

Where might it be?
The rusty hatchet he used
to behead the rooster
that chased me across the lawn
when I was six, in Illinois,
on that fine summer day.

Grabbing those piston legs,
he held that squawking beast
in one hard hand with ease,
and brought the hatchet down
on that loud bird's scrawny neck.
Then he flung the carcass away.

I watched it run across
the lawn's green grass
under tall old blue spruce trees,
and into my grandpa's flowerbeds,
full of color and life. His life's
blood spurted six feet up in the air.

Until he began to wobble and stagger
like a drunk on a toot.
Finally, he fell to the ground,
still at last. My grandpa
said, "go get that bird."
I did,

And I helped him prep
its carcass to eat.
Grandpa left his hatchet
stuck in the stump
he used as a chopping block.
I wonder where it went.

Change of Heart

(Four Haikus)

BY MILAN HAMILTON

Change is hard
Becomes harder
When so is the heart.

Change is hard
What to do
Soften the heart.

Change gonna come
Ready or not
Heartbreak.

No pain no gain
No grief no relief
Acceptance.

A Chair at the Table

BY MILAN HAMILTON

(A Haiku)

Empty chair noticed
One flower opens closes
Tears flowing freely.

Intimacy

by Milan Hamilton

I used to crave it
Thought I could brave it
But when it's approaching
I fear the encroaching
"Man the barricades –
Come to my aid!" someone cries.

A little understanding
Just a little understanding
Is all that I ask.
My wife penetrates
To the quick in a flash
"I understand you," barricades turn to ash.

Babies and Bathwater

by Milan Hamilton

How many civilizations have come and gone
As the universe moves along
While we humans pile up endless debris
Until we are choking on what we have made
Filling every ocean, every sea
With the waste of our throwaway society.
The thirsty Land cries out "Mother save me!"
There is no one to hear because everyone is busy
Making progress toward the magnificent extinction
Just like Lawrence Ferlinghetti told us
In the middle of it all comes the "smiling mortician."

Mercy

BY MILAN HAMILTON

Our neighbor has a dog named Mercy.
She is cute as can be.
I wonder if there's one named Clemency,
Or Sympathy, or Charity.
I never heard of any called Leniency or Pity.
The Puritans of old and New England
Named their daughters with all the virtues:
Faith, Hope, and (no pressure) Chastity,
As not so subtle reminders of their responsibilities.
Shakespeare's "What's in a name?" may be relevant.
I knew a girl named Rose once. And she did smell sweet.
I did some research and found that my name means "loveable."
I need to spend my time now turning that adjective into a verb.

God Save the Queen

by Milan Hamilton

Hi, I'm Buzzy. I'm a wild honeybee of the worker type and we just found this really cool tree branch to cluster around our queen, Labeezah. She's only six weeks old and she's really hot. That's what I was told anyway. My job is just to protect her and do all the other tasks, like taking care of all the fertilized eggs that those good-for-nothing drones have impregnated her with. Can you believe it? All they do is lay around all day waiting for sex-time? And then, we have to give the signal for everybody to go crazy and start strutting around for a chance with her and that's only about a dozen of the 400,000 or so of the lazy louts who get to spend any time with her, and we have to hang out and watch and then clean up the mess they leave. Then we have to tend to all the eggs and raise the kids. Our only sense of justice is the dozen lucky drones all meet their maker in the mating act, so that's something, I guess.

Anyway, I was saying, we just found this cool tree branch to cluster up. Then, I kid you not, this dude with a big pickup truck shows up with a camera crew no less. He starts shaking the branch so violently that most of our newly formed hive falls to the truck bed, including our hot queen. I don't know how but this dude in the truck kidnaps our queen. He's filming the whole thing as he forces her into this big box. Well, you know what happens next—pandemonium that's what! All the workers and drones are all over the truckbed and flying all around in confusion. Someone says: "She's in that big box thing." So everyone starts marching right into that box.

But hold it! In the confusion a couple of wasps just landed right by the entrance to the box. They are five times the size of any one of us. "May Day! May Day!" The call goes out. Two squads of about 8 to 10 form up immediately—all of them workers of course—not those cowardly drones of the masculine persuasion—fall into one of the phalanxes. We don't even wait for a signal. We are on those invaders like flies on honey. They are powerful but don't stand a chance. They must be hungry because normally wasps would give up and leave in a hurry, confronted by our overwhelming numbers. But they decide to stay and fight to the death. Bad decision—on all sides actually. Because when we are done stinging them to their demise, we too have given our last full measure of devotion to our queen. But that is what we signed on for. That is who we are. We are the worker bees. "God save the Queen."

St. Valentine was No Romantic

by Milan Hamilton

St. Valentine lost his head in century three
Not for some romantic notion
But due to his devotion
And the miracle of sight restoration
Which is how he got to be a saint.

Geoffrey Chaucer made the love connection
Much later—a millennium in fact—
Making the astute observation
Of birds engaging in the mating act
On that headless Saint's day celebration.

Some French Duke languishing in London's Tower
Wrote his wife he was "sick of love,"
Was first to say, far as we can tell,
"You're my valentine."
Shakespeare penned love's tragic side
Romeo and Juliet made all too clear
And lovestruck Ophelia beside
Called Hamlet her dear Valentine.
So when did February 14 become
Captive to chocolatiers
And industrial, mass-production,
cards for every romantic seduction?

Finding love is hard these days—
I've given up searching—
Not looking for the pony in that pile—
I'll just be going natural now—
Love itself will not go out of style.

The Dead and Restless

BY NIKKI HARLIN

Everyone can tell that you're dead.
Since you drag your twisted foot

around the city. Arms outstretched
to nothing. Holding your guts

in your purse. Though you can still feel
fear: You're afraid of secrets

swarming your body long after
the skin grays and how you may deserve

the drops of saliva falling from the stray
dog's mouth before you're devoured

alone. Still, nothing can keep you
from seeking out flesh and moaning

woefully when you find it in parking lots
and other public places, broad daylight

damning you. But feels like kissing
your first brains and shame

was the first appendage to shrivel off.
Your smile, held up by staples,

is infectious and promises a home
for fingers and bone. When you finally

get him alone, indeed it seems he's the only man left.
As you tongue his neck your eyes go slack
and the worms in your heart start to dance.

El abuso del hombre hacia la mujer

by Doralba "Dora" Harmon

Mi nombre es Dora y por naturaleza soy amante de la justicia y en medio de tantas y tantas injusticias como las que presenciamos todos los días y en todas partes del mundo, una de las que más me hace hervir la sangre es la injusticia contra las mujeres. Por ser mujer y como la gran mayoría he sufrido el abuso por parte del hombre que por ser superior en fuerza física, su insaciable anhelo de poder y control, perversidad sexual y falta de sensibilidad y nobleza, las mujeres hemos sido sus víctimas usadas y acusadas desde épocas inmemoriales.

Los registros más antiguos de estos abusos comenzaron con dos de las instituciones más antiguas y que aún sobreviven. La santa iglesia católica apostólica y romana desde hace 2,000 años y la musulmana desde hace 1,400 años. Todas dos creadas y dirigidas sólo por hombres; han sido las religiones de todos, pero la mujer nunca ha tenido ni voz ni voto; todo lo que se le permite hacer es escuchar y obedecer ciegamente los mandatos órdenes de sus superiores. Yo nací dentro de la iglesia católica y por eso conozco algunos de sus mandatos, como amar y obedecer a tu esposo, estar ahí en las buenas y en las malas y si te pega y maltrata verbalmente cada vez que se le antoja, sufrir con paciencia los designios de Dios y nunca dejarlo porque lo que Dios ata nadie lo desata.

Cómo es posible que Dios nos designe semejante infierno? Por este infame lavado de cerebro, millones de mujeres han sufrido los más horrendos abusos físicos y emocionales y miles han muerto asesinadas por los hombres que dizque ante Dios prometieron amarlas y cuidarlas hasta que la muerte los separe. ¡Otro mandato! Hay que tener todos los hijos que Dios mande, no a los anticonceptivos, entonces parejas pobrísimas teniendo 10, 15 y más hijos, viviendo el infierno del hambre, la miseria, la enfermedad y la ignorancia. No al aborto y conozco a una mujer con cuatro invalidas, y porque cuatro? Porque tenía que obedecer las órdenes de no evitarlos, no abortarlos y no podía dejar de satisfacer sexualmente al marido, porque ella está ahí, es para amarlo y servirlo. Tenía que sufrir con paciencia los designios de Dios y de y de paso los cuatro invadidos tienen que compartir el mismo infierno de la madre, tiradas en una acera al sol y al agua, pidiendo limosnas para poder sobrevivir.

Pero entre más católicos traigamos al mundo, más crece la Santa Iglesia en poder y dinero. El tribunal de la Santa inquisición establecida en 1184 por el papa Lucio III, el cual se extendió por todo Europa y luego fue traído a las Americas en 1252, fue autorizado para usar la tortura y obtener la confesión de los reos, hasta el año 1821. Fueron cientos de años donde hombres, mujeres y niños fueron asesinados por los Templarios, que eran ejércitos pagados por la Santa iglesia católica y países aliados para exterminar a los ateos e impíos, quemando pueblos y ciudades enteras y a su paso violando mujeres y niños con la cruz en una mano y la espada en la otra....y todo en nombre de Jesus. Las mujeres fueron asesinadas lenta y dolorosamente en las hogueras por brujería. El jurado era compuesto por las autoridades eclesiásticas. Los representantes de Dios en la tierra, las condenaban a ser quemadas vivas por no creer en los mandatos de la Santa iglesia; de la misma manera exterminaron a los Cátaros, Rosacruces y muchas otras organizaciones religiosas y millones de indígenas en nuestro continente que se negaban a aceptar a otro Dios que no era el de ellos. También le prometió la iglesia que a todos los que entrarán al ejército de los Templarios, todos sus pecados les serán perdonados y al morir irían derechito al cielo. Es exactamente lo que hace el ejercito musulman hoy en día, ISIS les prometen que encontraran 72 vírgenes esperando por ellos cuando lleguen al cielo y aun en pleno siglo XXI, todavía hay quién cree semejantes estupideces y ahi estar arrodillados orando cinco veces al día y el resto del tiempo, asesinando a hombres, mujeres, y niños en nombre de Alá y lo llaman la guerra Santa. Pretenden exterminar a todos los impíos, que somos el resto del mundo que no creemos en Alá de la misma manera que ellos lo ven.

También en pleno siglo XXI existe el salvajismo despiadado y cruel del abuso del hombre hacia la mujer, cuando en países como Jordania, Turquía, Irán, Irak, Yemen y Pakistán, una mujer de la que el marido sospecha, o se queja de las palizas del marido.... debe ser ejecutada para limpiar el honor de la familia. Tiene derecho de quemarla viva su padre, su hermano o su cuñado, cualquier hombre de la familia. Cada año se registran más de 5.000 casos de crímenes de honor porque los que no se registran son muchísimos más. Las mismas madres asesinan a sus hijas al nacer, cuando sus maridos no quieren hijas mujeres.

Squad Filal sobrevivir al crimen de honor y hoy radicada en Suiza y después de 27 operaciones todo su cuerpo, su rostro aún es una pesadilla, anda con máscara y peluca, no solamente para ocultar su deformidad, sino también su personalidad y anda con guardaespaldas porque aun no la perdonan. Ella, como su madre, asesinó a siete de sus hermanas al nacer, ahorcándolas con el cable de teléfono y con la ayuda de su tía porque su padre no quería más hijas mujeres. Esta mujer publicó su historia en el libro "Quemada Viva".

Yo siempre creí que el amor de una madre para sus hijos era un lazo tan fuerte y sagrado que nada ni nadie podía romper. Pero al ver madres que son capaces de traer al mundo a 10 o más hijos a aguantar hambre, dolor, y miseria, otras que los traen sabiendo que vienen con incapacidades físicas o mentales, a vivir un verdadero infierno y las que son capaces de matar a sus hijas solo porque el marido no las quiere, entonces me doy cuenta que el lavado de cerebro, las ideas sembradas desde nuestros primeros años de vida por las religiones y la idiosincrasia delegar donde nacemos, son más poderosas que cualquier otra cosa sobre la tierra. Las primeras enseñanzas que nos llegan son de nuestros padres y por ello lo tomamos como la verdad absoluta y como se nos enseñó obediencia y respeto a nuestros padres y superiores, no teníamos derecho a pensar, ni mucho menos a opinar.

Yo tengo 82 años y hace 64 años que quise ir a la Universidad a estudiar abogacía, precisamente para luchar por los derechos de la mujer, pero mis padres me dijeron que la universidad era solo para los hombres. Las mujeres pertenecen al hogar criando a sus hijos y atendiendo a sus maridos y este fue el primer abuso del que fui víctima. Por supuesto, ignorancia es sinónimo de esclavitud, entre más ignorantes seamos, más fácil es para las iglesias y la Sociedad en general usarnos, abusarnos y esclavizarnos de todas las formas posibles como la realidad lo han hecho durante los últimos 2,000 años.

No teníamos derecho al voto, en muchas civilizaciones el esposo era escogido por los padres y en otros casos ella era vendida al mayor postor por unas cuantas veces. Se les negó el derecho de la mujer a sentir el placer natural en el acto sexual, entonces desde niñas les cortan el clítoris de sus partes privadas. El placer es solo para el hombre. Hay lugares en África donde la madre con un leño encendido al rojo vivo le queman los senos a su hija cuando estos empiezan a desarrollarse, para que los hombres no se las llevan tan jovencitas de sus casas. Acabo de ver en la televisión que en San Juan De Chamulas, en Chiapas, una mujer de raza india casada a la edad de 14 años, porque el marido le pegaba decidió dejarlo, el aviso a la policía y la encarcelaron con una fianza de $24,700 pesos mexicanos. El maltrato, el abuso y el asesinato de mujeres en México, tiene el indice mas alto en nuestra continente y tiene tambien el indice de católicos mas alto del continente.

En pleno siglo XXI muchos siguen viendo a la mujer solamente como un objeto de placer, y negocio y entonces nace el más aberrante crimen y abuso del hombre hacia la mujer, la trata de placas, niñas menores de edad traídas de Suramérica, Centroamérica y México, algunos veces vendidas por sus propias madres, otras veces engañadas con ofertas de trabajo o con promesas de modelaje dinero y fama y por venir de familias donde muchas veces el padre es un borracho que maltrata tanto a la madre cómoda lo hijos y donde hay diez o más hermanos viviendo el infierno del hambre y la miseria y lo único que tienen en abundancia es ignorancia, entonces tanto la madre como las hijas son víctimas fáciles de los depredadores que las atraen por miles, para abastecer el más horripilante, macabro y asqueroso mercado sexual, pagado por las peores carroñas humanas en Estados Unidos y Europa, los países más avanzados del mundo en tecnología, dinero y poder, pero su avance moral o espiritual está en pañales.

Acabo de entrar a una organización para ayudar a redimir las vidas de estás pobres mujeres y en el primer día de entrenamiento me di cuenta de que la magnitud del tráfico humano es de 32 millones de dólares al año y que ahora sobrepasa el tráfico de drogas en el sur de California.

Designios de Dios dicen, como si Dios fuese un ser tan malvado que las han designado tragedias, dolor y miseria a todo el que se le antoja. También me enseñaron que Dios no manda más de lo que puedas soportar; porque entonces tanta gente se suicida bajo el peso de una tragedia que no fue capaz de enfrentar? Aprendí que mis errores no son pecados que me condenan eternamente a un infierno de llamas, sino que son lecciones que tengo que aprender para crecer como ser humano. El miedo es una de las emociones más fuertes del ser humano y por eso desde muy pequeños nos sembraron el miedo al infierno para hacernos creer todas las estupideces que nos enseñaron.

Hoy en día ya se que tanto el infierno como el Edén me lo creo yo misma a través de esa maravillosa mente que Dios me dio y el libre albedrío para elegir. No me asombra tanto que los hombres nos hayan usado, maltratado y abusado por tantos años, porque mientras uno se deje siempre habrá quien lo haga; lo que realmente me asombra es que lo hayamos permitido, que nos hayamos dejado maltratar por tantos años, porque si analizamos la realidad, en primer lugar somos mayoría, en segundo lugar somos tan inteligentes como ellos y desde que ganamos el derecho a votar y a ir a la Universidad. Ahora tenemos mujeres en altas posiciones de liderazgo, en las políticas y la ciencia que antes era solo para los hombres.

Hoy hay mujeres sobresalientes y destacadas en todos los campos del conocimiento humano, hasta astronautas e inclusive una Santa en plano siglo XXI y que realmente mereció el título, la Madre Teresa de Calcuta. Tenemos la fortaleza, la inteligencia, el conocimiento, el liderazgo y la maravillosa capacidad de reproducirnos que ellos no tienen, y con unos cantos sementales y bancos de semen, podríamos crear una Sociedad maravillosa donde el amor, el respeto y la armonía reinarán.

Otra Atlántida…. pero mientras tanto cada una de nosotras debemos luchar por cultivarnos intelectualmente y no permitir que nadie, ni por ningún motivo nos abuse. El amor propio, el orgullo y la dignidad son elementos esenciales para hacerse respetar e inculcar este principio en nuestras hijas en vez de la sumisión y la esclavitud ante un hombre o una ideología. Como madres es un deber romper con esta fatídica costumbre en nuestra sociedad, de mirar a la mujer como a un ser inferior que solamente sirve para tener hijos y brindar placer a los hombres.

Astraphobia

BY EDNA HELED

Driving towards Yosemite National Park, enormous lightning scares the shit out of me. I stop immediately and turn the car around.

The thunderous explosion that follows is my husband's roar: *"What?! Back?! You're messing up our whole trip's schedule!"*

"I don't care! I'm not driving us straight into a thunderstorm!" I bark back. I know I am risking my marriage.

Five miles later lightning strikes again. This time bigger, stronger, closer. I stop, turn around, and silently drive us to the park. If we're bound to get killed by lightning, at least let it be in the right direction...

Forked Lightning

by Edna Heled

He wanted right, she wanted left. He wanted new, she preferred what was left. He wanted an apple, she wanted a pear. He wanted far, she wanted near. "Forked Lightning", that's how they always appeared.

Then, they were 'bubbled'.

No right, no left, no north or south - but the park by their street is so perfectly nice! Pears and apples are all out of stock but don't they both think that bananas rock?

And when summer ends and thunderstorms start, forked lightning at the window is the loveliest sight.

To watch, cuddling, together.

The Little Old Man

by Edna Heled

I adored him. Every evening walking up and down the street for two hours... seemed like mission impossible at his age. The little old man never missed a day. Rain or shine, dressed in a Glow-in-the-Dark jacket, he carried his crooked bones along. Such an exceptional man surely deserves his long life!

One day he saw a handyman's van in my driveway, and shifted his body towards my house asking for his business card. At close distance I saw a bitter, grumpy, beak-nosed woodpecker-man, like a nightmare from kid's horror movies.

He still walks every day. I stopped admiring.

The Terrible Winter of '75

by Richard Hess

I practiced OBGYN in Fairbanks for 41 years, but I still remember the winter of '75. Fairbanks was so wonderful in the summer, but the next winter the temperature dropped to 60 degrees below zero and stayed there for the next three weeks! I have written some rhymes to commemorate this.

The summer in Fairbanks was so much fun
Watching ball games neath the midnight sun.

It was not too hot, and not too cold.
Each day a new treasure to behold.

Then winter came and it got cold
and colder and colder.

I remember it well, how can I survive
This horrible winter of '75?

This was nature's cruel trick
Making ice fog so thick
How can anyone stay alive?

Yes, we had some ice and snow
For three weeks the high temp – 55 below!!

If you must go out, you'd better beware
You will not survive – unless you are a polar bear!

The farther down the temperature goes,
The faster you'll frostbite your fingers and toes.

Spring will be coming; we know that for sure
But we must survive this – there is no real cure.

I am now freaking out; this cold is a bummer
It was so nice and warm when I came here last summer.

But now things are changing, new forces are forming.
We feel the effects of global warming.

In Fairbanks they still see the ice and the snow.
But rarely a day even 40 below.

I fear that real soon, there'll be no one alive
Who remembers the winter of '75!

Saving The Galaxy – Again!

BY RICHARD HESS

Young Bart Goodheart was very nervous as he approached the house. The evil Psylon Empire was launching new attacks and threatened to take over the Galaxy. Bart had been sent by the Federation Council to find the one man who could lead them to victory – Luke Skywalker. As Bart got to the door, he saw that it was a very old house. What is a nice guy like you doing in a place like this? he wondered. Anyway, there was no time to waste, so he knocked hard on the door.

"Who the hell is that?" a loud voice demanded. "If you are Jehovah's Witnesses, go away! If you are Girl Scouts, I don't want any more cookies!"

"Sir, I am Bart Goodheart, and I come with an urgent request from the Federation Council. The Galaxy is threatened, and we need you to save us!" "All right, you can come in and sit on the floor. I have no other chairs because I am here all alone. Last year I saved the Galaxy from that evil guy, Darth – what's his name? Actually, I feel kind of sorry for him. When his mom sent him to school every day – Evil School – she always dressed him in black. What kind of mom would do that? Although that was the official school color – black!"

"After the last battle where we defeated Darth what's his name, all the other Jedis left. Where did they all go – Disneyland? I was so bummed out I retreated to this old place. And how did the Federation thank me? Did I get the Jedi of the Month award? NO!! I know all you get if you win are some worthless action figures and two free meals at McDonald's, but it's the idea behind it, kid. Who got the Jedi of the Month award anyway? Some little snotnose kid from Alpha Centuri. So, I retreated here to sulk and contemplate this lack of respect. Just get me my wine and my Prozac!"

"Kid, would you pour me another glass of that red wine? My thanks to Ernest and Julio! And bring me that bottle over there – it says Prozac 20 mg. With the wine and the Prozac, I should be feeling much better."

"But sir! The Galaxy is threatened by the evil Psylons – you must come with me immediately!"

"So, now they want me? Tell them to get that Newby kid from Alpha Centuri, Mr. Jedi of the Month!"

Bart was perplexed. What could he do? He tried to humor Luke. "Sir, everyone knows those awards are really popularity contests. People just vote for their friends." Luke replied, 'I don't know why people don't like me. Mom says I am terrific. Of course, all moms say that to their kids. To quote the late, great Rodney Dangerfield, I don't get no respect."

"Sir, everyone knows you are the best Jedi in the Galaxy. Surely, you will be elected into the Jedi Hall of Fame five years after you officially retire. First ballot, no question! They just wanted to throw some crumbs to the kid. But we must get going, please! Uh…Sir, you are gobbling down those Prozacs like they are M&M's." Luke replied, "Between the wine and my Prozacs in an hour I should be really chill! But okay, I will go with you. It's the only way to get you to be quiet! Where is my lightsaber? I can never find that damn thing when I need it! Oh, here it is – under the bed. If you can't find something, always look under the bed. Okay, kid, let's go! This saving the galaxy stuff is getting old. And I probably still won't get Jedi of the month!"

Adversity is Good for You!

BY RICHARD HESS

I practiced OBGYN in Fairbanks, Alaska for 41 years. This is a true story about my first winter there.

Old man winter and his helper ice-fog are making a serious attempt to kill me! I am in Fairbanks, and it is the winter of '75. We are in the grips of a terrible cold spell with temperatures down to 60 degrees below zero. That is the real temperature, not some wimpy feels-like temperature where the wind blows for 5 seconds, and it feels like…. Please. I am not impressed by that. The weather report is given by a meteorologist. Why are they called that? – when was the last time you heard one of them talk about meteors? She (it is usually a very attractive young female) tells us that we should feel sorry for those poor people in Minnesota because the temperature there will go down to 10 degrees above zero. You think that is cold? Hearing that makes me want to throw up! Here in Fairbanks, it is 60 degrees below zero at night, but during the day it does "warm up" to 55 degrees below zero. And this incredible cold spell will last for 3 weeks. Not a good time to be homeless and sleeping under the Wendell Street Bridge. Your body will probably be found next spring when the snow melts. They say about an athlete who is calm under stress, "He has ice water in his veins." At 60 below, I wonder if that might actually be true. What is the freezing point of blood?

What to do? I spend a lot of time at the hospital. The hospital is always warm. And if a mom-to-be comes to the hospital in labor, I don't have to drive through the ice fog to get to the hospital; I am already there! Cars do not exactly thrive in this weather either. We have engine heaters, and we keep our cars plugged into electrical outlets when they are outside. But inside the car it is **so cold!** You run to your car to start the engine. But the engine will have to run for several minutes before you can take off. So, you stay in your car, curled up in the fetal position while you wait. I can't feel my fingers or toes, but I know they must still be there! Lord have mercy!

Now all this is but a memory- though not a pleasant one! Because now we have global warming. This has catastrophic effects for the earth, but winters in Fairbanks are now much warmer. It rarely hits even 30 below. This is why us old-timers must keep telling this story of the winter of '75. Like old Eskimos telling their kids stories about how their brave ancestors went out in small boats to get the Great Whale. Now the village would have food, thanks to their heroism. I suspect the story got better each time it was retold.

And now cars have remote starts. So, from a nice warm building you can just point this device at your car in the parking lot – and it will start! Wait a few minutes and you can get into a nice warm car and drive off! Jim Lundquist, an old family practice doctor at the Clinic, told me that once a guy left his car in the parking lot in first gear. When he remote-started the car, it took off across the parking lot and hit another car. I am not sure if this story is true, as Jim was given to telling me stories that were not always, "the truth, the whole truth, and nothing but the truth." But maybe that really did happen!

Now people may ask you, "What is that cord coming out of your car?" You can tell them that when you were in Alaska you would plug your car into an electrical outlet to keep your engine from freezing at night. It makes for an interesting conversation piece. And then maybe you can tell them about the winter of '75.

Breathes there a man alive
Who remembers the winter of '75?
Those who lived through this were stupid or bold
Perhaps we were both, if the story be told!

A Barnyard Transformation: Celena's Magic

by Connie Jameson

Before Celena's Poetry Class:

Farmer Brown - kind, caring and concerned. He loved his animals, provided them food to eat, water to drink, warm places to sleep and fields in which to run and play. But lately, his critters seemed a little less frisky, a little less frolicky, a little less…happy.

"Of course, I care for their bodies," thought Farmer Brown, "but what about their minds? They need to have food for thought and exercise for their brains. Aha! Celena's poetry class."

Gathering his animals around him, Farmer Brown shared his plan. Soon the barnyard was all a-buzz and it wasn't just the bees.

Learning About the Class:

Horsefly volunteered to check out the class.
"I can use my natural talent of 'fly on the wall.'
Then I'll come back and report to y'all."
Everyone wondered what Fly would learn
And anxiously waited for his return.
Fly's report: The poetry class is interesting, informative and fun.
Miss Celena is smart, kind and helpful.
However, she rather prefers that poems not rhyme.

Responses About the Class:

Some animals were concerned about non-rhyming poetry:
I can't imagine that — said Cat
It's become our habit — said Rabbit
I'm afraid I'd fail — said Snail
Yes, just my luck — said Duck

But that's how we'll grow — said Crow

I hope she's not cruel — said Mule

I bet she'll be nice — said Mice

Of course, of course — said Horse

Just try — said Fly

Oops! I mean just endeavor, just persist (trying not to rhyme, you know)

Off to the Class:

Horse said he'd be the "Steed in the Lead"

Cow was ready to get a'moovin' and a'hoovin'

"Okay, I'll take a gander at it" — said Goose.

"We'll come, too" said the Goat family — Nanny, Billy and the Kid.

Soon there was a parade of animals on the move.

With a clomp, clomp, clomp of hooves

And a swish, swish, swish of tails — off they went.

Farmer Brown watched with a smile on his face and hope in his heart.

After the Class:

Upon their return, Farmer Brown was overjoyed. It appeared that Celena and her class had performed their magic.

Now, Horse stands in the pasture, head held high, wind blowing through his mane. In his mind, he is now Pegasus or Unicorn or Winner of the Kentucky Derby. Cow slowly chews her cud, big, brown eyes staring at the horizon, her mind deep in creative thoughts.

As Pig rolls in the mud and Lamb kicks up her heels and Dog chases his tail, it is with much more gusto, more joy.

It was, indeed, a Barnyard Transformation and all thanks to CelenaDiana Bumpus!!

Fourth of July 2021

by Marlene Jones

Rocky shivers and pants heavily all day even though we give him the correct dosage of trazodone hydrochloride prescribed by the veterinarian. The loud, popping fireworks frighten our dog. Bob and I watch the news on television while trying to comfort him with hugs, stroking his fur and calmly talking to him.

At 8 p.m. things change. A deafening boom scares the three of us. Rocky gazes into our eyes with fear. The earsplitting sound comes from behind our house by the sliding door leading to the backyard pool area. My husband and I jump to our feet and rush to see how close the firecrackers are to our home.

The rear of our residence faces south, overlooking Berry Road and beyond to Martin Luther King High School, which is about four miles as the crow flies. Illegal pyrotechnics light up the night. The number of blasting rockets is overwhelming. They are the type set off at Disneyland or the fairgrounds. Beautiful, but particularly dangerous in a residential setting.

Bob sprints to the TV area to check on Rocky. I rush to follow him. Our pet is scooping up his dog bed in terror. "Rocky. Do you want to go for a ride?" I cry out.

He races to the garage and scratches my car door with his front paws. Rocky wants to escape the explosive noises. I grab his leash and vamoose to the gas station, believing that this ride will do him good. But no! All the way down Alessandro Blvd toward Moreno Valley, the same illegal fireworks dominate each side of the highway. The dog cannot sit still. Neighbors living barely thirty feet away from the gas station ignite the sky with the same kind of illegal fireworks. Chilling! Unbelievable!

Police cars drive up and down the main road without targeting any residents for forbidden firecrackers. I figure they do not have the manpower for the enormous quantity of offenders, and that law enforcement must prepare to handle worse problems should they arise.

Dang! My dog is a wreck! I drive home and stay up soothing him the best I can. Nothing helps much. Finally, at 3 a.m. Rocky sleeps on his doggy bed by my bedstead where I ultimately collapse.

Surreal

by Marlene Jones

An honest, caring, hard-working man passes away on April 30, 2004 at Kaiser Hospital in Bellflower. Our family is in mourning. He is my dear 87- year-old dad. Family and friends are saddened, but more so, Mom has lost her true love. She is beside herself with grief as her heart aches for him.

Embracing her small frame with affection, Bob and I assure her that we want her with us and bring her to live in Riverside at our home straightaway. She will be 90 in May.

Mike's old bedroom becomes his Grandma Yanni's boudoir. Her doctor recommends she keep her feet up as often as possible. Thankfully, our sectional sofa includes a chaise where she can watch the news, Jeopardy and Wheel of Fortune in comfort.

Mom and I are frequently challenged by Scrabble and Canasta. When Jeanetta, my sister, visits, she joins us. We learned these games from our parents. It gave us an opportunity as young girls to enjoy the games and become familiar with spelling and mathematics. As we get older, we continue playing them with Mom and Dad, relatives and friends.

In spite of her medical issues, Mom does quite well for herself by following her doctors' orders: stay on a diabetic diet, walk around the house with a walker for exercise, take prescribed medicine at the correct times and come into the doctor's office for check-ups.

Mom is a loving, caring person who always sees the best in people. I never heard her say an unkind word to anyone. She endears herself to others by her positive personality. People just seem to gravitate towards her.

Over the next years, I plan birthday parties, holiday celebrations and other get-togethers at our house with Mom.

I have fond memories of a trip back East to visit relatives with Mom and my daughter, Gina, in 2007. We enjoyed Broadway shows and attractions from Upstate New York to Philadelphia, Pennsylvania. I rented a van, put our luggage and rented wheelchair inside it and drove to most locations except Manhattan, where we hailed taxis. The wheelchair was folded and placed in the trunk of each yellow cab we took.

After the trip, Mom does remarkably well for months. Then what I feared the most happened. I'm sitting on the couch watching the news and I turn to face Mom. Sounds are coming out of her mouth. What's this? Jabberwocky? I do not understand a word spoken and am totally scared for her. 911 is called. Ambulance, fire truck and police car appear. Mom is swiftly driven to Kaiser Emergency by ambulance. Medical personnel transport her to a Care Unit.

We discover Mom had a mini-stroke that not only impaired her speech, but a blood clot lodged in one eye made her blind in that eye. Very scary. Days passed and finally, we drive her home. I rented a wheelchair and oxygen tanks with prescribed monthly tanks to follow. Prescriptions for various eye drops were now necessary.

When she gets home, Mom speaks correctly, but the loss of vision in her left eye is permanent. As she recuperates, friends visit our home. Mom enjoys talking, laughing and eating home-cooked meals with us all. Every morning she wakes up early to take her medications and makes her own breakfast.

Over the next two years, she had a few more mini-strokes at different times, but Mom always bounced back. The joy ended when she had a final stroke and was rushed to Kaiser Emergency. It was so surreal as I watched the medical crew pound on her chest to no avail. She passed away on November 7, 2009.

I miss her so much. My best friend, my confidant, my mom is with me always. No regrets. Just happy memories.

Retirement

BY MARLENE JONES

After over 40 years of establishing and working at our business, Jones Backhoe Service Inc., my husband Bob and I retired on April 1, 2019. Bob doesn't have to get up early anymore to drive heavy equipment to job locations and I no longer have any more office work once the corporation taxes are filed.

Once we leave the company, there's always something to do such as working on the house, yard, rentals and so forth. Spending time with each other, our friends and continuing our hobbies is awfully important, too. Bob loves going to sprint-car races, fishing, old cars, the Masons and meeting up with his buddies for coffee and chatting with them each morning. I prefer dancing, outings with friends and family, painting, Scrabble, Solitaire, the Rare Fruit Growers group and my writing class.

Living life is not much different from before retirement until eleven months later when Covid-19 put a wrench into our lifestyle. The pandemic ends socializing as we know it. Masking up, wearing gloves, disinfecting groceries, counters and floors, ordering online merchandise and food delivery becomes part of everyday life. Zoom takes the place of dancing, meetings and classes in person. We follow the rules and cannot wait to be vaccinated for protection from this virus.

Two fun diversions do occur during the pandemic. On May 17th, 2020, Bob and Mike, our oldest son, win the 38th Lake Havasu Fishing Tournament in Arizona. This is a special event for Bob, because he is the only participant that has never missed one tournament. He strives to win and came in second place with Dan, our younger son, in 2016. Then on January 16, 2021, we purchase a blue 1963 Chevy Nova Sport. I love riding in it to the beach with Bob who does fantastic upkeep on it.

Bob and I are very happy spending time with our caring kids

now that we're no longer working. We are proud that all our kids have jobs. My daughter, Gina, is a vet tech and loves animals. Dan is an Operating Engineer and runs heavy equipment. Mike is a Senior Project Engineer and sees that the construction jobs are properly prepared and completed. My life is good in retirement.

Wabi-Sabi Writing Desk

by Jessica Lea

veneer bubbled
worn
pieces broken off
wood bare and naked
exposed
raw

polish is just a stain
to camouflage

highlight instead through
mental kintsugi

leave unashamed

broken
yet whole

in spite of myself

Stealth Gardening

BY JESSICA LEA

I want to build a backyard forest

a temple
a visceral ode to creation
drown out suburban clamor
of
expectations
                    hatred
                              ignorance
invasive species of darkness

earth's star
reflected back
as
primrose
            sunflowers
                        subtly spreading seeds
in neighboring yards

now unsuspecting beacons
for the winged.

Fantasy Careers

BY JESSICA LEA

In another life
I am a
falconer
environmental scientist
farm hand
forest ranger
dude ranch operator
kayak tour guide

something
anything
except
dormant before a screen

log on
and
log out

VPN activated
and
deactivated

wondering
if I am touching
anyone
in the real world.

Ghost Rider

BY JESSICA LEA

solo convertible joyride

flash past
orange groves

on a back road

blanketed mountain backdrop

hair howling

snap

capture
her ghost
from 25 years ago

driving

Excavation

BY MERRILL LYEW

Goosebumps on his purple skin. He heard the motor rumbling, but at such distance he could not distinguish if it was a yellow caterpillar, or a green John Deere. The person in the white lab-coat running around in muddy boots must be the archeologist leading the excavation. What precious treasures could they be digging out? He strolled closer; water was spewing out from the bottom of the hole.

The rumbling ended as he ceased scratching his balding head, his pale fingers with bloody skull skin under the fingernails. He forgot what he was digging into his ever-vanishing memories for.

Nano and the Shiny Coins

BY JACQUELINE MANTZ

Marie, Estella, and Yuri pinched each other as their mom drove the brown Pinto hatchback up the dirt road. They piled out, running up the driveway into their Nano's arms.

"Buenos días, nietas, me han hecho falta toda la semana," he said.

"Hey Pop," said their mom.

The three girls did not understand his words but they felt the warmth of their Nano's hug.

"Love you Nano," they said. The three girls held their hands out like when they went to receive Holy Communion as shiny coins spilled into their hands. Their mom and Nano waved them to go as they spoke in rapid-fire Spanish.

The girls walked down the dirt road to Rodriguez Market. They pushed the door which tinkled as they entered. They stuck candy into the paper bags Mr. Rodriguez gave them. Marie pulled three ice-cold bottled Coca-Colas from the fridge and Mr. Rodriguez opened each of them with a snap. They walked home pouring Pop Rock candies into their mouths. The girls admired the Ring Pops on their fingers.

Their mom listened to Nano with her head cupped in her hands at the kitchen table when they walked into the house. Nano had a picture of Nana who died when their mom was fourteen on the kitchen table.

"Your grandpa is telling me how grandma used to help run their dairies. She handled all the money."

"Please Nano, tell us about Nana," the girls said crowding around the faded picture.

"Tu abuela era muy inteligente con las matemáticas. Como tu mamá…" Mom translated, "Your grandmother was so intelligent in math. Just like your mom."

The girls nodded, ate their candy, downed their Coca-Colas, and listened as their mom translated stories about their Nana, a few sentences at a time.

Joan Didion Died

BY JACQUELINE MANTZ

Joan Didion is dead. I learned of her death by text. Joan Didion died. Of late, I process differently, declining to comment on her death. For days I chose to stay silent of pen. Joan Didion died on December 23rd, 2021. Her death is marked on my calendar by the articles written about her on CNN, NPR, and The Washington Post. Joan Didion died of complications from Parkinson's disease. To pick up her books that lay by my bathtub felt unbearable. So I don't. I do nothing.

On December 29th, I want to eat breakfast. Joe's mom sleeps in the bed beside me. We are in Las Vegas in a room at Planet Hollywood. It is 6 am. The room is cold. Joan Didion wrote of 1967 Las Vegas. I reread "Marrying Absurd" and marvel. "This geographical implausibility reinforces the sense that what happens there has no connection with "real" life...But Las Vegas seems to exist only in the eye of beholder all of which makes it an extraordinary and interesting place, but an odd one in which to want to wear a candlelight satin Priscilla of Boston wedding dress with Chantilly lace insets, tapered sleeves and a detachable modified train," Joan Didion wrote.

Her words are everything Las Vegas lacks. Joan Didion built layer upon layer of truth with journalistic precision and a psychological keen sense. I ache for Palm Springs, for those books by my tub. So I drive home.

Bites of Life

BY JACQUELINE MANTZ

Daddy cooked a dry turkey, but his ham was legendary. He basted it with a magical sugar concoction. I didn't know then it just came from a silver foil packet. Maybe daddy put other spices into it. When the ham was baked the smell filled the house with caramel baking meat notes. The flesh of the pig oozing warmth and sustenance.

Mom made tasty Mexican rice and greasy "I want another" tacos but with her work schedule many days it was boiled hot dogs and macaroni from a box. I didn't mind as my childhood and even adult palate craved boxed foods, canned vegetables, and bread, lots of bread as it made me feel at home.

"John makes his own bread and slices the meat," Pam, my sister's best friend, sang loud when she watched my daddy make sandwiches. I take after my mom. My husband Joe cooks the delicacies or we eat out. Tuesdays I always bring home Rubio's fish tacos. I consider this cooking. Joe will taste a dish like shrimp chili gueros and replicate it with a delicate sure touch at home.

"I can do better," Joe muttered as we ate the shrimp stuffed chilis and lapped up the chipotle sauce with store-bought chips. When Joe spoke those words with such earnestness he reminded me of Jack Nicholson in *As Good As It Gets* and I wanted him to kiss me.

Joe's mom stayed with us for weeks these last few months and my resolve to be vegetarian faded as chicken mole, tacos dorado, and pozole all appeared on the dinner table in the evening. Cooking and I have issues. Whenever I cook, I want to eat. Whenever I eat, I want to throw up. Yet, I eat a lot and have kept the throw-up monster at bay, for now. This is just a gross way to explain that cooking gives me anxiety. It's just too much for me as my food issues run deep. I've worked on my food issues via therapy but it doesn't mean I'm cured or fixed or whatever. So I limit my cooking to simple stuff like eggs and sandwiches. Truly I appreciate Joe and his mom cooking for me at this stage in my life.

"Cuando cocinas mamá, me siento tan caliente y como en casa," Google Translator spoke to Joe's mom in a robotic voice.

"Thank you, Jackie," she replied. I wanted to write a poem today but instead I wrote about food and those people, those beautiful people who are intertwined in every bite of my life. I love you, my words are all I have to cook for you, and may you be nourished as you nourished me.

Save Me

BY JACQUELINE MANTZ

Dreaming
Fill up the pool with water
as assigned, add a turtle
she swims lazily by and looks me in the eye
within a glance
once dream now nightmare
water draining inexplicably
our turtle gasping for air
once green now brown mush, like coffee grounds
her eyes implore me

Save Me

As she heaves her last sigh
awaken and watch our world draining
drawing and sighing our last breaths
Save Me

Suspended in Wing

by Jacqueline Mantz

Yellow open buds of April
chubby bumblebees hang, black glistening wings
buzzing suspended, blue sky
green trapeze tree limbs

Chirp, sound of silence, silent silence,
sound between silence, chirp, chirp,
every two seconds another chirp

A yellow flower falls with five petal parts
airbrushed by mother nature's nail salon
red patterns
as I breathe

Pink mat covering red ants walking underneath me, on me
if I am still
Enough

Bring the Breath

BY JACQUELINE MANTZ

Breathing love in and out-hope hips grounded
left crack-right crack, creaky floor my body – my body – older,
   slower, 48er

Back to the breath – the breath, calm the breath, steady the
   heart flow

Douse flames – fires rain ash, force flight, democracy's cracks
   revealed-breathing in and out-grouting interior exterior
   cracks with love.

I Wanted To Write About...

BY MAE WAGNER MARINELLO

I wanted to write about how it was for me, a child in a small town in Southwestern North Dakota, about how my sister, Betty, and I would walk from our house to downtown where the wonderful Dale's Variety store existed. About how we would stand in front of the old-fashioned candy counter where its windows showcased the enticing variety of penny candy. What should we spend our pennies on? One of the tempting choices was small, jelly-like black candies, sugar-coated and shaped like a little boy.

Now, some 70 years later, it's even hard for me to write the words — and will be harder yet if I were to read them aloud, about how those candies were called "nigger babies." Betty and I knew nothing about prejudice or racial injustice then. I had never seen a Negro, as Black people were called back then, where Highway-12 cut through my small hometown, a single blinking light slung over the highway, blinking red for Main Street traffic and yellow for the highway.

I wanted to write about how, in contrast, I saw many Negroes when, nearly every summer of my chaotic childhood, my mother took Betty and me to Riverside, California, while my dad and two brothers remained in Dakota. My mother's parents and many aunts and uncles lived in Riverside. We would travel by bus, train or car.

When we were going by car, as we approached towns, I would see signs along the highway that said "Green River Ordinance* Enforced Here."

"Mamma, what does that mean?" I would ask.

And she would answer, "It means black people are supposed to be out of town before sunset."

It was something I could not comprehend. What was wrong with black people being in town after dark? By then, I may have been somewhat aware of Mark Twain's books where I had romantic visions of steamboats on the Mississippi River, and was most likely charmed when he wrote dialogue as we imagined Black people talked, like they did in Pudd'nhead Wilson." (pp10)

"...Oh, I's middlin'; hain't got noth'n to complain of. I's gwine to come a-court'n' you bimeby, Roxy."

Actually, I never heard anyone talk like that in real life.

(Recently, a college professor was fired for reading verbatim from Pudd'nhead Wilson, using the N-word. Hannah Berliner Fischthal, a 20-year adjunct instructor at St. John's University, a Catholic college in Queens, uttered the N-word once during a remote "Literature of Satire" class on February 10, 2021.)

I wanted to write about how my mother's parents lived on Prospect Avenue in Riverside in the late 40s or early 50s. I loved their house. I loved Prospect Avenue. I slept in the screened-in front porch where I fell asleep amidst the delicious, cooler night air.

The lady who lived next door to my grandparents worked at the lunch counter at the Woolworth store in downtown Riverside. In hindsight, I doubt the lunch counter was integrated at that time. I never even thought about such things.

I wanted to write about another vivid memory from one of those early trips to Riverside, My relatives dropped some of my cousins and me off at the Fox Theater downtown. I was the kid who didn't like movies, not even Disney movies.

During Pinocchio, I remember kneeling in front of the scratchy red plush seat at the Strand Theater in my hometown with my head buried in its cushion. I didn't want Pinocchio to be a bad boy and get donkey ears. I didn't want him to be swallowed by a whale! It was the same theater where I cried when Bambi's mother was shot.

The movie playing at the Fox Theater on that long-ago day was

Uncle Tom's Cabin, based on a book by Harriet Beecher Stowe. Two memories from that movie remain etched in my brain. If I was scared for Pinocchio, imagine my terror when Simon Legree lashed his whip at slaves working on the plantation. If I cried when Bambi's mother was shot, I sobbed uncontrollably when little black Topsy, sobbing just like me, knelt at the bed of an angelic-looking white child as she lay dying in her bed. It was the most beautiful bed I had ever seen, draped with white gossamer fabric, the sunlight shining through the window on Little Eva and the small black figure kneeling at her bedside.

I wanted to write about how, on one of our return trips to Riverside, my grandma and grandpa had moved from Prospect to Eucalyptus Avenue, right across from Longfellow Elementary School. I was confused about why they had moved. I liked their old house and the old street much better. Grandma said they had to move because the "coloreds" were moving into the old neighborhood. Even though I remember having some sense of shame, in those days, we did not question the reasoning of our elders.

After one Christmas and many summers in California, my mother left her unhappy marriage and her two sons in 1957 and took Betty and me to Riverside to live. I still had two years of high school to go. On one of our earlier trips to California, I met Sandy, a girl my age who lived a couple of blocks from my grandparents. She became my lifelong "best friend" until she died in 2017.

Because of Sandy, I was able to make the difficult transition from attending the small school in my Dakota home town where our graduating classes averaged 35 to Riverside's Poly where graduating classes numbered around 600.

Sandy told me about being in a Texas bus station where a huge star was embedded in the floor and the drinking fountains were labeled "colored" and "white."

I was incredulous at the idea of people drinking from separate drinking fountains because of the color of their skin.

I knew it wasn't that way for our Negro classmates at Poly. Even though Riverside neighborhoods seemed to be racially divided, there were no drinking fountains (that I knew of) labeled "white" and "colored." The California I knew was different from Sandy's memories of her visit to Texas — which is one reason I think I continued to live in my bubble, unaware of the deep-rooted racial prejudice in America, especially because I felt no prejudice toward anyone.

I wanted to write about the summer of 1958 when several friends and I spent a week at the beach in Oceanside, California. We stayed at a little trailer park up the coast from Camp Pendleton. And that is when I met a handsome Marine and we fell in love. We were married in the summer of 1959, a week before I graduated from Poly and a month before I turned 18. It was one of the happiest times of my life. (It was not unusual to marry that young at the time.)

When my husband's time in the Marines was up, we returned to his hometown in Southern Illinois. He had been looking forward to reconnecting with his friend, Phillip. When Phillip met me, he chose to call me a "God Damn Republican Yankee." I didn't even know what political party I might belong to at that time and I wasn't clear on why he called me that. But I wasn't used to being called a "God Damn" anything.

One night, Phillip, my husband and I went to a bar in nearby Shawneetown, a wild n' woolly town at the border between Illinois and Indiana. At 18, I was still too young to have ever spent much time in bars, especially one like the one we went to in Shawneetown. There, Confederate flags were part of the décor. I was sitting at the table alone when I heard someone at my ear say "I believe they are playing our song…"

Just then, my husband returned from the restroom and saw the stranger whispering in my ear. He was picking the stranger up by the front of his shirt, ready for a fight. The little band began play-ing a rousing version of "Dixie" and the crowd was singing and cheering and stomping their feet. Phillip danced on top of the table.

Time went on. We were still very poor and, by now, we had two sons, one born in 1962, and the other in 1963. I had been focused on having babies and being a good wife and mother, living bliss-fully in my bubble and budgeting everything down to the last nickel.

I vividly remember one day back then. I was ironing clothes as I watched the TV. Three Civil Rights workers had seemingly dis-appeared while on their way to states in the South to register Negro people to vote.

The search for them seemed interminable, especially now with much news coming from TV. There was talk of an "earthen dam" and the possibility of law enforcement being involved in their disappearance.

And that is what happened. Their bodies were found buried in an earthen dam. The killers were aided by someone in law enforcement.

That was the day my bubble burst, the day my illusions were shattered. How could this possibly happen in America, land that I loved?

And now, it is 2021. Apparently, we have learned nothing from lessons of the past. Many Southern States have recently imple-mented voting restrictions, undoing any progress we thought we made. We had a president who seemed to encourage white na-tionalism, driving divisions even deeper within our country. There are attacks on Jewish places of worship. Black mothers cry for their sons.

And now, I'm just too sad and weary. I don't understand how you can hate someone for the color of their skin or because of how they worship.

I don't want to write about any of it anymore.

**This is what Google had to say about the Green River Or-
dinance:* The Green River Ordinance originated in Green
River, Wyoming in 1931. This ordinance prohibited
door-to-door selling which had been a particular problem during the Great Depression. A former editor of the
Green River Star, Adrian Reynolds, said the ordinance
was less an anti-peddling ordinance but an anti-trespass
ordinance that confirms the right of the homeowner to
say who comes into the home. Other cities in the United
States enacted their own versions of the original
ordinance.

And this is what I have to say: In the racial climate of
that time, perhaps there were those who chose to inter-
pret such ordinances the way my mother explained it to
me.

Children of the Chaos of Change

by Ruthie Marlenée

Waking, dorsal side up, flat in the middle of the dusty rainforest, I find myself in quite the quagmire. And while I can see it's a rainforest (my eyes, after all, are on the top of my head) – or what remains of a rainforest – it's problematic in that I'm also a stingray out of water. I haven't always been a stingray, but now I'm having trouble breathing since my gill slits and my mouth are on the underside of my body, stranded in the mud. I taste the damp metallic flavor of the earth.

The full moon sucks back the tide as it sparkles across the exposed mudflats like tiny marshmallows sprinkled over cocoa. So it isn't too hard to imagine how I've gotten here since I happen to belong to a long line of freshwater stingrays surviving in the Amazon. How long I've been here, stuck in the sediment, I don't know, but I do sense an urgency to get back to the river before my gills dry up. That, or pray for rain.

Before long, carrying a big water bucket, a young sienna-skinned girl with straight obsidian-colored bangs and a face brightly speckled with burnt umber paint, stands above me. From her slender neck swings a necklace made of a tail spine I recognize from the remains my species. She seems familiar. My ears, so full of mud, but I think I hear her say, "You've come back for us. Just let me run and get the others."

"Wait, what are you called?" I cough, trying to clear the muck lodged in my throat.

"Bindi, the Jungle Girl." She examines me more closely. "And you?"

"Potamo," I answer without hesitation and confidently, never having been asked before, but knowing I'm from the family of Potamotrygonidae, one of the fishes related to sharks. "Bindi, may I please have some water?"

"Oh, yes, of course. Silly me," she says, dashing to the river's edge to ladle up some water. She returns to pour the murky liquid over me. It's refreshing, but I can only manage to slurp in what's puddled beneath me, including the sludge.

And then in the puddle, I stare at the reflection of my giant pancake-shaped face, grayish-brown and mottled with orange spots, spots like hers – the only similarity. I wonder how it's possible Bindi and I speak the same language.

"More," I plead.

This time she turns me over and pours water directly into my mouth. I swallow. "Thank you."

"You're welcome." She pivots to leave.

"Wait! Would you please help me back to the river first?"

"I will just as soon as I return with the others. We don't have much time."

"Others?"

"Yes, the children of the chaos of change," she says, tears making rivulets through the dappled paint on her cheeks. "It hasn't rained in such a long time. The trees are burning and we've run out of food much less any resources with which to survive. And now a strange pandemic is attacking our elders. The children are next to die. We have no choice but to return to the river before it disappears, too. Potamo, you are our savior."

"I'm no savior, merely a stingray. I wish there was something I could do." Sadly, I watch as Bindi returns to the ragged-toothed forest.

Later, as the sun sets over the sparse treetops, a flock of parrots burst out of the smoldering jungle like a bloom of long ago tropical flowers. Behind them dash more dark-skinned children in assorted painted faces. One boy with stick straight black hair, serrated bangs and a shark's tooth necklace picks up a rock and throws it at me, striking me smack between my eyes. Another boy pokes me with a stick.

"Arildo, Renato stop it!" Bindi yells. "He's here to save us!"

Disoriented, bruised and tasting the blood dripping from my left eye, I can barely hear the boy called Renato yell, "Yeah, right. Fake news!" And then he kicks me before picking me up by my venomous stinger tail. As he lasso swings me over his head, I reflexively sting him in his hand. He screams loud enough to wake all in the jungle, dead or alive. Renato lets go and I land in the river with a splash.

I gulp in the water. Clearing my sinuses, I then gargle and rinse the silt from my mouth before slithering away. Surfacing safely in the middle of the river, I can see Renato hobbling away along the shore, a tail between his legs, and Bindi standing at the edge clearly distraught, waving for me to come back. "Don't leave me. Please, take me with you."

Later, as the tide recedes, again I find myself lying flat in the mud, the moon glistening across the marsh. With no one around to help me, and sensing I need to get back to the water quickly, I feel my body thrust up from the morass. I look down to see my spotty, earth-colored hands pushing up from the bog. The next thing I know, I'm standing on my own two legs.

Bindi, carrying her water bucket, has returned with the children. "Oh, Potamo," she cries. "You've become one of us! Now it's too late." She sobs and then holds up the bucket where I think I can see my reflection. But it's only the image of me before I'd grown limbs.

"It's Renato," Bindi says, pointing into the bucket. "This is what happened to him after you stung him. We're bringing him back to the water."

When Renato and I lock eyes, he suddenly becomes enraged, splashes out of the bucket, whipping his tail and stinging me, before stinging all who surround him, including Bindi.

In excruciating pain, I know what to do and without time to spare. "Follow me," I yell, my heart aching where Renato stung me.

Bindi, head flattening, arms withering, follows. The children, tails between their shrinking legs, limp behind her until they are all knee deep into the river.

Twilight, the moon wanes, providing just enough energy for the transformation. And then before the tributaries and rivers begin to evaporate, the children of the chaos of change have made their way back to the sea, back to where the water has always been in their DNA, back to where they surface only long enough to witness the rainforest blazing on the horizon, the embers floating into a star-filled sky.

"Welcome home, my children."

A Sewing Machine

by Terry Lee Marzell

Sewing occupied a very important part of my youth. Those who remember the late 1950's and early 1960's know that we girls almost always wore dresses, and that those dresses were almost always made at home. Hardly anyone could afford to buy all their clothes ready-made, like we do today.

I still remember the childhood dresses my mother made for me. My favorite one featured a white bodice, a fitted waistline, and a flared red-and-white checkered skirt. The dress was sleeveless, but Mom had used leftover bits of the skirt material cut on the bias to finish the armholes and neckline, and she hand-stitched my initials in red embroidery thread in the upper left-hand corner of the bodice. Another outfit she made for me consisted of a dress with long, puffy sleeves made of a very shiny fabric. This garment could be worn by itself, or under a gold-colored, ruffled pinafore, which she also created. Or the pinafore could be worn with other dresses made from the same pattern. My mother was clever at sewing garments that could be used to create multiple looks with just a few coordinated pieces.

You might be surprised at how young I was when my mother first began to teach me how to sew. I was maybe seven years old when she helped me sew a simple shift. Together we laid out the fabric, pinned the pattern pieces—I think there were only four of them—to the material, and then she did the cutting. She showed me how to baste the seams together, and then how to use her sewing machine to carefully sew the straight lines that created the permanent seams. The sleeves were not set-in, they were actually part of the pieces that formed the front and the back of the garment. Because they were more difficult, Mom sewed the front and back facings around the neckline. Then she pinned the hemlines into place, and I sewed them myself by hand with a simple slip stitch.

I imagine the method my mother used to teach me to sew was the same method my grandmother employed to teach her to sew. Maybe my grandmother learned this way from her mother, too.

When I was in junior high school, every girl was required to complete a year of courses in Home Economics—one semester of cooking and one semester of sewing. Neither my seventh grade nor my eighth grade sewing courses required overly-challenging assignments, although, I have always found putting in zippers difficult, even with the aid of a zipper foot. Also, I have always had a hard time with button holes. Accomplished seamstresses are probably surprised by this, because both are rather basic sewing skills. When I was younger, I usually put my zippers in by hand, and Mom helped me by hand-stitching the button holes. When I became an adult, I cheated a bit and paid a tailor to complete these tasks for me. The amount they charged me to do this wasn't much, and certainly worth it.

Alas, my eighth grade Home Ec teacher wouldn't allow me any shortcuts or assists in her class. For my end-of-semester project, I selected a three-piece suit consisting of a fitted A-line skirt, a three-button jacket with long sleeves and a collar, and a simple, scoop neck sleeveless blouse. The blouse was no sweat; I churned that out real fast. The skirt, though, which required the installation of a seven-inch zipper, nearly got the better of me. My teacher insisted I complete the task by machine and using a zipper foot. Although I tried my best, she was dissatisfied with my efforts. She made me rip that zipper out and re-sew it so many times that the fabric was literally shredding. Finally she accepted my work, not because I had succeeded in measuring up to her expectations, but because the garment would not survive another re-do. The collar was very tricky, as I had never attempted one of those before, but I managed to get it done successfully. When it came time to do the button holes. the teacher didn't even argue about that; she let me do those by hand. I think we were both tired of that project at that point.

By the time I was in high school, I devoted a good deal of my summers to sewing my wardrobe for the upcoming school year. Because I didn't have a whole lot of money to work with, I bought fabric and notions on sale, and one or two new patterns, choosing designs that offered several variations. For example, a dress or blouse pattern may have a sleeveless version, a short-sleeved version, and a long-sleeved version, all in the same envelope. I always bought Simplicity patterns, because with Simplicity, the pieces were interchangeable. I could take the sleeves from one pattern and build them into a dress or a blouse from a different pattern. I used the same pattern for all my new clothes, and often bought remnants to add touches of variety.

In those days, my family didn't own a sewing machine, nor was I taking Home Ec classes in school, so I did all the sewing by hand. Not just the zippers and the button holes. All of it.

Right before my junior year, on my sixteenth birthday, my grandparents took pity on me and gifted me with a basic Kenmore sewing machine, mounted into a sturdy walnut cabinet. This was a good choice for me because I could sew in my room instead of at the kitchen table, and this meant I didn't have to inconvenience the family with my sewing mess. The first project I created with my new sewing machine was a floor-length formal in strawberry-milkshake pink featuring long, sheer sleeves trimmed with cranberry-colored ribbon which I fashioned for a school affair. After the event, I shortened the hemline and wore it as a party dress. The pink fabric was a rather bold choice for me, because my mother always told me pink was not a flattering color on me, so I never wore the hue.

But I loved my little sewing machine. In the 70's, I used the Kenmore to sew my costume for the Renaissance Pleasure Faire. In the 80's, I used it to sew a dress for Scottish country dancing—a fully-lined floor-length dress of white eyelet trimmed with a green ribbon around the waist. In the 90's, I crafted dining room curtains and a matching wall hanging for my apartment. And I also used that sewing machine to create a pieced-quilt crib blanket in shades of lavender, featuring two rows of lace hand-stitched around the perimeter, for my husband's first grandchild.

Today, it seems that sewing has almost become a forgotten folk art. I confess I personally haven't done very much sewing in the last two decades, either. But I still have that basic Kenmore sewing machine my grandparents bought me for my sixteenth birthday. It's been 50 years since they gave it to me, and it still works! Every time I look at it, an entire lifetime of sewing memories and sewing creations, spring to mind.

My Introduction to French Cuisine

by Terry Lee Marzell

When my husband, Hal, and I toured France in 2015, I was introduced to the gastronomic delights—and quirks—of French cuisine. Nearly every meal I had there was delectable—a feast for the palate—with one or two notable exceptions.

For my first dinner in Paris, enjoyed in a sidewalk café for which the City of Lights is so famous, I ordered a quiche, fully expecting the fluffy egg dish so often served by that name in America. What I received was a tuna pie. By tuna pie, I mean, specifically, tuna fish baked into a pie crust. True, the tuna was succulent and flavorful, and the crust was buttery and flaky, but I found the dish, served without vegetables or salad, rather plain, both in appearance and taste. By no means would I pretend to be a critic of French cooking, but no matter what I'm eating, I like to see some vegetables, preferably green ones, on my plate. Some pearl onions and plump firm peas or a small salad would have been a welcome addition to that particular entrée.

Another meal I considered a miss was a bouillabaisse I ordered at a seaside restaurant in the town of Arromanches, Normandy. Bouillabaisse is a soup made of various seafoods mixed with tomatoes, garlic, and orange peel, and this one came highly recommended by Ian, our tour guide. When the soup was set before me, I approached the tureen with great anticipation. However, one spoonful of this witches' brew and I was ready to toss the entire bowl back into the ocean. If I didn't know better, I'd swear the chef had simply gone down to the tide pool with a ladle, spooned fishy seawater into a pot, brought it to a boil, and thrown it on the table.

A couple of days later, our tour group rolled into Carcassonne, a charming medieval village in the southeast part of the country. All day, Ian had been singing the praises of a regional dish known as cassoulet. Ian's recommendation had me salivating in anticipation. I had no idea what cassoulet was, but I couldn't wait to try it. At the appointed hour, Hal and I appeared in the hotel dining room. I eagerly ordered the cassoulet, but Hal, who is not culinarily adventurous, was uninterested. He made a safer choice: chicken breast with fettuccini noodles.

When my meal was served, I took one look and, well, I was trés disappointed, to say the least. Cassoulet, apparently, is a fancy French word for navy beans. I was well acquainted with these small, white beans. Every kid raised by a man who completed a stint in the United States Navy is well-acquainted with white beans. My stepfather, Arlie, was such a man. He liked his navy beans best paired with ham hocks and boiled to within an inch of their lives. To compensate for the lackluster flavor of the beans, Arlie salted the mushy, greasy mess liberally. Suffice it to say, his cooking was not the inspiration of Le Cordon Bleu.

The version of cassoulet set before me paired the beans with duck, sausage, pork, and mutton. This French dish is humble fare—the food of country peasants—and therefore, whatever leftover meats are available in the kitchen are thrown into the pot and simmered all day. Yay. Despite my disappointment and the less than exciting ingredients, I did find the concoction edible, and I was hungry. So I swallowed the beans and then promptly forgot the meal.

Strangely, once we returned to the United States, this was the one French dish I couldn't get out of my mind. Before long, I decided that I simply must try to recreate cassoulet at home. I began to research recipes online, and quickly came to the conclusion that there would be difficulty in serving this meal to my husband. The man does not eat anything in the pork family, he doesn't eat mutton, or duck. He likes his meats very lean—nothing fatty or greasy. And he steadfastly refuses to eat most varieties of beans. White beans are not among the varieties he favors. Furthermore, my quest to create an edible cassoulet was complicated by the notion of flavor. Navy beans are notoriously bland. The delectable flavor of the French version of the dish is supplied by the meats and their fatty components. How could I create a recipe that would overcome Hal's culinary taboos and also offer a savory taste?

After a great deal of deliberation, I created what I hoped was a pleasing recipe. Instead of the recommended four cans of cannelloni beans, I used only one can. Let there be just a suggestion of beans, not an avalanche, I reasoned. For the meats, I used chicken thighs, Andouille chicken sausages cut into coins, and turkey sausage crumbles to give a variety of textures to the dish. I added flavor with a generous measure of bella mushrooms, fire-roasted tomatoes, white cooking wine, and chicken broth. Six hours on low in the slow cooker, and voila! I had proudly produced my first foray into French-inspired cooking.

Truth is, I genuinely enjoyed my version of cassoulet, but would my husband find the dish acceptable? In my house, the test of a successful recipe is how many servings the man will consume in a single sitting. One serving means: he doesn't much care for it, but he's hungry, so he'll choke it down, don't serve this again. Two servings means: it's edible, OK to serve again, but not too often. Three servings means: the dish is delicious, add it to the regular repertoire.

My concoction was a hit! Magnifique! I christened my new recipe "Cassoulet Marzell" and proudly inscribed it into my personal recipe book for future dining pleasure. Vive la France!

Calling Out

by KaShawna McKay

I can't come in today,
I'm sick.
Sick of being proper and quietly compliant.
I can't go out in the world today,
I'm sick.
Sick of being nice when I feel dark and defiant.

> I can't talk right now,
> I'm sick.
> Sick of biting my tongue and minding my expression.
> I can't explain it any clearer.
> I'm sick.
> Sick of systematic oppression.

No, you can't touch my hair,
I'm sick.
And it might be the last thing you ever do.
I can't tolerate your ignorance today,
I'm sick.
Sick of being Me when I have to deal with You.

> I can't be civil and composed today,
> I'm sick.
> Sick of being guarded but not protected.
> I'm sick of being bound by these chains.
> I'm sick
> of feeling tied down and disconnected.

I'm sick of censoring my rage.
I'm sick of stifling my pain.
Sick of watching the world swerve all over the road
while I'm expected to stay in my lane.

> You'd like me to shut up and calm down,
> but I'm sick.
> Sick of protesting to a revolving door.
> Sick of freedom that isn't free at all.
> I'm sick.
> And I can't hold it all in anymore.

Dyslexia

by Mary McLoughlin

A round peg in a square hole adrift
    Unable to decipher the letters
    whirl and float
A disability or a gift?

Love of learning do admit
    Support and fortitude to keep trying
A disability or a gift?

Learning to read melds and shift
    Now reading to learn.
A disability or a gift?

To reach the summit
    Pushing to overcome.
A disability or a gift?

A talented mathematician with grit
    A teacher who understands and leaves no one behind.
A disability or a gift?
    A round peg in a square hole adrift

The Ceili

BY MARY MCLOUGHLIN

Semi-circle of musicians ready
    Dancers form a square of 8
1, 2, 3, the music begins the room is alive
    Dancers move to the beat

Dancers form a square of 8
    4 couples swing in unison
Dancers move to the beat
    Ancient reels and jigs, layers of sound

4 couples swing in unison
    Smiles and 'hups' fill the room
Ancient reels and jigs, layers of sound
    Immersed in the moment, this is the world

Smiles and 'hups' fill the room
    Musicians play as one, absorbed
Immersed in the moment, this is the world
    2 quick taps on the bodhran, just 8 beats to go.

Let's do another one!

My Life in 6 Pages

BY CARMEN MELENDEZ-GUTIERREZ

I was born in a little town in the middle of the island of Puerto Rico. I came to this world with the help of a midwife (comadrona), madrina Castula. It was a hot summer day, as told by my family members. I was the middle of five siblings, two older brothers, a younger brother, and a younger sister. Growing up around my grandparents and cousins, life was tough but we were happy. Life was simple. For the first 7 years of my life I was raised in the neighborhood of La Loma (el barrio). I lived in a few houses with my grandparents: Papa Juan and Mama Ramona. Ramona Marquez was my grandmother. She was very special and fundamental in my upbringing, unfortunately she died young. She died on October 12, 1969. About my father, I can't find it in my heart to love him or forgive him for all the suffering he causes my family. I mean my mother died when she was 52, I always think that indirectly he killed her "a cuchillo de palo." I do not remember any happy moments with my father. He never was a father, supported us or gave us advice, on the contrary he was an abusive father and husband. He even stole from us. My mother was the first wife. When my mother was pregnant with me, he got another woman, who had a daughter months after I was born. And guess what, he named her second daughter Carmen, just like my mother and me. He named my half-sister from another mother after my mother to make her feel better for having a "corteja", so he said. That tells you how ignorant he was.

When I was 7 we moved to town, to the projects (el caserio). The people in my hometown were friendly and kind. I remember living in the "caserio" and seeing a whole new world compared to living in a farm-like atmosphere. I got tough by necessity. Walking home from school occasionally I encountered a bully named Nora.

My joy was to visit my maternal grandmother in Pinas, another community in my hometown where my mother grew up. I remember the hacienda 'Las Posas", my maternal grandparents' home. It was remote and as progress showed they built a house by the main road, but my grandfather Pablo and his two brothers: Visitacion (Becho) and Tio Jacinto continue working the hacienda. I will go with my uncle Jose Manuel to bring "fiambreras" with lunch to them. On the way there we go near the "cascadas" and play with the water. I love it that every Sunday all the family will gather for a meal. It was the best memories playing with my cousins.

In 1969, I was 15 years old when my dear grandma, Mama Ramona, died. I remember Titi Narcisa traveled from New York for the funeral. She was so beautiful and bitchy. Later I learned she was a pinup girl and a singer in the 60's. She married some Aguilar guy from Mexico, who was later famous. Titi Narcisa died in a fire in New Jersey with 6 or 7 of her grandkids. That was such a tragedy for the whole family. I remember Titi Lydia went to New Jersey for the funerals and brought many newspapers with articles of this awful event.

I graduated in 1972 from High School and went to graduate school for 6 months to study drafting but had to stop due to financial hardship. I really wanted to study pharmacy but was unable to get into the university again due to financial hardship. I asked my dad to use his military benefits to sponsor my studies and he refused. Later, I went to a vocacional school and studied Banking Service, and started working for Banco Popular de Puerto Rico, a major financial institution on the island. I worked for Banco Popular for 3 years, 1974-1977. I started in Hato Rey, La Milla de Oro. I worked at the vault (La Boveda), with Mr. Ruiz-Chaar, and Mayito. I have the best memories of those years. A lot of good stuff happened to me. I met Jaime and Papo. I also worked as a "relief" teller for the Metropolitan Area, visiting 26 different branches. I was working at LD, (Loan Department) in

Cupey Center when I met Papo. He was the love of my life. I also met Gerardo, Papo's best friend. I was fired from this job because I was always late. I was late for work almost every day, but this was not my choice. No matter how early I woke up trying to win time, I was traveling from Comerio to San Juan and the transportation was awful. I was good at what I was doing. I got many achievements and was praised constantly by all my customers, co-workers, and superiors.

During this time I was able to buy a house in Bayamon for my mother. My oldest brother Junior and his wife Milagros lived there with us. Unfortunately we lost that house. I was the only one working and "no pude con la carga."

In 1979 I joined the PR National Guard and went to training in Fort Benjamin Harrison, Indiana, where I met my husband who I married in 1980. Meeting Pedro was a "love story". After I finished a class at the Administration Building in Fort Benjamin Harrison in Indiana, I was walking down the stairs when I saw this guy that mesmerized me. I was attending Finance Training for the PR National Guard. He was walking up the stairs, me down, our eyes met and continued looking at each other for a while. Cupid did his duty! We did not speak a word. He was hot! Eric Estrada lookalike! Later I learned he was also Puerto Rican. I continued walking to my room, when there I started telling my roommate Rita how I just met the guy I was going to marry! She laughed at me, made fun at me and told me "you are so romantic". Days passed and I saw this guy at the mess hall (at this point I still have not talked to him). He looked at me, I looked at him, another spark! This time he smiled at me and I froze. I felt stupid. Weeks later Rita had a date and hooked me up with her date's best friend. Rita's date happens to be the guy I met walking down the stairs. I ended up being with that guy and Rita was so mad at me. Years later I married this guy.

March is a special month for me. I left Puerto Rico on March

18 of 1980. Got married on the 22nd of March, 3 days after I arrived in California. I was supposed to visit and stay with my friend Shelly during my vacations but never made it to her place. Instead she took Pedro with her to the airport to pick me up. It was a surprise for me! Pedro received me with the most beautiful red roses arrangement. He took me to dinner at a very nice Chinese food restaurant in the Hollywood Hills, then to his apartment where I had the most amazing experience. I fell in love with the guy all over again. I went back to Puerto Rico to quit my job and to pick my favorite things to move to California. I remember the day I said goodbye to my mom. The radio was playing Michael Jackson's "Rock With Me." I lived with Pedro in his apartment in Covina, CA for a little while and then we rented a really nice place in Rowland Heights, CA.

I got pregnant but lost my first baby. I was unhappy that I left my sick mother behind, I think that had to do a lot with my miscarriage. I left PR because I was so tired of being responsible for being the only one taking care of my mother. My two older brothers did nothing, my two younger siblings did less. So I left far, far away to California. That same year I had to go back because my mother got Pneumonia. She died while I was there and I stayed for her funeral. She was 52 when she died. That caused me such trauma that when I reached 52, (and because every time I went to Puerto Rico people in my family commented on how much I looked like my mother), I thought I was going to die. In that year, 2006, I traveled, on my own, in my little Toyota Corolla car, from California to Florida. I called it the "menopausal rampage"

I had my first child Gloriani in 1982, she was born in the Army military base of Fort Ord, California. From there we moved to Hawaii where my second daughter Monica was born in Tripler Army Hospital. We were living in the Army base Fort Shafter. While living in this house on Macomb Dr, my sister Annie and nephew Felix came to visit in Hawaii.

After I left my husband, I left Hawaii and went to live in Riverside, California with my two daughters, my sister and my nephew. Every night we watched a soap opera called "CRYSTAL". One time they announced that the characters of "Crystal" will be in Riverside at the place now known as the Fox Theater. I always wanted to be a reporter so the night of the show, me and my sister dressed up really fancy and went to the theater pretending to be reporters. They never asked us for any identification, we had a camera and for some unknown reason they let us go in and mingle with the stars. I took pictures with me and all of the stars. I still remember the thrill!

2000 was a special year. I went to Puerto Rico for my Class Reunion, I had an encounter with an old friend and had a passionate 2 week affair, then came back home to California.

All my life I LOVE making movies but 2001 - 2002 was my peak! I made a few movies, and met some celebrities. I still dream about making THE ONE.

2018 seems to be the year!

Being a single mother was not easy. I struggled to communicate with my family with the best words I could so they won't take it the wrong way. It makes me so mad that my kids did not respect me. I felt that as a mom I was not strict, firm or strong enough to stand up and discipline my kids.

In my family the oldest living is my brother Junior, but he is in Puerto Rico, but in California I am the queen! I am the oldest Melendez in California. In Puerto Rico I have the most amazing group of friends in my hometown, my classmates. Even after more than 49 years, when I graduated from High School, I still keep in touch with my childhood friends.

I am so proud of my sister and myself. We came to this country as "jibaritas'" and we survived. We raised our kids by ourselves. We were able to create many achievements. Today my heart is broken because 2 years ago my sister died suddenly. No one expected it. One Sunday we were having lunch and going shopping and the next morning she died of a heart attack. I often wonder what would have been if I would have stayed in Puerto Rico, but this is the path that God chose for me. I miss my island, but my loved ones are here. Would I ever go back to live there?

Barbara Meyer

BY BARBARA MEYER

I have been suffering from Dementia for several years and was told it was the Alzheimer type. I have had almost no short-term memory for years. I have also been diagnosed with rather severe scoliosis. I am bent forward a lot and sideways. My shoulders are rather far to the right of my hips. My primary doctor says I should walk at least 150 minutes per week. My husband Marvin would like this to be in our backyard in the early morning hours, rather than me sleeping in! (Tell your daughters of this problem if they marry a farm boy.) My work in our home is pretty much limited to cleaning sinks, counters and dishes. I do not like to be left at home alone. Fortunately, I have a daughter, a son-in-law, a grandson, a granddaughter and two dogs a block away and they all like me!

A Pot in Our Bathroom

by Barbara Meyer

Some people are concerned about having a seat at the table, as I was growing up, we often had a different problem! We were a family of six with a single bathroom that was, as usual, equipped with a single toilet and sink, in the same room. That would be a difficult scheduling problem without the added problem that was ours. My dad, Steven Otis Porter, was an alcoholic that also worked a regular job. He often closed the bars at 2 AM! The beer intake likely added to his need to spend time draining it off. In addition to this problem, due to his shortage of sleep, he would often fall asleep on that one and only toilet! The other five family members often needed it, and the sink, to meet their schedules.

It was a great relief when my mom, Alta Peters Porter, divorced him, learned to be a defense plant inspector and bought a home for her family. Otis was an excellent auto mechanic and he did one good thing, he maintained his ex-wife's cars for most of his remaining life. Oh, he also helped his son-in-law, my husband Marvin, exchange the engine in our red 1952 Ford convertible. He was a terrible husband and father but an excellent and generous auto mechanic.

My Trip of Childhood & Youth Nostalgia

by Marvin Meyer

It has been many years since we have visited the place of my birth, childhood and youth in Western OK. It would be nice to do so again, although I fear that much will be different. Many of the people that I knew are dead but there will probably be a few still vertical or seated in a wheelchair. All housing rental units that we built have been sold. These were always the spots that we hooked up our little motorhome. We still know the present owner so we might still be able to park there. Also, we still own the farm but there is no electricity there. I would travel to our farm, my birthplace farm, the country church and its cemetery. A cruise around the towns of Weatherford and Clinton, OK would be interesting and of course time would be spent in the Clinton cemetery where my mom, dad, sister and brother-in-law are buried.

When I leave that area, I would like to follow the route that I traveled at age 16 driving a truck hauling a very tall, wide and heavy combine. I also hauled the wheat from the combines to grain elevators as we worked the custom combine event from Oklahoma up state route 183 into North Dakota. When I get into Kansas, I would take the Yellow Brick Road east to Wichita and try to locate where my uncle and aunt, Henry and Anna Sawatzky, lived. My future brother-in-law also rented a small apartment in their basement and they both worked at the Boeing Aircraft plant. I would also like to find the backyard house that my sister Blondina and her husband Leon Town were asphyxiated in.

Now I would go back west and resume my wheat harvest route. Our first night was probably in Kansas, there was an overnight dust storm so I was not able to see the color of my red car. How did my car get there? My job was driving dad's truck with a combine on top of it! The combine was 13' wide over the truck cab and it extended about 5' past the rear of the truck bed. I was not about to leave my car at home so I fabricated a long towbar and towed my car along with us. As I recall, our first stop, unloading and harvesting was done at Gurly, Nebraska. My car came in handy here as the engine in my truck failed. I pulled it, dropped it in the car trunk, got a rebuilt one and installed it. One day's trucking was lost by this problem. When we ran out of wheat to cut in this area, we loaded up and headed north again. The normal pattern was to travel a little further than the ripe wheat, arrange for a job, unload and begin harvesting. This time we went to Lemon, South Dakota and it began raining! The grain cannot be thrashed out of the head when moist, so we waited for a week or so. My car was again of great joy.

Somewhere along the route I would like to observe the area that I had to do a balancing act with the top-heavy loaded truck. I was on the outside of a flat curve (no superelevation) and the truck was leaning precariously as I kept it on the road. It did not tip and I did not go off and down the slope. Later I topped a long steep downhill and saw a bridge at the bottom. It was one that had the support structure over its' top. Therefore, I knew that we had to stop, flag traffic and creep across it as our wide loads used almost the entire bridge width. I was able to stop a few feet behind our other loaded truck but my front brakes began smoking badly and I had trouble standing as I exited the cab. I had been on the brakes, then lowering to the next gear and on the brakes again all the way down the hill. This was really critical as it would have wrecked both trucks and combines, and the primary cause would likely have been the extra push of my car in tow!

Each night of the entire trip, we placed a tarp over the truck beds and slept there. As we went north and fall was coming it became colder; a little snow fell and we had to break a little ice off our pan to freshen up. After we finished harvesting this area, we headed north again to the area west of Minot, North Dakota. The fields were much stonier there than our OK ones.

While there we met an OK farmer from south of our place and his story was very interesting. He farmed in both Oklahoma and North Dakota! He would plant his winter wheat in the fall in OK, then go to ND to run a rock picker through his fields prior to planting spring wheat there. Back in OK, he would harvest his wheat in late June, do custom harvesting as it ripened going north. He eventually ends up at his ND farm in the late fall, harvests his ND wheat and heads back to OK unless he chooses to work up into Canada before going home.

When finished here we decided not to go on to Canada, so we loaded up and headed down south to OK. We had a very strong headwind for much of the way home, I could never get into my higher gears as we were pushing the 13' wide combine header into the wind. On this trip that I would like to take, I would not return to OK but would head west and scope out Wyoming. I would like to move there.

Perseverance

by Marvin Meyer

I cannot think of anything in my life that took an abnormal amount of perseverance. I have been very blessed with good parents, good opportunities and good schools. The only thing that I believe I can take credit for, is that I tried to take maximum advantage of every opportunity that was available to me. In looking back, I am sure that God was directing, maneuvering or blocking while I thought I was in control!

Now allow me to talk about a life that required perseverance. That would be my parents Otto and Lena Meyer. Mom lost her mother at an early age and lived under two stepmothers after that. Her father was a very hard taskmaster and very little a father. Dad lost his father at about age nine, his fourth grade year in school was his last formal education. Dad used books to help teach himself carpentry. He had complete confidence that he could learn anything that he chose. He later taught himself to be a brick mason and home designer. Many custom homes in and around Clinton, OK were designed and built by him. In his late years he even did the plumbing and electrical work. He designed and built a few houses with only the help of a bit of labor, he performed all the construction trades. This allowed everything to fit perfectly without any conflict between the trades. Dad also maintained all our farm and family vehicles. I can only remember him hiring a mechanic to overhaul the engine of one tractor and the "so called mechanic" did a terrible job. Do you wonder why I am such a compulsive do-it-yourselfer?

Through their years of marriage and raising two children, things were very rough. The dust bowl was rolling through during several of these years. At the time, we were living on the dirt "Brick plant road" with many trucks passing as they hauled clay to the plant. The dust was so bad that mom placed damp towels or rags along the base of doors and windows to keep the dust out. She also placed my sister and I in an interior closet to protect us. During this time, many farmers gave up and ended up in the Bakersfield area. Dad always farmed but could never have survived without his building construction abilities.

Living on and farming the land is a way of life for many, even if they are forced to learn another trade to survive financially. There were many prayers for rain and a few for the rain to stop before the farm washed away. Also, when the wheat comes near ripe for harvest there was and is always the threat of hail. I can remember harvesting a few bushels of a new crop before hail came and Dad lost a year's investment in the mud. He and the rest of the farmers borrowed money and bought more seed, fertilizer and fuel to try again for a harvest.

Mom and Dad persevered through many health issues, with no medical insurance: it began with my breech birth which caused Mom a fallen stomach, Mom also had life threatening asthma, their daughter fought life threatening pneumonia and Mom battled cancer for four years before it got her. Dad taught his only son to be a journeyman brick mason and then lost half of his family in three months. Three months after his wife died, his only daughter got married and ten days later they were both asphyxiated in their home.

My Very Happy Memory with Daughter Janetta

by Marvin Meyer

When our oldest daughter was about to graduate college with her bachelor's degree, she announced that she wanted to spend the summer in Europe. She asked me, her father, to go with her! When you hear this, your mind immediately says, "Sure, she wants you to pay for it". That was not her desire, she had earned and saved her money for the trip. It was very difficult for me to get my work caught up and to get six weeks of leave. But I was so honored to have a daughter that wanted her dad with her on this momentous trip, that I made it work. As we were in LAX waiting for our plane, I recognized the pastor that married Barbara and me. I spoke with him and his wife and learned that they were on their way on our airplane to visit their daughter Carol! She had been a close friend of ours as we dated. We were able to meet her on the East Coast.

A male friend of Janetta's had agreed to meet her at this airport, he did, took her to lunch and our plane was ready to depart but she had not shown up. In the absolute knick of time, she made it! That would have been a disaster! What was I to do? Remember this was before cell phones. Her cousin was expecting to meet us at the airport in Germany! We made it and had a wonderful meal but I was wiped out from the ordeal and jet lag. We got Eurail passes, packed our backpacks and hit the rails. We slept on trains, used bed and breakfasts or youth hostels as we traveled. We normally made a loop of a part of Europe, taking 1 ½ to two weeks for each. Then we headed back to our base to clean up and do laundry before heading out for another loop. I believe our first loop was through Scandinavia. I can't remember what came next but we ended up in Switzerland, Ireland and Italy. We traveled mostly by train but were on several ships, ferries and a cog rail train. Most of our time was in Germany because of my heritage. We visited my grandmother, Katie Mueller Meyer's church, village and cemetery. It was odd to see swastikas on many grave markers! We did three of these loops before I headed home and she went to England for another six weeks.

It was a wonderful time; we had a lot of neat experiences including seeing Oberammergau. That took a lot to arrange! We were in a hostel and learned that they locked the place up tight at night and did not open until it would be too late for us to catch a bus and get there! It was very dangerous for them to lock us in all night. As a professional safety engineer, I discussed that problem with the management, so they made a special effort to let us out early and even sent lunches with us! The bus stop that we knew would take us to our destination was a rather long way from the hostel, so we ran as fast as we could, made it and then laughed as the bus drove right past our hostel!

I felt like the most honored father to have a daughter that wanted to travel with me. What a wonderful time. We each paid our own way for the trip. Our children have been fantastic in desiring to be financially independent.

Nopales: La Planta de Vida

BY ROSE Y. MONGE

Alaina Bixon, quoting Brillat-Savarin, said: "Tell me what you eat, and I will tell you who you are." This quote resonates with me from Alaina's food workshop last year. During the class, we explored food sustainability and food sources that find their way into daily meals. As we're in the midst of dire global warming, I start to think about the repercussions of climate change. How can we avert the consequences? No easy answer.

When I think about the meals I ate in childhood, I recall Mom cooking with the most humble of ingredients. Her gentle hand continues to guide me as I try to recreate her recipes. Last year I wrote about a staple at our meals, flour tortillas. This year, another Mexican staple comes to mind, the ubiquitous nopal or prickly pear cactus-genus Opuntia. There are 300 species of the genus growing in a wide range of climate conditions. It has yet to garner the respect it justly deserves.

This humble staple is one of the fundamental symbols of Mexico. Why so? The following website provides some insight:www. survivingmexico.com

"It is considered la planta de vida (life-giving plant), as it seems to never die. Fallen pencas (leaves) form new plants, therefore an apt symbol of the life-rebirth cycle found in the most ancient of Mexican myths. Legend has it that the first nopal grew from Copil's heart, the son of the Moon Goddess, Malinalxochitl."

The legend continues with tragic consequences. Copil believed that his uncle Huitzilopochtli, the Sun God, had abandoned his mother and attempted to murder him. "Huitzilopochtli defeated his nephew and removed Copil's heart, which was later buried. The next day, the first nopal appeared, complete with the thorns of a warrior and flowers that blossomed with the love Copil had shown in defending his mother. This nopal was discovered by the wandering Aztecs. Atop the nopal was an eagle, devouring a serpent, over a lake, the sign the nomads had been waiting for."

It's on this site the Aztecs settle to establish their empire. The myth or legend is so iconic that it's depicted on the coat of arms in the Mexican flag. If you are not a fan of myths or legends another explanation of the origin of nopales might be in order. This website asserts that nopales are likely a native of Mexico: www.gourmetsleuth.com/articles/detail/nopalitos

"It has been noted that the nopales were grown and eaten as a vegetable in Central Mexico, since before the Spanish arrived. The Spanish explorers took the plant back to Spain and the plant spread throughout North Africa with the Moors. The plant is currently grown throughout Mexico as well as parts of the United States and in many areas of the Mediterranean."

I was born in the Sonoran desert – Agua Prieta, Mexico. Nopales are part of the desert landscape and every home has a cactus "garden." Before Dad fashions an ocotillo fence around the house, nopales surround the small adobe house built by my Tata (grandfather) and Dad. As Dad owns a milpa (small farm), the "farm to table" concept is alive and well, guiding Mom's food preparation. Eating nopales is as common as eating corn, squash, tomatoes, and peppers. I'm five years old when we immigrate to Riverside. The cactus growing in the Hispanic neighborhoods makes me feel at home.

There are two food crops derived from nopales – the "nopalitos" which are the cactus pads used for cooking; The other is the prickly "pear" (tuna) or fruit of the cactus which is used for juices, jellies, candies, teas and alcoholic drinks.. Who knew that a desert plant could be so versatile?

Mom is my nopales "guru" with her wide array of recipes. However, I don't recall any recipe for the "tuna" or pear fruit of the cactus. Preserving nopales in Mason jars is a yearly ritual in our family. The process requires skill and patience as this is a long process. Cutting out the espinas (thorns) from the cactus pads is arduous and challenging. Trust me! Those tiny thorn pricks are painful! After removing the thorns, Mom cuts them into rectangular slices before boiling them with salt, garlic and onion until they're tender. After removing them from the stove, she washes them with water several times as they tend to get slimy. Afterwards, she places them in jars which receive a second boil to seal the jars. When she hands me jars to take home, I feel I won the lottery.

When unexpected guests arrive, Mom has plenty of Mason jars in her pantry to prepare a delicious meal. She adds them to eggs, poultry, and soups. Once we immigrate, she expands her creativity adding them to whatever protein was at hand. But she always returns to those dishes that remind me of my childhood. Mom's nopales with chili colorado (red sauce), and nopales with dried shrimp patties are my favorites. Tender grilled nopalitos mixed with pico de gallo makes an exquisite smoky salsa.

Today with the growing interest in cultural cuisine, nopales either fresh or in jars are found in many grocery stores. That's the good news. But nopales may be an acquired taste. Some people like them; some don't. It reminds me of those who say they like or hate avocado or cilantro. Do nopales have a distinctive flavor? I think so but it depends on preparation and the ingredients in the mix.

Over the holidays, a Facebook post advertising soap made from nopales intrigued me. As I was writing about nopales, I Googled the website. The brand name Nopalera was created by Sandra Lilia Velasquez. As we know, inspiration comes from unexpected places. She wrote that her inspiration came while eating eggs and nopales at her parents' home. At the time, she was making organic plant-based soaps.

"Nopales have been around my entire life, and I feel we take them for granted. They are there against fences and along the sides of freeways. They are this wonder plant because they need nothing," says Velasquez. "All they need is dirt to grow, and they're not only good for your digestion, but you can make textiles out of them and apply them on your skin the way you would apply aloe vera." And as the adage goes, the rest is history. Her soaps are now available at Nordstrom and boutiques nationwide.

And there's more. John Staughton wrote the following in the article: 11 Impressive Benefits of Nopales | Organic Facts (July 9, 2021). He cites that nopales can "help in weight loss, improve skin care and heart health". Additionally, it may "improve digestion, boost the immune system, optimize metabolic activity, improve bone density, promote good sleep, and reduce inflammation throughout the body."

We all have to eat, but what do we eat in the future, in the face of global warming and climate change? How can we grow food in less than ideal conditions? It changes access, availability, stability, prices, food supply and safety. Every culture has signature regional dishes based on available food supply. Let's respect Mother Earth and seek innovative ways to use the food sources that have sustained us for years. The humble nopal stands the test of time.

Are nopales truly the "plant of life?" You be the judge .A hardy plant that flourishes under the most difficult of climate conditions, provides sustenance both as a vegetable and a fruit needs our respect. The health benefits alone deserve our attention.

As an aside, Mom judges the authenticity of a Mexican restaurant by whether they have nopales on the menu. Perhaps this assessment is a tad harsh, but I smile thinking of Mom when I notice nopales on a menu. (November 2021)

Summer 1986 in Mexico City.

by Rose Y. Monge

Sally's phone call surprises me. Meet us in Mexico City, my sister tells me. I thought you were in Managua visiting your friends for the summer, I respond. We are, but we want to spend a few days in Mexico City before heading home. Can you join us? It's the summer in 1986 and just like that, my summer plans change.

You may be wondering what connection my sister has to Nicaragua. In 1981, my sister and her husband Tony opt to leave their teaching jobs in San Francisco to support a socialist, political party, the Sandinistas in Managua, Nicaragua. Why they feel compelled to go during a civil war intrigues me. Other family members are in shock, especially Mom.

Mom worries about the constant media accounts of the bloody scrimmages and death toll on both sides: the oppositional militias known as Contras supported by the CIA against the Sandinistas for local control. When Sally informs Mom she's pregnant with her first child, imagine my surprise when she decides to fly to Managua all by herself!. She stays for several months after my niece, Rosita is born but Sally and the family remain until 1983. Mom breathes a sigh of relief when they return to their teaching jobs in San Francisco.

Back to the phone call. I'm on summer break from Poly HS where I'm a guidance counselor and never been to Mexico City. I gladly accept my sister's offer and make flight arrangements. Sally and her family plan to arrive a few days before me to secure lodging. I'm giddy with excitement to see my family but also to see more and learn of my native land.

I plan to leave from the Tijuana Airport and not LAX to save a few dollars. I just bought a beautiful new car, a red T-Bird, and every penny counts. When I tell my parents that I'm going to

Mexico City, they're thrilled for me. My dad agrees to take me to the airport and pick me up upon my return.

It's a beautiful sunny morning in July when Dad picks me up. He's a great story-teller and regales me with stories of his childhood as we approach the US-Mexico border. I love his stories and now I regret not writing those stories down.

Once we reach the border, as expected, traffic is bumper to bumper. Dad patiently navigates through congested traffic. I learn as a youngster that nothing really bothers Dad unlike Mom who worries about everybody and everything. I sense that Dad enjoys the power of my new T-bird. We finally arrive at the airport. We hug our goodbyes and I hear Dad tell me "que Dios te bendiga" (May God bless you) when I exit the T-Bird.

Now to find my bearings as my plane leaves in an hour. The airport reminds me of a lively beehive, people scurrying to-and-fro in every direction around me. I finally pass through customs at the AeroMexico terminal and board the plane. In short order, every seat is taken and we're packed like sardines. The first few hours are fine once we're in the air. Unexpectedly, the pilot announces that a summer storm is on the horizon and to brace for some turbulence. Truer words were never spoken! I try to relax but I feel like I'm riding in an aerial roller coaster throughout the rest of the long flight.

My seat companion is a chatty older male who apparently sees my discomfort and tries to distract me. To this day, I don't remember anything I say to him. I nod occasionally as not to appear rude but intermittent thunder and lightning intensifies my misery. Squeals and gasps from the passengers add to my distress. I pray for the rain to stop.

Closing my eyes doesn't help and I don't recall eating anything during the flight. By the grace of God, we land without mishap. This international airport is huge, hectic and confusing. How will my brother-in-law Tony find me among the masses? Minutes feel like hours. Finally, I see Tony waving in the distance. After greeting him, we queue up to pick up my luggage. He tells me he has a taxi waiting for us and after 20 minutes or so, we're on our way.

The taxi ride from the airport to our hotel with the conglomeration of cars honking, the traffic violations at every turn and air pollution leaves me speechless. The Tijuana ride pales by comparison. I whisper a prayer as we exit in front of the hotel. Tony gathers my luggage and directs me to the second floor stairs. Once inside, my niece Rosita yells out Tia Rosie is here! She runs towards me embracing my legs. Sally cradles baby Loreta on one arm and hugs me with the other .Afterwards as I hold the cooing baby, I take stock of my living accommodations.

The suite is unlike any other hotel room for its spaciousness. The huge windows that reach the 12-foot ceiling are impressive. Rays of sunshine filter through the transparent, lacy curtains. The sleeping quarters consisting of two large beds are separated by oversized sofas. I see a large rustic table with several chairs near the entryway. The furniture appears worn but comfortable. I notice a tiny bathroom adjacent to the front door. How did you find this hotel, I ask Sally. I got lucky. It was the last and only available hotel near the Zona Rosa, she replies. The Zona Rosa is walking distance from the pulse of the cultural, entertainment, governmental and financial center of Mexico City.

Rosita keeps tugging at my blouse. I'm hungry, she moans. Yo, tambien (Me, too) I sigh. .We can walk to the restaurant nearby, Tony replies. Great idea. Let's go, Sally exclaims. My summer adventure is about to begin! (November 2021).

Job Hunting with Chopsticks

BY BARBARA MORTENSEN

It is terrible to know that you are not only underpaid and over-worked, but even worse to know you are undervalued! How to remedy this? I posed this question over lunch with a friend, a guru in Human Resources. We were in Los Angeles, going through the LA Times classified job ads (pre-Google) when we came upon an ad for an International Consultant for a presti-gious company. But the company was, per its phone number, in San Francisco. My friend offered a challenge and a bet: Call, and once you have reached the correct person, you have 5 minutes to get yourself an interview with an all-expense paid trip to San Francisco.

I won the bet and next thing I knew, briefcase in hand, I was flying to San Francisco! The dilemma was whether to wear my eyeglasses or contact lenses to the interview. I worried about windy San Francisco and opted for my aviator-style coke-bottle spectacles.

As I went up the corporate interview ladder, I found the job was truly going to be international and very challenging. Right up my alley!

Lunchtime was fast approaching, and I made another bet with myself: "Self," I said, "I bet they will take me to lunch in what they think will be a challenging food experience for me." I won the second bet too. I was invited to lunch at a well-known Japa-nese restaurant. Once again, I said "Self, they will want to see if I know what to do with sushi and if I know how to eat with chop-sticks." (Not only do I like Japanese food, but I can eat as well with chopsticks as I can with a fork and knife.)

When I sat down to lunch with my potential new boss and the worldwide controller of this vast company, I opened and prepared their chopsticks for them. As we ate, through the corner of my eye I watched them watching me and my table manners. The conversation revolved around job duties, experiences I had had – normal interview questions and lunch chit chat.

Suddenly the controller pointed his chopsticks at me and asked, "What would you do if you were sitting at a dinner in a foreign country you had never before visited, with people you didn't know, dressed in unusual garb, and your attitude and demeanor were crucial to the welfare of the company AND (here it comes), you were served a bowl of soup with a large eyeball floating in it?"

I put down my chopsticks (properly of course), took off my coke-bottle spectacles and replied, "You see these glasses: If I take them off, I can't see anything at all, and it wouldn't make a difference to me what they served in that soup bowl or what was floating in it."

I got the job, and a week later I was on another plane with my new boss, on our way to Australia.

What's for Dinner

BY BARBARA MORTENSEN

They say one picture is worth 1000 words.

Well, I will give you the words so that you get the picture!

In my kitchen is a large walk-in pantry, filled with condiments. I have a large built-in kitchen cabinet with large shelves next to my stove. It is also filled with condiments. I have a center island with drawers, which are filled with condiments. I have a huge French door refrigerator. Guess what – it's filled with condiments!

It's usually late afternoon when I ask my husband what he would like for dinner. His favorite food and his usual answer is "ANYTHING."

Unfortunately, ANYTHING is about the only dish I don't know how to make. What to do? I figure out how much time I am willing to spend in preparing a non-specific anything meal, what it should taste like, and what kind of side dish I could add to this mystery meal.

I begin to think about what I have in my huge freezers (yes, I have lots of those too!) that will defrost quickly. I also check one of my refrigerators for fresh vegetables I may have on hand to go with "Anything."

Arms loaded, I go to my condiment closets and start making my selections. I put a little of this and a little of that and then add some more of this and that into a pan until I like the aroma. Now I engage my husband once again.

"What kind of side dish would you like? Rice, pasta, potatoes?"

"NOTHING!"

"What do you mean, nothing?"

"Nothing, because I don't want you to go out of your way for me."

So the "nothing" item I usually select is rice because I like rice! I begin to mix my anything and my nothing decisions and add heat. After I stir and cook – VOILA, in a short time, a delicious, healthy, tasty and aromatic "ANYTHING MIXED WITH NOTHING DINNER!"

Sometimes, after we dine, my sweet husband even thanks me for "nothing."

La Reina De Beaumont

by Cindi Neisinger

The warm milk with a sprinkle of cinnamon and an egg, the whole egg—including the yellow yolk and its attached white string moquito—swirled in my cup.

My Great-Grandmother Viviana Aldaco called it un Ponche. The Eggnog-like delicious, nourishing recipe was passed down through the generations, originating in Mexico on my mother's side of the family. It was handed to the children in our family before we ran out the door to school. This cozy drink was served in a random mug, with a dash of love and a connection to the past. Whenever I smell cinnamon, it brings back memories.

In 1912, my Great-Grandmother Viviana lived in Beaumont, California. An unofficial Mexican community called Chancla. It was a long way off from her ancestral home in Guanajuato, Mexico. I found her picture, in a box in my mother's closet. On the back it was dated April 1912 in Beaumont, California. I looked her up in the 1920 US Census, yes, she was there. But, why? In those days Beaumont was a community of agricultural pickers and packers. Like Riverside had its oranges, Beaumont had apricots. The 10-freeway had not yet been built. There were still horses, more than cars. It was our migration history and a stepping stone into the land of milk and honey. El otro lado.

People didn't have much, but they had familia. They worked hard in the fields and packing farms. For fun, they would go to a festival once a month. It meant bringing a pail of savory frijoles refried in lard, and a bag of fresh handmade, brown speckled flour tortillas to eat throughout the day. A full day of fun on the Morongo Indian reservation, welcomed by the Cahuilla Indian Tribe, it was a long walk but worth it.

Great-Grandmother Viviana, I wish I had more information about how you ended up in Los Angeles, where my mother was born. I see you in this picture, like a queen with her court. Any concerns or anxiety about this new land are hidden in your regal smile, as your children and family are gathered around you, including my Grandmother Isabel. You look so content and happy.

Your daughter, my Grandmother, Isabel Gutierrez bought a small neighborhood market and a home in Los Angeles in the 1940s. I see how you imparted so much frugality, common sense and wisdom on her. My mom says she would can every fruit and vegetable from her garden. A deep cleaning was done on Saturdays—all drawers were emptied and organized. Outside, weeds were plucked and the grass was mowed. The yard was raked of leaves, especially around fruit trees and the regal Magnolia trees. My mom says even the dirt was cleared of rocks or debris. It was called tierra limpia or clean dirt.

The ripple of prosperity is still felt and seen through six generations. My mother, Dorita, opened a beauty shop with her inheritance, which paid off her one acre home in Riverside, CA. I bought my first home with the encouragement and help of a down payment from my mother. I paid it off. The trickle down of prosperity will probably end there because houses are too expensive now. Today, we are keeping the acre of land in the family. This is all because of you, my dearest Great-Grandmother.

I see in this picture how you cared about your appearance and the girls had beautiful bows in their hair. I see your hair is coiffed in stylish finger waves. I can almost feel the stiff, freshly starched and ironed dress material. I remember my mother ironing our clothes...with a damp rag, hot steam forcing the wrinkles to comply. We always have an ironing board set-up in our homes.

Did you know, Great-Grandmother that you gave us the love of music? I know my grandmother played the piano and my mother too. To this day I can hear my mother and see her hands quickly glide across the keys, pounding a boogie woogie and simultaneously using the foot pedal. She loved to play your song called, Un

Marinero. A joyous tune.

I want you to know that although you prayed the Rosary after dinner every night with your children; two generations on their knees, two generations sitting on the bed – that's four generations times ten fingers each — having slid across the Holy Rosary beads. That's a lot of prayers. So many prayers and grace from generations past to the future. It will probably end with me, the last of the Catholics and last to pray the Rosary. So sorry Great Grandmother.

I imagine hearing your voice...something like the blended voices of my Tias; Helen, Patty, Mary and my Mother Dorita. A low unexcited tone, hardly no inflection. Soft, calm and sweet. But, like in the picture your eyes – that smile – says it all. Live, love and laugh. I feel your essence in the flicker of candles we light in your honor on Dia De Los Muertos. I hear you in the

Ave Maria Song that has been sung and played for generations, it resonates and echoes off the walls of our Catholic Churches, for many weddings and funerals. I feel you in the traditions, recipes and even when I eat a sweet, juicy, orange-brown freckled apricot. Great-Grandmother Viviana, I see you, I see you...in this photograph I found, La Reina De Beaumont from 1912.

I want to acknowledge and thank author and playwright Denise Chávez of New Mexico for the inspiration to honor my Great-Grand-mother Viviana Aldaco. I participated in Maestra Chávez's amazing "Wise Latina Workshop Series: Dando la Bienvenida." In response to a 15-minute writing prompt, I drafted a spirited and heart-felt story about Viviana Aldaco. Additionally, I appreciate the opportunity to enhance and finesse my Great-Grandmother's tribute in Tesoros de Cuentos creative writing workshop. Thank you, Frances Vásquez.

Dear Ground Squirrel

After William Carlos Williams

BY S. J. PERRY

If your path had been
a tic straighter
streaking to
your burrow,

you'd probably be
eviscerated among
clippings in
my grass catcher.

I'm so relieved
I won't
have to clean
that up.

I dwell in a House—taken over

After Emily Dickinson and Julio Cortázar

BY S. J. PERRY

I dwell in a House—taken over—
By them I cannot see—
I live here with my Sister—
And they who never speak—

The oaken Doors conceal them—
And we—choose not intrude—
To save our Books—or Banknotes—
The House is theirs—for Good—

And we don't choose—to stop them—
When they crowd us to—the Street—
But rather save—their House—from Thieves—
By throwing away—the Key—

Dad's Greatest Hits: A Father's Legacy

BY CHRISTINE PETZAR

The man couldn't help himself—puns, wordplay, and just-plain-silly jokes were a daily occurrence. Driving home from church and approaching our house he'd announce, *"Hey kids, I'm a magician. Watch me turn a car into a driveway."* He'd then swerve into our driveway for dramatic effect, groans coming from the three of us in the backseat.

Fairy tales weren't exempt. Cinderella was in love with *Prince Chow Mein.*

The Big Bad Wolf *huffed and puffed and blew the house down... because it wasn't built to FHA specifications*—did I mention that he was a civil engineer? I was a teenager before I realized that FHA specifications weren't part of the story.

Even Christmas was not spared. The season for me officially starts when *Winter Wonderland* plays for the first time and I hear him singing his version: "*Later on we'll perspire....as we dream by the fire.*" As for The Night Before Christmas, after the line *"He ran to the window and threw up the sash"* my father would make a gagging sound. In our family we still read it that way, much to the chagrin of other relatives and friends who might be present.

Dad made us listen to Spike Jones records—long before Weird Al Yankovic. The manic "Cocktails for Two" (clink clink) and silly take on the opera "Carmen" (with Don Schmo-zay) are classics. He loved Stan Freberg singing "The Yellow Rose of TEX-as." Then there was the slow-paced comedy duo of Bob Elliott and Ray Gould—the Komodo Dragon sketch being my all-time favorite. Comedy was part of our cultural literacy.

He was in the cement marketing business—I always say he gave me a lot of concrete advice (insert groan here). Once, to promote the use of Riverside white cement, he had special labels made for bottles of white wine. Instead of a bucolic scene of a winery in the countryside, he had an artist create a lovely pen-and-ink drawing of the cement plant with the words *"Riverside White...Always White, Always Dry."* It was a big hit with clients.

My father died at age 73 of Parkinson's disease—too young. But his legacy lives on. My daughter and I make a game of creating silly new words. Her contribution: *mug puddles*, the water that accumulates on upside-down mugs in the dishwasher and the reason you unload the bottom rack first. Two of my contributions: *ridiculophotophobia* (the fear of appearing ridiculous in the background of other people's snapshots) and *holidated* (that one neighbor's house on the block with Christmas lights still up in March).

But my best effort was on the radio show Car Talk. The names of the Car Talk "staff" were the worst puns and my dad loved them—the law firm of *Dewey Cheetham & Howe*, their director of future planning *Kay Sera*. There was also a character named *Quasiautomotive* and one day I mused out loud to my husband, *"I wonder if he's known as the Hatchback of Notre Dame."* The rest is history—I sent a letter in with that suggestion, they read it on the air and guffawed. I have it recorded, ready to inflict my NPR fame on anyone within earshot—there's even a CD with that title. They read my letter in January 1994 and my dad died that October, so he got to hear it. He was so proud (and a little jealous, I think).

No matter what else my family chooses to write for my obituary, they have strict instructions to include the fact that I coined the term *"The Hatchback of Notre Dame."* My father's legacy lives on. I'll be here all week (badda-bing).

Work

by Janine Pourroy

The buzz of work surrounds me, like electricity.
Hissing sometimes, sometimes whispering behind my back
like two girls in a junior high school hallway
hands covering their mouths, eyes flickering, darting, landing
on all the work yet to be done.

The work dozing by the broom.
The work idle in the cupboard where we keep the gin
and the Swiffer.
The icy *clink* of reward at work's end
and the stillness of a duster, waiting in the dark.

Sturdy Legs

by Cindi Pringle

Sturdy middle-aged legs
feel strong as bollards
ground her
hold her space
stand rock steady

She doesn't worry
about a white cat twisting
between her ankles
when she's not looking
down at her feet

Balanced when jostled
she remains upright

Her determined gait
ignores curled toes
jammed in high heels
sturdy legs ache
as she drifts to sleep

* *

Spindly twelve-year-old legs
don ice skates
wobble over bumpy
frozen creek ice
ankles buckle

Knock-kneed, pigeon-toed
she doesn't comprehend
her mother's compliment
on her dancer's legs
men find appealing

Dainty ankles betray her
when she stumbles, tumbles

Roller skatin', hop scotchin'
jump ropin', bike ridin' legs
walk six blocks to school
trudge through thick, wet snow
cramp at night with growing pains

* *

Sturdy senior legs
didn't get their confidence
without effort
every-other-day
at the gym

Leg press, stationary bike
leave legs feeling
strong, invincible
powerful as Tina Turner's
signature stance

Miss a few workouts
legs are restless at night

Gotta keep movin'
health monitor says
she hasn't walked as far
today as yesterday
in a race with herself

* *

Aged flesh and bone
cast the same shadow
as the dancer's legs
of her youth
thin ankles, curvy calves

Downhill dog walks
now precarious
dodge puddles, cracks
feet thrust as brakes
throttle her pace

Look up, look down
she's observant to be sure-footed

Her tread diminishes uphill
as if thigh-deep in water
legs heavy as tree trunks
embark on fewer hikes
welcome Birkenstocks with socks

Pesticide Facials

by Edgar Rider

I came to the door with powder over part of Kipling's face and by her nose area.

She was ranting and raving about boyfriends she brought over to the house, even said she would shoot one and then herself rather than be put away. She went into the next room making funny noises, screeching noises and squeaking noises. I went closer to the bathroom and saw her standing up but doing something in front of the mirror. She was picking at her lips making painful noises and grunting sounds, "Ooh oww." What was she doing that she couldn't figure out? Was it a convulsive act? Insanity?

Went back and got my phone from the bag and called an operator. "Hello, I think my roommate is on something, not sure if I should call the paramedics or the cops. Do people call 911 for this?

"No sir, if it is not an emergency you have to dial the police department. I will connect you."

Soon I was on the line with the police operator. "I think my roommate is on something? Can someone come over? She has white powder over her face. "

"Ok sir, we will send someone over."

Thought she was on coke and was going to have some kind of seizure. Cops came and they were ready to call for an ambulance. The officer came into the room, "Where is she?"

Another officer appeared behind him. Went in front of him and into the next room. "Ma'am are you okay with what is going on? Have you taken anything?" She brushed by the officer and came out of the bathroom and appeared fine. She was carrying a bag of what was called Diatomaceous earth.

" I am fine, I have just been using this. It helps get worms out of my lips." For those unfamiliar, Diatomaceous Earth is a pesticide that kills bugs.

The two officers started discussing her claim that she was using it as a facial . One officer said "I never heard of such a thing, that is just kind of strange".

The other officer had a different opinion, "I have heard of a few people giving themselves pesticide facials ."

I was in shock and disbelief and thought for sure she was overdosing. My immediate perception of the diagnosis was wrong but what else could I have thought? The officers left because they could do nothing about putting Diatomaceous Earth on your face and especially your lips . I Googled it and found out there was such a thing as a pesticide facial. But there was no evidence that you should use it to get worms out of your lips. It seems like she had used something as true and blew it out of proportion so that her interpretation was valid but she had gone to the extreme of pulling gooey things out of her lips that were hard to distinguish as either worms or pus. What would anybody else have done, if they just moved in and saw someone in this condition? Don't tell me they would assume it was some sort of bug detoxifying system. No big deal. The officers said to me there was nothing they could do. There was nothing illegal about putting bug killer powder on your face and rubbing it in your lips. I was relieved in the sense that she was not on Cocaine but still concerned that she was on the edge of sanity. However, I had no place to go so I calmly went to bed realizing she wasn't insane. Little did I realize this was only the beginning of living in a hypochondriac world.

Nobody

After Emily Dickenson and Edgar Lee Masters

BY ROBIN WOODRUFF-LONGFIELD

A shadow in a room, was I,
A filament — A star —
A vision in white finery —
A study in pure gossamer.

A nobody — by my own design,
Were you nobody too?
An observer of all life — divine —
From Snake to Hydrangea blue?

Our earthly lives afford scant time,
To decant its wonders like a wine,
So slowly into a golden cup —
To sip, before our time is up —

No — flowers fade — fields go fallow,
No further seasons are they allowed —
When our time arrives, we must depart
Though heavy may we be of heart.

When underneath the Port Cochere,
Death's phantom phaeton stopped,
The plaintive wailing, did I hear,
Of horses, as their reins were dropped.

No more, I knew, could I record
or contemplate this life —
I held my hand out daintily
As though becoming now, a wife.

Hillsides (after H.D.)

BY ROBIN WOODRUFF-LONGFIELD

Return to me all hillsides.
All vacant land,
Wild Burros
Winding through Orange Groves;
The yearnings and warnings
Of Coyotes
At sundown.

I have no use
For newly carved roads,
Or, anonymous tiled roof homes,
Creeping up hillsides
Like Kudzu.

Give me no habitats
Dismantled
By earth movers—

Instead,
Leave me
Hillsides
Green
And velvety,
In Winter and Spring,

Brown
And brittle
In Summer and Fall.

Leave Fire Season

To the warehouses—

Especially

Warehouses—

Cavernous,

Concrete

Circus tents,

Their pitchmen

Courting commissioners

Like carnies clearing the Midway—

Don't look too closely

As the latest Leitzel*

Crashes

Just beyond the forklift.

---

* Lillian Leitzel, early 20th century circus performer, who perished
in 1931, of injuries incurred while performing her Roman Rings
routine.

Another Yellow Brick Road

(Or: The Highway, Hamentaschen, and One Family's War On "Culture")

BY ROBIN WOODRUFF-LONGFIELD

When our daughters, Ariel and Mia were small, extra money was often scarce. Absolute dedication to my self-assigned role as their first teacher meant I obsessively searched for free or nearly free educational places that they, my husband John, and I, could visit together.

In the 1990's , The Calendar section of the *Los Angeles Times* was my favorite source of information for planning these expeditions. It directed me to events at museums, book festivals, and other family friendly places. Nearly everything occurred in the L.A. area. This meant at least an hour's drive from our home in the Inland Empire.

I searched for these events with the same intensity John and the girls displayed while attempting to hide the *Times* from me. For John and Mia, each westward excursion meant hours away from DVR recordings of their beloved Law and Order SVU and C.S.I New York. For Ariel, it meant less time climbing trees, skateboarding, or engaging in other activities likely to land her in the emergency room and me one step closer to the Prozac highway. I was determined to show all three of them that there was life and learning beyond our little town.

Because I appear to have been born with the circadian rhythm of a vampire, and a high level of distractibility, we never seemed to embark on these adventures until 1:00 or 2:00 p.m. Knowing that this meant less time in the destination I planned for them, my family was never exactly in a hurry to push me out the door.

Our Fuchsia Ford Windstar seemed capable of finding its way to the westbound 10 with no guidance from me. I saw the 10 as not just a freeway, but my personal Yellow Brick Road. Each time I caught the first glimpse of the L.A. skyline during our descent from Kellogg Hill, I felt like we all were about to enter the land of Oz. If only the rest of my family felt the same…

Upon our arrival at the days' destination, the same battle plan was enacted: upon entering the event, John and the girls would look for the quickest exit. It did not matter what I had taken them to see. I would not be surprised to learn that there were discreet transfers of cash between John and the first security guard who could direct him, Ariel, and Mia to the quickest route to the nearest cafe or food court. I am still surprised that none of my family ever set off an alarm in their frantic quest to reach the outside world. At least, I don't think that ever happened.

Things may have gone a little differently had I not treated everything as though I would be quizzed on it before being allowed to enter the next section. As though passing from one section to the other was the artistic or educational equivalent of Checkpoint Charlie.

It would often be closing time before I allowed myself to leave or was encouraged by a staff member to leave. My family would be awaiting my arrival at the cafe or food court. All three of them were anxious for the next part of our journey — the bakery at Canter's Deli. That was the price I gladly paid for getting all of them into the car and on the road in the first place.

We always left the bakery counter carrying white plastic bags that were full of little pink boxes filled with our favorite treats: one Chocolate High Hat, one Vanilla High Hat, two Black and whites, a one- inch piece of Racetrack pastry, and one cherry Hamantaschen. Our choices rarely varied unless we were also bringing back treats for my parents. Then, there would also be pineapple danish and a small loaf-shaped cake with the word "Banana" cursive- written across the top in yellow icing.

My parents lived near the 405, and we often detoured there to bring treats and allow my parents time with their only grandkids. My father would want to know what I subjected them to THIS time. He would always ask the girls what they thought of it all, and about their favorite part of the day's experiences. Canter's was always what they liked best. Especially Mia, who would have much rather been just about anywhere else than L.A. That was fine by my father. He was much more comfortable teaching them how to play poker or bet on horses than ever setting foot in a museum or an art gallery.

"I'm teaching them math skills," he would say in his Yosemite Sam accent.

"Why did you drag those kids away from home AGAIN? I think you would take them to Hell if you knew you could make it a round trip!" was my mom's usual greeting.

"There's a big world out there — someone has to show it to them," was my Nice Daughter reply. "Home is for the faint of heart," was my reply when Nice Daughter could not be summoned.

I knew my time to expose Ariel and Mia to the world beyond their hometown would be short. As they grew older, their weekends would be focused on sports tournaments and sleepovers. I was determined to never miss an opportunity before those inevitable changes began. Even if it meant rousing them from sleep and gently guiding them to their beds once the van was once again in its own driveway.

What, if anything, Ariel and Mia took from their family trips to L.A., other than the part they played in keeping Canter's in business, is their story to tell. Their opinions of me have been consigned to the secretive, sacrosanct language of sisters. For that, I am grateful. What I do know is that neither of them could truthfully say "My parents never took me anywhere." I am even more grateful for that.

What Remains

(1995-2018)

BY ROBIN WOODRUFF-LONGFIELD

Baby teeth in ziplock bag
Plaster cast of five-year-old's hand
The Adventures of K'Ton Ton
Puffalump
Where The Wild Things Are
Plastic yellow Easter bunny
The Marvelous Land of Oz
Highlighters
Colored pencils
All Star jersey
Mizuno pitcher's glove
Glamour photo
Horse pedigree
Stress-relief candle
Neon green chucks
White jacket
Gray hoodie
Three tabby cats
One black cat
Inspirational quotations
Police report
Diary
Cell phone
Keys

Dance, My Life

by Marilyn Sequoia

...Stay! Stay!
Ballerina in my life.
Pirouette through
The aisles of my
Work-a-day brain.
Remind me of life lived,
Life loved,
Love's beauty.

Interrupt my work,
My thoughts,
My everything
With your grace.
Oh stay !

I stood on my front lawn the day school began in the Fall of '91, waiting for the Termite Inspector to arrive. How could this be — me not at school? I'd been burning out, so just last school year I tried voluntarily switching from high school counseling back to teaching. Everyone thought I was crazy — going backwards, they said. What they must think now that I would not be reporting to work *at all* this whole school year — in any capacity!

It all started a couple of years before when that male substitute teacher at North High was wandering around in the main office near my own tiny, cluttered counseling space. He told me he'd taken a year off from his full time job — 'for reflection.' I was astonished at the thought. You mean a person can actually DO that? Of course, it was exactly what I needed to do myself. I was in those menopausal mid-life years, when unexpected things just start bubbling up into consciousness. I'd read Murray Stein's Mid-Life and studied Carl Jung...learning about mid-life's offerings--like how one's inferior, long-ignored personality traits and shadow can demand recognition and expression, giving the opportunity to become more balanced — to individuate! Sure, the concept appealed, but that was not all, for these things were already actually emerging in me. That's why the emaciated ballerina came calling me to beauty and art — first in a dream, and later returning as a poem--the one partially quoted above bidding her to stay!

The year following that substitute teacher's off-hand remark, after my seven years of exhausting high school counseling, I did make the move to 'go back to teaching,' — partly because I wanted to start the new Peer Helper Program at North High, plus actually *teach* the classes for it. Maybe this would be my answer. But to do so, I faced a schedule I could not imagine surviving: English, Psychology, Math, plus the two Peer Helper periods! I recall standing in front of my first class that year, realizing that the energy I'd need for this school year was already spent. I was burned-out before I'd even begun. And all along, the Muses just got louder and stronger — pushing me, pulling me beyond these old, tired ways.

After that grueling school year, I traveled to visit my family of origin in Ohio — a large extended Bohemian-Catholic family. Some twenty of us were on a summer day trip to Cedar Point, the famed amusement park on Lake Erie. Cotton candy. Roller coasters. Hot dogs and taffy. Yet there I was, beside myself, deciding whether or not to call back to California, in mid-August mind you, to ask for a Leave of Absence — just a few weeks before school was to begin. I've never been a very good decider, yet I just could not sell myself out this time. I felt like I would physically die if I did not heed this yearning. There was such a deep call inside me — to silence, to a place beyond listening, to some yet-to-be-discovered self.

So, in the midst of the family's light-hearted merriment, I located a payphone and dialed my school district in California, telling them, in cryptic terms, of my request for a Leave of Absence. That it would be entirely unpaid was freaking me out for it was so unlike me. I had been working steadily for four decades — all my life since seventh grade. As a result, now I was virtually self-supporting. Although I had a fine boyfriend, he could not have financially borne this burden. No, this was mainly on me, my own life's decision.

And then it all happened: I got the Leave, and back in California, my dear colleagues began calling me. I answered the phone not at all, for I knew they would try to convince me to come back...and would surely NOT understand why I could not. I felt so out of place with their workaday world already. Someone later asked me: "What will you do all day!?" How could I tell them that this was a spiritual quest that could not easily be explained...except to my new therapist and my also quite spiritual mate, who psychologically backed me implicitly...and understood.

Poetry was calling to me. Poems had begun pouring out of me everywhere. I'd be driving along the streets and I'd notice a tree, and a whole first line would come...and I'd be writing it down while holding the steering wheel with one hand and the pencil with the other. I'd wake up writing poems, composing them during my sleep. And again, after a bout of Morning Pages or journal writing would come another poem, like the one about the crows heading for their twilight convene at the river. It was nearly automatic writing, like God or some dear Muse was making these blessed words available.

The summer before, I had risked showing my writing to a friend who turned out to be a poetry lover herself... and she'd said to me: "You've been given a gift." At that moment, I remember gazing out the huge plate glass window of her North Hollywood apartment and feeling surrounded in beauty — the clouds, her Oriental rug, my tea cup, the poems. How precious were those words to hear. Was it true? It felt so. All these experiences served to move me along the path...towards a Self I had not known. All 'She' needed was space, quiet, and a place of her own, but mainly *time* — without serving others — for a change.

As I write this today, I notice that it no longer feels like the biggest risk of my life, for I can now see that I was being led, nudged, and coaxed along that road at every turn. At the time I had felt a sense of rightness, but also the anxiety of being without my salary. I got creative about the money with help from my *in-loco parentis* friend figuring out how I might access some funds, by borrowing from my life insurance policy. I did tutoring on the side. I volunteered at UC Extension to pay for my classes at Regular UCR. There I encountered gifted and encouraging poetry teachers as I sat, age 50, amidst my classmates, all in their early 20's! The professors were my age, contemporaries, and became my champions during this glorious year off. And so I learned, and wrote, and wrote, and was just filled with the spirit of poetry — like it was the most important thing in the world, and I was privy to it. I was in a rapture of gratitude. I was in love with words, and in a classic mid-life experience. Dance, my life!

After a while, I began to wonder about publishing, but found this endeavor to be premature: I did look into a very thick volume of "Poets and Writers," for publishing ideas...and got overwhelmed. This was not the time to go there; my poet's mind could not deal with such details now. And anyway, other gifts kept opening up to me instead. For example, in Yellowstone National Park, the following summer, I met the Writer-In-Residence there, when I appeared as the only audience to her first Poetry Reading, held at that old stone hut at the West Entrance to the Park. It turned out Keti was from Los Angeles, and soon, back in California, she introduced me to a local group called "No Limits for Women in the Arts." I started attending their monthly meetings all over Los Angeles, surrounded by artists of all genres, and soon found myself doing poetry readings in LA and environs. Advocacy was appearing all around me.

Slowly, though, I began to feel the poem-composing slipping away, for I did not stay solely upon that poetry track. The precious singular year off work for writing had been risk enough, and the best thing I'd ever done for myself and my life. Yet I found I needed to, financially, return to my former profession, in September — just one year later. Painfully, I began to sense the poems disappearing, although I thankfully still became ecstatic at the pink blossoms on those African orchid trees in Central Middle School's quad. My mind, though, became more specific, more filled with the jots and tittles of work-life, with details, more "to-do lists," more planning, more outer, less inner, less calm, more stress. So the precious Gift appeared to be waning, and I quietly began mourning its loss. It seemed I was losing "poet's mind" — that vast openness that allows quite careful looking, and deep listening.

Once in a great while the will to write came back to me. Here and there I'd take a class or go on a writing retreat, or do 'writing practice' with a friend. I have enjoyed sharing my favorite poems aloud here and there, plus in a chapbook and later as a little souvenir folder for my last big birthday celebration. I am proud of the published ones. Yet the old poems, many confessional, now seem dated to me, and although I love them, they seem out of time, about feelings at an earlier stage of my life, old struggles and all. They make a record of a life lived, yet I'm not sure they include enough of me anymore. So starting this Inlandia writing class feels very alien, yet I just begin regardless, and this prose appears. Once in a blue moon a poem comes forth in me, just popping out — like the recent one about my mother's make-up (make up). It just came quietly and I am grateful. So today I write about the biggest risk I ever took in my life. It involved all of my being at the time — body, mind, and soul — and was, so far, the apex of my life. As I type these words for my new writing class, I wonder what now? Or hopefully even…what's next?

Make-Up

BY MARILYN SEQUOIA

I kept my mother's make-up,
That tin of rouge and shadow
Free from Estée Lauder
When you buy lipstick or perfume.

I kept the lipstick too which
She always applied lightly
With her little finger and
Then an mmmmm of her lips.

She plucked her sparse eyebrows thin
Lying on her bed with just
The right sunlight exposing
Their want.

My mother, she grew grey
Only in her last few months of life,
Always a bottled champagne blonde,
Nighttime rollers, into her nineties.

Jessica, the dear, did up her hair
In bubble grey for her casket —
Our beauty dressed in periwinkle
And that gold crystal rosary I gave her.

The make-up wears thin on me now
The color almost gone as she is.
I don my own life and wear her

Under my thinning skin.

Taking her with me as I
Move beyond her world
Beyond her space
Beyond, even —
Her makeup.

This Little Piggy

BY KRISTINE ANN SHELL

My husband, Bob, and I live in a relatively new housing development in North Redlands. It's a family-friendly neighborhood. Plenty of teens, kids, dogs, cats. We're a block from the new high school and less than a block from a large park with walking trails, a baseball field, and a playground. We know most of our neighbors, their kids, and their pets by name, and few of us, if any, worry about our own safety during the day or at night.

Still, I'm a little uncomfortable around our neighbor, John Peterson, who lives two doors down from us. John, his wife, Marie, and their three teenagers are likeable enough. It's their humongous pet pig, Posie, that makes me uncomfortable.

Why couldn't John and his family settle for a dog, a cat, a parakeet, or a gerbil? What are they doing with a 300 pound, black and pink pig?

Every afternoon, I walk to the bank of mailboxes at the corner of our street. Right past John, who sits on a lawn chair in the shade of his garage while his pet pig Posie naps at his feet. And that's when my imagination runs wild. Is Posie an attack pig or Christmas dinner? Is Posie docile or pigheaded? Can a pig Posie's size outrun an old lady like me? Should I stay on the sidewalk or approach John? Speak up or remain silent? Will Posie get upset if I wake her from her nap? What's an old lady to do?

In the interest of self-preservation, I've learned more than I've ever wanted to know about pigs. Thank you, Google! Seems most pigs have lousy eyesight and poor hearing. Good! But pigs have a keen sense of smell. So, I won't be wearing perfume when I walk to the mailbox. I've also learned that pigs don't sweat. So, they suffer outdoors in hot weather. In fact, pigs can become agitated and irritable when it gets hot out. So, what is Posie doing in

Southern California? Wouldn't Posie be happier living on a farm in Iowa? I know I'd be happier if Posie lived on a farm in Iowa.

And another interesting fact about pigs: like humans, pigs often dream when they're sleeping. So, it's another hot summer afternoon in Southern California, and I'm on my way to the mailbox. John's sitting in his lawn chair. Posie's napping at his feet. And I'll bet you anything, Posie's dreaming about that farm in Iowa.

Oracle on Madison

by Ben Simmons

Inland, I learn the names of presidents
and that every crack of thirsty ground,
is a vessel, grateful and afraid of rain,
my lungs fill with dust on a December morning,
and where I walk my shoes mark the asphalt,
in a parking lot on Madison copper brown.

Inland, in a parking lot on Madison
I see her twitching, an oracle,
without prophecy and threadbare
doodlebug her way to oblivion.

She promises the love of god,
the way a cloud promises a flood
with each coin, I put a face to a name
and listen to the radio forecast
our tomorrows and rain.

It's An Easy Life

BY BEN SIMMONS

I held the small brown cube of sugar in the teaspoon and watched the crystals swell like little tears and dissolve. The kitchen's electric hum settled in the background. I didn't want to be there. I never liked just sitting in a stranger's house. It was the part of the job I hated the most, just sitting there. The dusty lampshade hanging above my head gave the kitchen the color of milky tea. On the table there was a ceramic fruit bowl, two linen placemats and a small clock. I stared at the clock as I waited. Behind the clock's hands was a faded portrait of a sheepdog circled by numbers. It made me angry just looking at it, watching the minute hand roll past the dog's ear.

I was out of the city; I didn't normally work out of the city. I can't remember why I was there. The regular agent was sick maybe. Keane always told me that I would do well in the country.

'Do well in Newbridge. They're your kind of people out there. Country people,' he told me. Newbridge isn't the country really, but any place outside the city, *there be dragons.*

I had left my lunch in the office, so I was hungry. At the other end of the kitchen the lady was chopping mushrooms and onion, the dull click of the knife mixed with the clock's tick. The kitchen was homey, and the walls held three elegant paintings that leaned forward from long masonry nails. She wasn't a wealthy woman. There were traces of decay around the place; chips on the teacups that you'd feel on your lips before you saw them, the yellowing white painted walls. My guess was that the kitchen was the only warm room in the house.

She cut the onions into thick rings and placed them onto a plate of flour before resting them on a sheet of baking paper on the counter beside her. Each time she pressed the blade downward her body shifted from left to right, then back again. She wore a pair of old jeans and brown jumper, a husband's maybe. I didn't think it was her jumper. Even though the sleeves were rolled up, her arms were completely covered. She paused to wipe the tears gathering under her puffy eyes.

'Sorry… this makes me feel like a fool,' she said.

'I don't mind,' I said.

I rearranged the brochure and the contract on the table in front of me. Her name was Yvonne Brown. She was fifty-six years old and declared that a friend had told her about the company rather than advertisement. They always ask these things now. This was my last house call of the day. I knew that I had spent longer in the house than was recommended, but it was raining outside. There's nothing about rain in the company handbook. The kitchen was filling with steam; it was making me tired. Mrs. Brown placed the cook's knife on the counter and dropped six halved potatoes into a pot of boiling water resting on the stove. Each potato splashed in the water, displacing the bubbling water onto the gas flames.

'They send you out in all weathers! You're just like the postman.'

'I don't have a van,' I said.

She laughed slowly and walked toward me drying her hands on the worn tea-towel tucked into her belt. She winced with each squeeze and her eyes narrowed on the contract. The table rocked gently on the tile floor as she sat. I re-adjusted the paperwork, marking the signature line with a small cross. Without hesitation she scribbled her name across the line.

'It's a good deal' she said 'I made the appointment yesterday and they sent you straight out. I hope they pay you well for coming all the way out here.'

Together we went though what she was signing, and I explained that she could change her mind in the next ten days. As I pointed to the small square of text, she tilted her head toward the door-way. Mrs. Brown eyes narrowed again. I knew she was waiting for somebody.

'Are you okay?' I asked. In the short silence her eyes closed. I felt bad sitting there in this woman's house and she was being nice to me for no reason. I was just selling her something she could get over the phone. She wasn't looking at the contract anymore. Her eye's opened again. They were blue eyes and terrified, like she saw a child go under a bus. Just for a flash, the lines on her face and her eyes aligned for a moment, in memory of some terrible thing. I followed her gaze to a small table filled with family photographs.

'If now isn't a good time I can just leave the contract with you. You can finish it over the phone.'

We resumed our silence again and I drained the cooling tea from the cup. The rush of the sweetness filled my mouth.

'That's my son. He's about your age.'

I wiped my mouth and turned to look at the photograph. Her son was handsome - *she told me so.* In the photograph her son was dressed in a graduation gown and wedged between Mrs. Brown and another young man. They looked happy. In the handbook it says I should talk to her about her family, and I wanted to know about her family. If I had the courage, I would have asked why she was happy in the photograph and not happy now. I just felt that I was a big fat liar if I was selling something at the same time and it's hard to do two things at once.

'His name is Charlie. He works out in the business park.'

I thought they were beautiful together.

The handbook says I should have closed the sale and moved on by now. I knew that if I left without a signed contract, I'd lose my commission. Keane was clear when he shuffled me into his office earlier that morning.

'I don't care! I've given you good leads, but if you don't close any today you can sleep in tomorrow. I don't want you here if you're not pulling your weight. It brings everybody down. We all got to make an effort to keep up morale and be able to make things happen.'

Keane paused then began to pace behind the desk in his small corner office. It was like watching the class bully forget his lines in a school play.

'You know you're not putting a gun to their heads? You end up talking people out of it the way you go on! Have you tried just saying nothing? Try that today! Go out, give your pitch, and just shut up then. Okay? Maybe smile and give your face a holiday.'

I think I took the job because I liked wearing a suit. It's so stupid if you think about it. I didn't want to sweat for a living, but I was sweating in that kitchen. Everybody in the office was sold on the idea that this job was just a stop along the way to something better. Keane wanted to be a gym manager. I said I wanted to start a magazine just to fit in, but I never had a job I wanted. I'd just settle for going to sleep knowing that I wasn't an asshole. Keane was my boss, and I might have liked the guy if I had met him in some other place, but we met across his flat-packed desk.

The kitchen windows that looked over the backyard had steamed up. It was getting dark outside, and I shifted in the chair and folded my arms. I could hear some movement in the house. Mrs. Brown didn't seem to notice.

'Why do they ask if I'm married? I don't think that's their businesses!' she asked.

It wasn't their business. The handbook says all information is important for business. 'That's just for customer demographics. Leave it blank if you like,' I offered.

We had not spoken very much since I arrived, but for some

reason she asked if I liked my job. Perhaps she was being polite but there was a quiet sincerity in her voice. I just avoided the question. In the handbook it's straightforward on that: *always present a positive image of the company.*

Mrs. Brown folded her copy of the contract, and I gave her my card in case she had any questions. We both stood, the table between us, and shook hands. I'd get my commission. Together we left the kitchen and moved toward the hallway. I heard the soft click of the front door. A moment later her son was standing in the doorway. He carried a ladder and his jaw clenched at the sight of me.

'Who's this?'

Yvonne startled in her chair, smacking her knee as she rose. Charlie looked at his mother and back at me.

'We're finished here, Yvonne. Remember, if you change your mind just call the office,' I don't know why I used her name.

'Charlie, this gentleman's from the electricity company. I showed you the brochure,' she said, rubbing her knee.

What scam are you selling? Must be an easy life, talking to whoever is stupid enough to let you in the door.' There was a little hate in his voice. Charlie placed the steel frame of the ladder against the wall, stood aside leaving the path to the door open.

He placed the steel frame of the ladder against the wall, stood aside leaving the path to the door open. I wondered if I should introduce myself as I left, but I didn't. I stepped onto the footpath and the door closed behind me. I decided that I would sleep in the next day.

Albatross

by Lynne Stewart

My nerves are frayed like a hole-y old sweater worn-out and unraveling. We thought we were ready to put some normalcy back in our lives. A trip to a local coffee shop was a great adventure, until we entered with our masks secure, to find signs reminding us of all the coronavirus safety precautions we must take while dining and all the changes to the establishment's operating procedures. Every other table and booth are out of service with a sign explaining the principle of safe distancing. Servers are donning surgical masks, face shields and plastic gloves as they distribute abbreviated disposable paper menus. No more communally shared condiments or seasonings on the table. Instead, we are given our own individual share of minuscule packets of salt and pepper and little plastic or paper cups with a selection of our very own condiments.

The supermarkets have a line outside the store of shoppers standing single-file, six feet between each person in line. The line to enter Costco stretched clear around the building when we went for groceries early in the pandemic. Even today, I stood in a line outside Trader Joe's. As one or two people left the store, one or two people were allowed to enter. I was in line outside in the hot summer sun for fifteen minutes. The store is now providing large portable canopies every few feet for shade while waiting in line.

Nearly everyone I encounter outside or inside is wearing a face mask. These have become fashion statements with every color, pattern, style and logo imaginable. I am still adapting and adjusting to the complications of communicating effectively through these barriers. I, and many of my friends, have hearing deficits to begin with, so the advent of mufflers muffling our voices is a challenge. Also, my eye glasses tend to fog up under these germ stoppers.

However minor the details are individually, they add up to a major alteration of the status quo. Using FaceTime for a doctor visit, Zooming a religious meeting, not being with family and friends for months, etc., etc., is eating away at my equilibrium. At first, I enjoyed home time and accomplished some long-delayed household tasks. I've become disinterested in these home projects.

I am too old and set in my ways to handle the subtle and overt changes the pandemic has imposed on me. I have been coping for years with my ever-narrowing world due to the simple reality of aging. It has taken conscious effort to get used to living with chronic and deteriorating conditions. This goes hand-in-hand with functional limitations and a shrinking of my exposure to the world of youth and middle age. There is anger in me over my situation that I better not ignore. This confinement has become an albatross.

Another Blank Sheet of Paper to Author

by Lynne Stewart

Another blank sheet of paper to author, not of the past, but of the present, the here and now. This will be a treatise on the fluidity of time. The moment changes to the next and the words attempt to reflect the vacillating, tumbling modification. To reflect on what's been written above is to hesitate and venture out of the present. Go on documenting the current experience without reflection on the past. Continue to stay in the moment of the feeling.

Abdomen is backing up to the chest. Throat is clogged and sadness gathers everywhere. As I stop to feel the feelings and reflect on the meaning, I find only pain. A hurt so deep that it penetrates to my core being, and spews out to the most distant edges of my body. Not the joy and happiness I encounter now, living my life to the fullest, but the pain of loneliness and agony to connect with a person the way I connected once.

That is the past. My endeavor now is to be here, be now. When I am present to myself, I am not wanting to live in this world without the love I felt once. Tears come and the present becomes the past. Don't reflect on what has gone before. Stay here in this safe and comfortable apartment with friends all around me and my son realizing his life fully.

Stay with the abilities and skills you have to express and know yourself. The past haunts in moments of reflection. The tears are here and now. The pain is today. The agony of aloneness lives fully in my soul. The memories flood my body as I stay here. The act of writing brings up the past to cause me grief. The lump in my throat, the trembling in my stomach, the pressure and tingling on my skin, all here and now. It is residue from the past. It does not reflect my life as I live it today.

The matter at hand is writing in the present. The present does not mirror the past. Now, the present is safe and comfortable, filled with people who love as they can; filled with activities of leisure and supportiveness.

The meaning is in everyday acts, primary of which is in the *love we show to each other.* The past looms again. The past when there was no meaning and I did not know of *goodness and mercy.* It is pleasant and fulfilling to love now that I can. This gift is to be passed on.

Thank you to all my teachers who crossed my path when I was able and ready to learn; all those persistent and wise instructors who knew so soon in their lives what was important.

I am in the here and now with residue of the past staining my heart. The blessings of the moment are shaking those same tears loose.

The past is intertwined with the present. It is for us to separate them from each other, so that we can be fully here and now, no longer enmeshed in the sorrows of the past.

Discovering Boys

by Lynne Stewart

Memory: Hormone driven boys were exciting in a new way. I had a figure that my Yiddish speaking relatives called, "zaftig." The English dictionary defines zaftig as: "[a woman] having a full, rounded figure." The Yiddish to English dictionary defines "zaftik" as "juicy, succulent."

Make of that what you will, the boys liked to tease me and flirt with me because of my shape. I was a "good sport" about the teasing by laughing it off and keeping them at bay. I liked the male attention and the feeling that they thought I was attractive and fun. I allowed no touching connected with our bantering, even though the jokes had sexual innuendo and intent.

My high school grade point average went from 4.0 to 1.8 in my senior year. I failed Physics, Public Speaking and English Literature my last year. I would not have graduated with my class if I had not gotten A's in two previous summer school classes.

I met more high school and college boys at B'nai Brith and AZA socials. B'nai Brith girls (BBG) and AZA boys were members of clubs created in synagogues to give Jewish teenagers an opportunity to meet and socialize. The socials were held in the parents' homes.

Richard, my first steady boyfriend, was a freshman in college when I was a junior in high school. We met at an AZA/BBG social. We went "steady," that is dated no one else during our year-and-a-half as a couple. The custom was that I wore his class ring either on a chain around my neck or on one of my fingers big enough not to lose it. As I recall it was the index finger. He was my date for all my senior year special events, such as the class trip to Disneyland and of course, my senior prom.

We broke up when I began college the following September. I entered Los Angeles City College (LACC) where I could fulfill my lower division work to transfer to a four-year university. I wanted to become a school psychologist.

I was encountering a similar following of male attention at LACC as I had in high school, but it had become annoying, a little scary and possibly dangerous. Junior college had recent high school graduates attending, but also older students.

The annoying part was that I was not highly skilled in anticipating and averting serious advances. I was also more focused on achieving my academic goals and less interested in kidding around.

The scary part was that these were not high school boys with budding sexuality, these were men expecting more than clever repartée and innuendo.

A danger came when my World History teacher made advances. I not only had to discourage him without jeopardizing my grade, but I had to contend with accusations from classmates of favoritism and not legitimately earning my grade.

Reflection: After seven and a half decades living in this body, I can still remember how I felt, thought and behaved in the past. My body has undergone changes through growth, decline and trauma. Biological changes out of my control have challenged my equilibrium. I had little ability to control the reality altering impact undergone during the surge of hormones that starts at puberty. Growth, decline and trauma occur at a speedier pace than my ability to acquire knowledge on how to make effective coping decisions. The slower paced acquisition of information, experience and skills that ultimately leads to understanding can be decades behind the original reality altering experience.

Back then, I had little respect for myself or any other female. I thought about my femaleness in the ways of the times and according to the norms and practices of my family. Among these were that girls and women were not as smart, respectable or reliable as boys and men. All the paternalistic stereotypes, biases and attitudes were my early legacy.

During the teasing and being the object of their jokes in those teenage years, I thought this was an expression of their liking me and finding me attractive and fun. Later I came to see the boys' comments and behavior as disrespectful, degrading, objectifying, and victimizing. Today, I realize the boys and men were also victims of the social and cultural norms of the time.

These attitudes and practices still plague much of humanity. If opposite attitudes such as, kindness, empathy, respect, humility and gratitude are not adopted as a norm among our species, the ongoing violations of the soul of humanity have the potential to destroy our species and the earth itself.

Edward Kay Villegas Stowers:

My Brother, My Friend, My Hero

by Scharlett Stowers Vai

My brother Eddie was my hero. He nurtured me from the day I was brought home from the hospital to our house in Casa Blanca, even though he was only about seven or eight years old. I was a small, sickly baby — born in 1952, a Morphine addict with a heart murmur. My mother had been hospitalized with pregnancy complications and was given Morphine for her excruciating pain. During my childhood, my brother protected me from taunts by my sister Emma, who was four years older than me.

Most people called my brother Eddie. I called him "Ese," a term I heard his buddies call him in Casa Blanca. My brother's full, real name is Edward Kay Villegas-Stowers. He was born on January 3, 1945 in Riverside to his mother Lillius "Sugar" Alexander-Stowers. His biological father was SSgt. Ysmael "Smiley" Reyes Villegas. But, because of the societal norms of the day about race, they could not discuss this open secret, even though all the Villegas family and elders in the community knew the truth of who Eddie's real father was. Sadly, Eddie and his parents are now gone to correct and openly embrace the truth.

My brother's father was killed on March 20, 1945 in Luzon, Philippines during World War II, on the day before his 21st birthday. Ysmael is a local hometown hero and was awarded the MEDAL OF HONOR for his courage and bravery beyond the call of duty. My brother was only three months old and my mother was devastated.

Growing up, our home was then called Opal Street in Casa Blanca. Eddie's bedroom was down the hall from mine. My parents' room was on the other side of the wall from the girls' room. I slept on the top of a bunk bed; my little sister Janice slept on the bottom bunk. Older sister Emma had a twin bed across the room from us. Once, I rolled off my bed in the middle of the night. There was a wooden safety bar across the side of my bed, which was supposed to protect me from falling over the side. But, because I was so small, I slipped under the bar and landed on the floor — Crash! No one responded. I was stunned for a few moments as it was quite a drop. Then, I realized I was lying on the floor in pain. Before I could cry, my brother had heard the crash and quickly ran in to rescue me.

He picked me up and held me close to his heart as he always did — beating so fast. The pain I felt went away once I was safe in his arms. He carried me down the hall to his room and tucked me into bed with him, and we snuggled closely to help me to go back to sleep. My parents never responded. Not even after Eddie told them what had happened. Why?

When I was seven years old, I broke my right leg. I couldn't walk; Eddie would carry me on his back. I couldn't go to school or go out to play with my best friend, Robert Barajas. I couldn't even take a bath. I hated sponge baths. One day my brother came up with a new invention. He put my broken casted leg in a plastic bag and bathed me head-to-toe. He was so awesome. I loved him so much; no one would ever love him as much as I do.

When I was 10 years old, my brother got married. I was quite upset; I felt he was being taken away from me forever. He was just 16 years old.

When I was 11 years old my brother had a son, Edward Brandon. My nephew became my first baby. He was my heart. I was very mature for my age and was allowed to babysit him when my brother and his wife went to mass on Sundays. I was so excited and happy that I was trusted to take care of their baby. We bonded right away. Later, my brother had two daughters, Christina Marie and Angel Sheri. Soon after, my brother got divorced. We were separated from the kids for a short time. It was emotionally devastating for me. From time-to-time they were allowed to visit with us. Brandon loved the music I played for him. One song and artist was his favorite, "You'll Never Get To Heaven If You Break My Heart" by Dionne Warwick. It started out: *La, la, la, la, la, la, la, la*. He would always say, "Scha, play la la; play la la." I wore out that album playing it over and over for him.

In the 1960s, I was in junior high school. I went through a lot of pain, turmoil, and abuse from my mother, and older sister, and especially the Black girls at school. I was fair skinned with green eyes, so they hated me — my brother supported me through this difficult time. Now, it was the age of Hippies and the Vietnam war, my brother received a letter from the United States Army giving him notice that he was drafted. Eddie did not believe in killing people and refused to go to war in Vietnam. He planned to go to Canada but a friend told him he could fight this with a special lawyer named Michael Green from Santa Monica, CA. Friends and professors at UCR held fundraiser dances and raised the money for his defense — he was declared a conscientious objector.

I loved the cultural changes. Everyone was cool. I so looked forward to the weekends. That's when I was allowed to spend the whole weekend with my brother.

Eddie understood me. He helped me deal with the changes I was going through becoming a teenager and my mother's abuse. I made sure not to get into trouble, especially with my mother. It felt like I was walking on eggshells. I even held my breath the whole week. I was a victim of my mother's whims. When our mother got mad at him, I wouldn't be allowed to see him, much less to go with him anywhere. Who knew for how long this restriction would be?

My brother knew how to humor her. Sometimes, he'd clown for her by imitating comedian Flip Wilson's "Geraldine" character to change her mood. Sometimes, we'd go stay overnight with our grandmother Nang Nang, our nickname for her, in spite of our mother's mood. There, we got to be with each other. It was safe neutral territory, even though it was just next door.

My brother had all kinds of friends: from plain to the unusual. All were welcomed at both our home and at grandmother's house. They all called her "Granma." They came to visit even when my brother wasn't around. One day, I went over to Granma's house and out front there were a lot of choppers — Harley Davidson motorcycles, also sometimes called "hogs." There were "Hells' Angels," a motorcycle gang, kicking it with Granma on her porch. You never knew who you'd meet through my brother. I love and miss those awesome days.

I met some really cool people at University of California, Riverside (UCR). Some were even UCR instructors. They all treated me like an equal even though I was just a high school kid. I was invited and was allowed to go to the dances and concerts on campus, too.

I loved it. Hippies were opened-minded adults, they taught me many things as did my brother. I loved being with my brother. He made me feel safe and appreciated for just being me. When I met someone on campus and elsewhere, if they found out I was Eddie's little sister, I was treated extra special. I felt on top of the world. It helped me to cope with my mother when she was in a mean mood with me, and with all of the other traumas in my life.

As a senior in high school, I wanted to go to college. It was more exciting than high school, which bored me. I decided I wanted to go to the university. There were so many courses of interest and you were free to choose your course of study.

I went to summer school two years in a row, so I could graduate a half-year earlier. It was worth the sacrifice. My brother was so proud of me, even though mother kept trying to discourage me. She said I wasn't smart enough for college. But, my brother always encouraged me to do it. He told me, "I know you can do this; I'll even take classes with you." He gave me the self-confidence I needed. I was soaring with excitement.

In January 1970, I graduated high school and the first thing I did was register at UCR. For a moment I was devastated. The man in admissions, John Coleman put up several road blocks to my being able to be admitted. I thought I'd die. I worked sooo hard to graduate early. Later, I was introduced to Dr. Carlos Cortés, Chair of Chicano Studies Department, who became my adviser. We spoke for three hours only in Spanish. I lived all my life in a mostly Chicano Barrio, Casa Blanca, and I am both bilingual and bicultural. He was impressed. He told me that I didn't need to get in as a Black student — that I could get in as a Chicana. He helped me cut through the red tape, and thanks to Dr. Cortés, I was accepted at UCR.

With the help of my brother, whom I always called *Ese*, I earned straight As during my first quarter at UCR. I proved to both my mother and John Coleman that I did it. I was elated and proud of myself, as was my brother.

In 1971, I got married and had a daughter, Erika Ana Elizabeth. A year later, I got divorced. I was worried about being a single parent, but my brother encouraged me and helped me with my daughter. The love they had for each other was as strong as the love my brother and I had.

I learned so much from my brother. He turned me on to music, art, literature, and open-minded thinking. Eddie made me aware of bands like The Beatles, The Rolling Stones, and Bobby "Blue" Bland. Later, because of him, I became a fan of singer-song writer, Marvin Gaye, who is my favorite spiritual guide. Eddie taught me about jazz, rock, and even classical music. My brother was everything to me. I dearly love and miss my brother and I thank him for helping me to be the best me that I am today.

LOVE YOU, ESE!

Correspondence

by Heather Takenaga

Bells tone the end of
Children's play
Below, colors of life scatter,
Passing farewells for this day
You watch by the windowsill
Like a budgie
You repeat the glimmers of words
From other lives, of others' wishes
Scarlet skies
Highlight your lips
Your ocean blue eyes reflect the
Calling of the night

Consumed by hope
I cover your hand
You tilt your head at me
A smile on your face
I wonder
If the twitch I feel
Is a flicker of you inside
I'm afraid to ask
Praying instead
We remain this way, linked,
No lights in the room
Till darkness claims us both

To Whom It May Concern: In The Event of A Death

by Heather Takenaga

Once every one or two days, please poke behind the couch with a stick.

If you feel a bump—which has a 99.999% chance of happening—please say, "Get up, Heather." If there is no response from the unmoving mass, please rub and ruffle the mess of hair.

Under any circumstances, do *not* untangle the knots. Or you'll awaken a banshee.

Do kick the mass in the event of a stench. Please say, "Take a shower, Heather."

Please have patience with the glares and insults. They're a mask. Defend yourself with a pot of green tea, a mug, and a big fat book. Extra points: bring an empty notebook and a fully-inked pen. Slowly and quietly, back away.

If the sun is blinding or if the sky is stained red, please kick the tangled mass awake. Leave something plant-based to eat and drink. Open a window or part the curtains.

Should there be monsoons or storms stampeding outside, do not attempt a rescue. Please prepare a set of dry clothes. Keep the windows and doors unlocked. Wait for drenched footsteps to come back inside.

Every night, check the floors. If you see the shivering mass, please cover with a blanket. For your safety, please do not attempt to move.

Leave a smartphone next to the weeping mass. Walk away if classical music and booming strings do not appeal to you. Sit and relax if they do.

Repeat the above instructions for three days. With luck, the mass will accept being a person again. Apply extensions as needed.

Additional instructions for dealing with the person emerging from the mass:

Whenever possible, please do not ask me "Are you okay?" unless you are armed with tissues and do not care for the purity of your clothing. Or the rest of your day.

However possible, refrain from telling me something along the lines of, "It's life, it happens every day, everywhere—" unless you're intending to kill the person and revive the mass.

Wherever possible, please do not share with me "I'm sorry for—" because there's a good chance that even if you *are* sorry, you're implicating yourself for something you had no control or responsibility for. Even if it happens you may have played some part, *shush*. It's a band-aid over an endless pit where loss has made its home.

Tell me instead how you feel. If you don't feel anything, tell me that too. If you don't know, tell me that too.

Silence can be empathy too.

But to the boldest and bravest of the heart, mass or person, do not hesitate giving hugs. Hugs are always respected and appreciated.

Mirrors

BY HEATHER TAKENAGA

You would not want to read about
The little girl who never told
Her father

        She loved him

That she was never kind to
Her father

        She ignored him

Because she was never with
Her father

        She hated him

Since she was never the one for
Her father

        She left him

And she didn't know that
Her aunt watched
Her father
Cry

    To her how
        his little girl
            his little flower
                his only child

                never would say it

      how he

hoped

    through

       the ten hour slog
          the five hour jams
            the three hour naps

       she'd
       love

           him

It was only when the cicadas sang again
To the aubade of his memory
that she told

Her father
      She loved

Pandemic Blinks

BY HEATHER TAKENAGA

Lucia hopped from her hoverboard, her gravity boots activating when her toe hit gravel. She ran across the terraformed lawn of her grandmother's pod, waving her ID card at the entrance and lowering her mask in the sanitization airlock. The girl brought in the delivered food rations.

Her grandmother was at her usual spot. Facing the blue star, the home planet before the Great Migration. Lucia handwaved at the wireless tablet and set up to record her homework. After their usual pleasantries, she asked her grandmother.

"What was COVID like, Grandma?"

Her grandmother smiled.

"Like this, except with more people."

There wasn't a single part of Hayden that didn't hurt. Their loved ones, their wallet, their body, their sanity—fluttered away like endangered butterflies. This was the third time they'd awaken in this darkness, the heartbeat before daylight.

Hayden reached for their drained smartphone and swiped the screen. Their fingers flicked through their files. They pressed a sideways triangle. Their mother, who couldn't speak anymore, sang back to them.

Hope is on the way.

Their fingers curled into the sheets. The digital 3:30 AM blinked out of sight. They breathed. Phase three. They pressed again.

Hope is on the way.

Rhys saw red. Unlawful detainer was what the letter said. Tell that to his cheeky landlord who slid the envelope under his door. A week after his brother died from this damn virus, and this? Not today.

Rhys stomped to the landlord's office—apartment, really—and pounded on the door. It opened a crack. Colorful threats greyed his throat to the landlord's watery eyes. Somehow the old man shared news of his beautiful wife of forty years. Emergency call. Labored breaths. No available beds. Didn't say goodbye.

Rhys toed through the crack and crushed the sobbing old man in a hug.

The Amazon

by Elizabeth Uter

At first she stood on a mudbank, then near a Walking Palm to look,

this unsung hero and she knew no ordinary soul was berthed in
 the rain soak

of the forest and like the slow-coiling waters hedging it

that shared its name, for miles, as far as her long-glassed eye
 could see

river unrolling river, unhurried, towards the edge of time itself,

keeping the secret that said, no man can rest here.

She dug and delved in the emerald floor as that was her trade.

She waited until the depth of shattered mud on her spade

cleared and in the space before her, a treasure trove.

She leant in close, so close she almost kissed the gone-forever,

long-dead lips of the warrior queen she'd made a constant dream of.

Had loved in night visions before she even knew herself and
 now as real as she.

A twisted neck, mouth canting to the side, frown between soft
 eye sockets,

hard and empty now from an age of endless sun turns, lost in
 earth's middle,

sling-wrapped and curled tight as a nine month fetus.

And more, in the surrounds, her tribe, unknown sparks of life,
 100 graves

to mark their presence, to say, 'yes, we once lived bereft of men,'
 legend has it.

In the black, unmade earth bed, the Amazon, legs bowed from
 ceaseless riding,

a quiver forty arrows strong beside, and death, an iron dagger, bronzed with age

encrusted in her chest. This armoured amor, soulmate, the dig-
ger's find of a lifetime.

All Ruined

BY ELIZABETH UTER

I am all alone,
forgotten, lost to the memory
of those who used to tread my
stairs, slide across my floors
marbled, polished.
The corridors leading
to rooms grand as if everyone
a ballroom.
I remember the dancing,
the lightness of feet, of ladies twirled
in a Viennese whirl.
Myriad windows watching the grounds,
arrivals, departures
throughout the years,
centuries, revolutions come,
whether of sun, moon
or people seeking freedoms.

All have trod the path that leads
to me.
Gardens styled as if a
lesser Versailles, sundials
- antique brass, on vinestone
pedestals, one for all the yous
who have gone before,
far-flung to the four quarters
of my vast lawn-arenas.

Politicians striding like gladiators
seeking deals away from prying,
public eyes - I see you in my dreams,
still see the worlds that you
have grasped; burned with
greedy hands seeking more, more, more.

Mazes, one two three,
children playing hide and seek
running in to supper, faces flushed
with gifts from fruited trees,
apples tickled pink from the touch
of lovers, peaches dripping down
the cheeks of others and the teeth, the teeth
digging deep into the flesh, eyes rolling,
closing in ecstasy of relishing the best
- pears, plums, strawberries -
the humdrum ones that everyone loves.
Berries to bury your tastebuds in.
I have even seen harvests of lemons
that have soured the face
of the many until honey
from the hives was added
- thyme-soaked as the bees
always seemed to prefer
to rest on these.

When the good folk tire of my
grounds they come in through
the chateau doors - I consume
them all, savouring the disparate

flavour of men, women, babies,
both the old, the young
- I have the tang on my tongue
of each of you.
Aaaaaaaah
How your fingers tickle,
tracing my ornate walls,
you wondered at my beauty, grace
- that was then but now
blitzed, beyond repair
almost raised to the ground,
I am born again to ruin.
Gone to seed when even you
new strangers, tourists peer
within
or scurry by.
All of you, once here
can never leave,
even with my sides caved in.
I capture your images
and sigh for you
forever in my mind.

In Ruins 2

BY ELIZABETH UTER

There are endless
doors leading to
this space of dereliction,
it is bleeding despair
- graffiti splashed like spoiled fruit
across lofty walls and floors.

Light squashes through open,
broken windows,
glares in with no desire to stay,
a squat place, factory-like,
unloved, because no one's
home today, no yesterdays,
not even reluctant tomorrows.

Here, on a summer's day,
the lush green spines
of surrounding fields are bending,
breaking inwards through one,
two, three empty window frames.

The life force here is dim,
dull, alone as a suitcase left
forgotten on a lost luggage rack -
overlooked an eternity.
Maybe workers once prowled
the mouldering grounds?
Machines, oils, metallic
shifting hands, cogs, gone.

Perhaps livestock once
tramped uneasy feet within
this abattoir of fading
dreams? Maybe the building's
breath has oozed through the cracks
and all purpose now is done.

When Darkness Rushes

BY ELIZABETH UTER

Three are neighbours looking in at you
under the cover of night,
looking where there is nothing to see.
There are curtains dripping
in the wind, following silently,
falling like ice against open windows
in the cold, cold blow of a night
that might never end.
Often in my child's laughing eye,
the world swings higher at night,
no longer blinded by the day.
For eyes have not yet been made
to look at this sun; have not yet learnt to
nose in its direction.

It reminds me of the man
with a lighted lamp, searching
in daylight for an honest man,
peering into faces aided by the lights,
but, seeing nothing; like a blossom
warming its heart in the sky, unaware
of its roots underground;
like a laugh awaiting its joke, heedless
of the mind that must come before.
The night is day to darkness
and the day, the dark, to light.

Seasons adrift, senses confused,
days shrugging by, full when fullness
should be dead and barren when plenty
should reign, inappropriate by colour,
sound and not design.

And now, the last few drops of day
usher sleep in and in the silence
it lives a while clinging to its heart's edge
and then forgets its name.
When darkness rushes in
a shutter falls, the room is dim.
As old as the first baby arising
from the womb: 'you cannot look without
until you look within.' It's written in stone;
I forget the name of the stones,
but they make me shiver as they stand up
warm against the breathing,
evening sky.

Bird Watching

by Gudelia Vaden

Watching the assortment of birds: Blue Jays, brown sparrows and yellow finches with red beaks, on neighbour, Diane's wrought iron fence. Morning light scatters across the horizon and trickles down my narrow horizontal patio. Shattering into the blue mosaic water fountain, as they come for their early breakfast. She hangs large aluminium bird feeders filled to the brim with seed. Luckily, she can still find bird seed at her favorite store despite the pandemic.

However, I particularly watch a red breasted robin that flies to my patio from Diane's purple and pink flowered Jacaranda tree. He is a brave one to come for my breadcrumbs so close to the door. Sometimes I have bread left over from our breakfast and let it harden in my Whirlpool oven with the dial on off. It usually takes a day or two for the bread to be just right, but worth the wait. I was told that soft bread would make them choke and eventually kill them. The robin must think this is a special treat for him, as he happily chirps, while feasting on multigrain bread. After filling his tummy with crumbs, he hops and flutters his wings to the Martha Washington fuchsia coloured geranium garden. He picks earthworms from his sharp beak in the dark and moist soil. It pleases me that he is getting a balanced diet. He is my friend and I feel that we have bonded. The best part is he lets me get close to him, as I greet and talk to him each day.

There is something mesmerizing about bird watching. I can feel my blood pressure drop and a sense of peacefulness come over me. I am in tune with God's feathered creatures. After filling their tummies, fluttering their wings and flying into the clear azure sky, chirping and tweeting melodies that is music to my ear. Their song, so beautiful, so perfect and flawless. Birds that sing for their daily bread.

My First Inlandia Workshop

by Gudelia Vaden

In 2014, I put my temporary disability on hold and shuffled to my first Inlandia Writing workshop on crutches. No one could have been more excited. I wanted to jump up and down with the enthusiasm of a child opening presents on Christmas day, but knew it would be impossible with a fractured ankle. How could I possibly have fractured my ankle?

One dark and moonless night, just before midnight, dressed up in a full length purple sequined gown, coming from a party at the Officer's Club at March Air Reserve Base, I raced to turn off the ear-piercing alarm. Instead of losing my slipper like Cinderella, I made a daring leap, only to catch my foot on a gate, and stumbled onto the hard tile floor. When I stood up, it felt as if pins and needles were stabbing my ankle. Tom, my husband, rushed me to the emergency room. The doctor placed a splint on my ankle and because it was a Friday, I would have to wait until Tuesday to have an orthopedic surgeon put a cast on my leg. The doctor's orders were to not dance or put pressure on my foot for at least six weeks.

I thought, what do I do now? I enjoyed line dancing and now that has been put on hold. I can pursue my passion for writing. Writing is an important part of my life. It is much more than putting words on paper. It is a form of communication. It becomes personal, if not magical, like entering a new dimension. I, like most writers, was searching for inspiration.

Saturday morning, a friend told me about a workshop which was held outdoors at the Riverside Plaza. We were met with hugs and handshakes by the facilitator, Gayle Brandeis. Her brown eyes, like sand at a beach, sparkled as she spoke and her curly mahogany hair with plum highlights shimmered in the sunlight. Her warm, ear-to-ear smile made us feel at home. We sat in caramel, oversized comfortable cushions on a wooden lounge. Juices, fruit, cookies, and water were provided, as well as yellow legal-sized notepads and pens. We were all set for this writing adventure, hoping it would be just as fun as a trip to Knott's Berry Farm.

The sun was shining, the birds and sea gulls were not only chirping, but flying about, just waiting to catch a morsel of someone's food dropped on the ground. It was a windy April day. So windy, I could have flown a kite!

It does not surprise me that one of our prompts was to write about the wind. I could feel the Santa Ana Wind, not only as it blew my hair into my face, but made breathing difficult and my throat raspy. Handheld packages of shoppers were strown in the wind, strollers shuffled around, and children were crying in dismay. It was obvious the wind had shown its torment. Knowing that, what would I write about? I created a poem about the wind. There was no right or wrong, Gayle just wanted us to write without pressure. She encouraged us to choose our own writing topic. How liberating to explore and be creative! The students were all engaged in writing. There were opportunities to read our pieces aloud. I. shared my poem and received compliments. Some wrote prose, poetry, and short stories.

I did not want this workshop to end. The two hours were magical and empowered me to be a better writer. I enjoyed being with other writers. The unfortunate experience of breaking an ankle turned out to be a blessing in disguise. This first experience attending an Inlandia workshop was so much fun that I knew it would not be my last.

Tesoros de Cuentos

by Frances J. Vásquez

It began with a spirited Unity Poetry event featuring **Juan Felipe Herrera** near the Mahatma Gandhi Monument on the Main Street Pedestrian Walkway in Downtown Riverside. At the time, he served as California State Poet Laureate and professor at the University of California, Riverside. He motivated an attentive crowd by declaring, "Value our parents' and grandparents' stories...value your own stories, and most of all...Celebrate your beautiful voices. Share your voices." We spoke afterwards about my grandson Oscar's Capirotada story. Juan Felipe encouraged me to write about it, which I did later in a creative writing workshop, and Inlandia Institute published it in an anthology of work from the workshops.

Juan Felipe's event inspired me to form a bilingual, bicultural writing group — in the Chicano(a)/Latina(o) community to help develop their literary voices — endowed with a rich oral history. Ideas ruminated in my imagination to elicit the treasure trove of stories held in the hearts and memories of "our gente" through memoir writing workshops. Five years ago, at my direction, we launched the first Tesoros de Cuentos workshop during 2016 National Hispanic/Latino(a) Heritage Month. We conducted the workshops at the SSgt. Salvador J. Lara Casa Blanca Library in the heart of Riverside.

In a friendly and supportive environment, participants wrote down their memoirs. We aspired to help give voice to their stories about family, school, tamaladas, fiestas, and their neighborhood. Sweet and savory recollections unraveled. We also convened talleres to help edit and finesse their work, which culminated in submission of wonderful stories in the 2017 Writings from Inlandia Anthology.

The Inland region has significant, and in some localities, a majority Chicana(o)/Latino(a) presence and history. The main theme for the fall 2021 Tesoros de Cuentos workshop was "Recuerdos" — to memorialize and honor significant members of participant's families or from the community. Our initial goal was to fulfill a commitment I made to *Cuentistas* at the funeral repast of beloved late participant **Jennie Rivera** — to memorialize her major accomplishments that benefited Casa Blanca. We mourned her untimely death and her friends wanted to honor her. Then, the COVID-19 global pandemic hit...and the rigors of the 2020 quarantine...

During 2021 Hispanic/Latino(a) Heritage Month on October 8th, we convened in person at the SSgt. Salvador J. Lara Casa Blanca Library to initiate the fall workshops. It also happened to be on the birthday of the late **Morris Mendoza,** who passed away on January 27th, and whose noble spirit surely accompanied us in the library. How serendipitous was that? Morris was a beloved community leader and the first person to sign up for Tesoros de Cuentos workshops five years ago when I addressed a Casa Blanca CAG meeting.

Our first guest speaker, **Travis Du Bry**, a professor of Anthropology, discussed best practices for conducting and writing oral histories. We discussed effective writing techniques, including Ekphrastic writing, and how to compose various memorial tributes. Participant and guest speaker, **Carlos Cruz** provided context to his proposed mini-museum exhibition of Casa Blanca artifacts.

Gracias del Corazón to the class of 2021: **Cindy Mendoza Collins, Carlos Cruz, Kimberly Olvera Du Bry, Bob Garcia, Doralba Harmon, Roberto Murillo, Cindi Neisinger, Lillian Solorio,** and **Scharlett Stowers Vai.** These remarkable Cuentistas shored up their courage, energy, and commitment to articulate their beautiful literary voices — some for the first time and surviving a challenging COVID-19 pandemic that affected us personally in myriad and even lethal ways. Participants wrote about their elation and joy upon hearing the vote by the Trustees of the Riverside Unified School District Board of Education to name the imminent new neighborhood school: Casa Blanca Elementary School.

Participants used Ekphrastic techniques to write descriptive narratives of their photos and a vintage flyer. As a result of family interviews, some learned new information about their beloved abuelitas: one migrated from México during the Mexican Revolution to become an entrepreneur and la Reina de Banning; another also migrated during the Mexican Revolution and was a folk medicine practitioner who applied massage therapies and remedios in Casa Blanca. One migrated from México all alone as a youth and later during the 1940s, dressed like a stylish Pachuca and became a local entrepreneur. One participant shored up her vulnerability to reveal sensitive long-held "secrets" to honor her late brother. Another person wrote about a meeting flyer, "Recibimiento de la Marcha" from 44 years ago; one reflected on the tremendous strength and fortitude of her late mother, la Generala in Colombia, and an essay on the institutionalized abuse and marginalization of women. Two members wrote about their leadership roles and reflections on the joyful, unanimous vote by the RUSD Board of Education to select the Casa Blanca CAG's school name recommendation, and more. All participants prevailed in expressing their creativity by composing compelling and powerful stories — with many more waiting to be written.

Sincere appreciation and thanks to the Casa Blanca Community Action Group for allowing me time at their meetings and for supporting our workshops. I felt privileged to have been invited as an honorary CAG member to write and speak about the historical origins of the Casa Blanca school at the November 18, 2021 RUSD Board meeting. Several CAG members and supporters addressed the Board with their recommendations. We were in the audience when the Trustees voted. We were all jubilant! Some shed tears of joyful relief, and the Board requested a group photograph with us, and asked that we submit our written speeches for inclusion in the new school building time capsule. As our Tesoros de Cuentos motto states: "Las palabras vuelan; los escritos quedan" — Spanish for "Words fly; writings endure."

Special thanks and appreciation to the personnel at SSgt. Salvador J. Lara Casa Blanca Library for providing a comfortable, welcoming meeting place for us to write and read compelling and powerful stories. Heartfelt thanks and sincere gratitude to the Inlandia Institute for their continued community service sponsorship and publication of our cuentos.

Sister Celine Vásquez: Stellar Guiding Spirit Full of Grace

BY FRANCES J. VÁSQUEZ

De colores, de colores / Se visten los campos en la primavera /... Y por / eso los grandes amores / De muchos colores me gustan a mí.
~ Traditional Mexican Folk Song

It was a glorious summer day in Los Angeles when we celebrated Sister Celine Vásquez's 25th Jubilee of the profession of her vows with the Sisters of Social Service. It was 1962 and celebrants joined hands to form a huge circle to sing *De Colores*, a traditional Mexican folk song associated with the United Farm Workers Union. Accompanied by guitarists, we sang joyfully. Sister Celine was a beloved paternal aunt and one of my early mentors whom I admired, loved, and respected. She stood up and worked for social justice and civil rights. She marched with César Chávez and Dolores Huerta in support of the farm workers.

My aunt was brilliant like the Stella Maris star and had a steadfast commitment to advocate for the poor and downtrodden. She was a gifted organizer and administrator. In about the mid-1930s she joined the Sisters of Social Service — a Catholic community of religious women based in Los Angeles. She professed her vows on July 26, 1937 (at the age of 21). It's the custom of many religious orders to forego material wealth and personal assets, and she changed her given baptismal name, Maria Brigida, to Celine as her forever religious name.

As the title of the community implies, the Sisters worked in the community as social workers with poor and marginalized people. Because of her impressive intelligence and talents, Sister Frederica Horvath, the Sister's Superior General, sent her to attend Georgetown University in Washington, D.C. where she earned Bachelors and Masters Degrees (probably in the early 1940s). She headed several ministries in California, Missouri, other U.S.

locations, México and in several countries. The last organization she helped found and headed before her untimely death was in Zacapu, Michoacán, México.

Brigida, as she was called in her youth, was my father's sister and one of six children born to José Maria Vásquez and Teodula Garcia. Brigida was born on August 15, 1916 in Highgrove — a small unincorporated enclave east of Riverside, California. Brigida was a builder... she built up people's lives, skills, and moral characters. And she literally built furniture at the school she attended until eighth grade — decades later she would actually help build structures in México. There were numerous Mexican children enrolled at Highgrove School, so they offered woodshop classes as part of the curriculum. I clearly remember a wooden desk she had handcrafted at school and graced my grandpa's dining room for decades.

An early memory of Sister Celine revolves around Easter. Growing up in semi-rural Highgrove, public recreational activities for children were scarce. Sister Celine resided at the Mother House on Westchester Place in Los Angeles. On Holy Saturday she organized wonderful Easter egg hunts and festivities and arranged for select children to attend. Imagine our joyful delight as we scrambled all over the Sisters' expansive front lawn in search of candy eggs. Some lucky kids won fancy foil-covered prize chocolate Easter bunnies — from See's Candies!

Sister Celine's generosity was welcome and enriching. My dad worked as a Mayordomo for LVW Brown Estate in Highgrove where the company operated a packing house, warehouse, and maintained several citrus groves. He received meager wages and our family was large, so he didn't have much disposable income. For Easter and Christmas, we were treated to nice new clothes. At Easter, my mother gave us lovely pastel-hued dresses with matching bonnets for us girls to wear to Mass. In those days, women and girls were required to cover their heads in church.

With our aunt's encouragement, we were endowed with devotion to our Catholic faith and religious practices.

In later years, Sister Celine brought us cardboard boxes of loose chocolates, in all varieties. The honeycomb crisps became my life-long favorite. We were so lucky! We eventually learned that the chocolates were "seconds" donated by See's Los Angeles choco-late factory — imagine Hollywood actors Lucy and Ethel's hi-larious antics at the iconic conveyor belt scene in the "I Love Lucy" television show. Sometimes the cardboard box included a container of chocolate sprinkles, which we used for baking cook-ies or melted for chocolate milk. Naturally, a box of See's choco-lates is one of my favorite gifts to special people for Easter and Christmas.

When I was a pre-teen, Sister Celine arranged for me to spend a week at Camp Mariastella in Wrightwood. The girls camp is nestled in the pine-forested heart of the San Gabriel Mountains. We enjoyed hiking, swimming, archery, crafts, and performing skits. We slept in small wooden cabins with other girls and ate delicious meals in a large dining room. Mariastella is still active and one of the few girls camps still around. The Sisters of Social Service operate it with a focus on outdoor recreation with an ecu-menical Christian setting. Later in life, I learned that the camp's motto is: "a place to come together, to recognize commonalities and to learn from each other through living together in a coop-erative environment." Oh, those ideals resonate with me!

As an adolescent, I looked to Sister Celine for answers to per-sonal questions I had about religion and Catholic doctrine. I trusted and appreciated that she was wise, knowledgeable, and non-judgmental. Her answers were direct, honest, and resonant: why are women not allowed to be Priests? I recall her explanation that it was not God's Divine Law, but Papal Doctrine.... Why are Priests not allowed to marry? Again, Papal Doctrine, not Divine Law....

For a time, Sister Celine was head of Catholic Youth Organization (CYO) in Los Angeles. During Easter break when I was 16 years old, my aunt took me to Los Angeles for an enriching opportunity to do volunteer work at the CYO office doing minor tasks such as filing and typing. I stayed at Stella Maris — a beautiful Victorian room-and-board residence for young career women that the Sisters operated. I ate my meals and slept there. While interning at CYO, I observed my aunt's astute leadership expertise and marveled at how efficiently and effectively she managed the office.

I wondered why my aunt chose Celine as her religious name and regret never having asked her. Research shows that Celine Chludzinska Borzeka — a religious woman from Antowil in the Russian Empire, now Belarus, founded the Sisters of the Resurrection in Rome about 1891, where she established a school. Pope John Paul II entitled her a *Servant of God* and initiated the apostolic process in 1964. Confirmation of Mother Celine's heroic virtue resulted in the Pope granting her the title of *Venerable* in 1982. She was beatified as *Blessed* on October 2007. The work of the 19th Century Celine surely inspired my aunt — I can visualize them together rejoicing in Heaven.

The Sisters of Social Service maintain ministries in many parts of the world. My aunt was one of the executive committee leaders to envision expanding their ministries to the state of Michoacán in central México. In 1963, they established their first community in Zacapu, located near the capital city of Morelia, where Sister Celine was appointed Mother Superior. Their ministries have included community development and training programs for nurses, community health, advocacy, education, and family programs. In about 1984, I was fortunate to visit the facilities in Zacapu.

My aunt told me that México has excellent centralized medical schools in Guadalajara, Jalisco where they train highly competent physicians and surgeons. At the time however, nursing care in

México was below par — thus, the rationale for the Sisters to establish a nursing school. Initially, they trained local young women to be nurse aides, and later provided more extensive training in licensed nursing programs. Sister Teresa Avila (originally, Eustolia Avila of East Riverside, CA) was part of the initial team of four Sisters charged with establishing the nursing school. Eventually, the Sisters expanded their ministries to work with the poor and marginalized people of Morelia and Tacambaro, Michoacán.

The last time I saw Sister Celine (and her younger sibling Virginia Vásquez) was at a family gathering in Highgrove in early or mid-September 1983. We met in the knotty pine-paneled living room in the little red house my Dad and his friends built on Church Street many years earlier. Sister was on vacation from her duties in México to help her sibling, Virgina, with the student exchange program Aunt Virginia had founded — Other Cultures, Inc. Sister Celine's eyes gleamed as she spoke excitedly about her imminent retirement. She was looking forward to taking classes at Marymount College to learn new pedagogies in the social sciences. At the time, I was about to begin graduate school at the University of California, Riverside and we discussed the theories of famous social scientists like anthropologist Margaret Mead and psychologist Abraham Mazlow. I remember feeling impressed and immensely proud of my aunt's desire for continued lifelong learning.

On September 23, 1983, our family suffered a horrific heartbreak. Our two beloved aunts, Sister Celine and Virginia Vásquez were tragically killed in an automobile accident in Idaho. They had been visiting prospective host families for the program's approaching arrival of students from Guatemala. We were all devastated! The deaths of our beautiful aunts shocked us, and changed the trajectory of my life at many levels.

Printed on Sister Celine's memorial card is the sacred inscription, "Behold the handmaid of the Lord...May she know the fullness of Life." She served brilliantly on Earth as God's devoted handmaid in the purest and most positive sense of the Biblical term. I believe that she blissfully experienced life's fullness. While I mourn and regret her passing, I feel some consolation that Sister Celine and Aunt Virginia were together in death. In eternal spirit, they are both beautiful Angels guiding us through our Earthly travails.

After my aunts died, I admit to becoming angry at God. Why? I questioned why these two blessed women, who lived exemplary lives in the spirit of God, died so horrifically while rapists and murderers roamed to spew hate on this planet. I struggled to understand the injustice. Sister Celine and Aunt Virginia contributed to the betterment of humanity. I began to question my faith and may have briefly veered off the Christian path. But, I never lost my way during this crisis of faith. Our enormous loss drove some family members into a dark abyss of anger, resentment, disunity, envidia. That is not what our aunts would have wanted — family unity was of utmost importance to them. A book, *When Bad Things Happen to Good People* by Harold Kushner was of tremendous help. It was gifted to me by a friend in Minnesota to help console me, and I have paid it forward many times by gifting it to friends who lost loved ones.

I cherish my Spring 2013 issue of SOCIAL IMPACT, a publication of the Sisters of Social Service. The Sisters honored the strength and resilience of the communities they serve and have worked with for 50 golden years. In the centerfold, they feature a pictorial-rich article celebrating the 50 years of ministries in México (highlighted on the left page is the work in México and on the right page, the Sister's work in Taiwan). One photo depicts the four founding Sisters as they leave for México: Celine Vásquez, Virginia Fabilli, Teresa Avila, and Mary Christa. They are wearing the grey street-length "habits" Sisters wore at the time. The article states, "Sisters have responded to the strengths and needs of local people in a variety of ways as social workers, nurses, parish workers, educators, and in other leadership roles." To be sure, the Michoacán ministries continue to flourish — as a memorial to Sister Celine's enduring legacy.

A few years ago, I planted drought-tolerant plants in our backyard. In sister Celine's honor, I planted a Chaste tree (Vitex agnus-castus), known to attract bees, hummingbirds, and butterflies. It bears celestial blue flowers — her favorite color which always blooms generously every summer, and in August for her birthday. Like her luminous spirit, the flowers are beautiful. I still visualize my aunt's radiant and serene smiling face wearing a light blue cardigan sweater. And I get misty-eyed when I hear the Mexican folk song, *De Colores*. To me, it symbolizes Sister Celine's joyous grace like the English verses sing, "Joyous, joyous / Let us live in grace / Spreading the light that illuminates / The divine grace from the great ideal. / And that is why I love / The great loves of many colors." I feel fortunate to have had her in my life and experienced my aunt's unconditional love and mutual respect. Indeed, she lived a beautiful life in the spirit.

If Sister Celine had been alive, I think she would have marched on the streets of Los Angeles in June 2020 in support of George Floyd — a Black man killed in custody by a Minneapolis police officer on May 25, 2020. She would have protested peacefully in solidarity with the rallies and vigils that took place in the aftermath of the crime. She exemplified a steadfast commitment to social change. She was a formidable woman — one of the many superlatives a journalist for the Los Angeles Times used to describe her in a newspaper story following her tragic accidental death.

I write about Sister Celine as an incredible component of our Vásquez family legacy that I want my children, grandchildren, nieces and nephews… and their grandchildren to learn they are descended from strong, brave, resilient people. Our ancestors were refugees of war who fled a brutal Mexican Revolution from Purándiro, Michoacán to live and work in Southern California to provide a better life for their young family. Their descendants must know from where and from whom they came from. Thank God for our Mexican ancestors for showing us the way.

+ Sister Celine Vásquez, MSW ~ ¡Presente!

Diplomas on the Wall: A Story of Perseverance

BY IRMA GABRIELLA VAZQUEZ-GARFIELD

Perseverance, perhaps it begins when, as a small child, you are sent to deliver your mother a cup of tea only to realize that no matter how much your 4-year-old frame shakes her, she will no longer wake up.

Or maybe when you are pulled from the safety and enchantment of your fifth-grade classroom and leave behind the light load of books in exchange for the coarse and crushing load of flour sacks at the Mercado's Bakery.

Perhaps it further develops as you wave goodbye to your wife, young family and hard-earned home bakeshop to immigrate as a guest, although not necessarily welcomed, farm worker (Bracero) in another land.

Certainly perseverance develops and finely chisels into your character, like the well-defined ripples in a bodybuilder's muscles as you pursue arduous years of 16-hour workdays while you earn the requisite amount to legally unite your family in what has now become your cherished country.

It takes the sweat of continuous perseverance to pay the bills and save for a house while acting as though your back isn't breaking in order to spare your growing children the temptation to abandon school in order to alleviate the heavy burden persistently clutching at your shoulders.

You don't tire of persevering, although perhaps others do, as you explain, yet again, to incredulous and perhaps jealous acquaintances that, YES, your grown sons and daughters are indeed *still* studying and will continue to study until *they*, and *only they*, determine that their academic hunger has been satiated.

Then, as years come to pass and each child and grandchild

graduates, your arthritic knees proudly and joyfully persevere the climb up and down various graduation stadiums.

Finally, at 98, there is the perseverance of a walker and labored steps as you slowly make your way across the hall where diplomas hang, announcing the long-ago births of the doctors, engineers, scientists, professors and teachers that your perseverance has engendered.

Macario C. Vazquez December 30, 1923 – January 26, 2022

Rest in Peace, Mi Querido Papi

Experience and Passion

BY JOSÉ LUIS VIZCARRA

So many go through a wasted lifetime

Searching for something they don't know what it is

Day after day, week after week, and they still in the same place

They see their health and income deteriorate

And there is nothing they can do

Their life is like being in quicksand

Slowly devoured, but screaming doesn't do any good

They ignored wise people and books that would have helped

They were competing in the rat race with a vehicle that is too slow

If the poor fools only knew that to be truly successful, you don't go in
the rat race

If you want to be truly successful there are only two assets to own

You better have years of experience and real passion for what you do

These people truly enjoy what they do

They are very rare and are true professionals that will complete their
work on time

Successful companies are lucky to have them

They invest money and time to locate the best

Those great employees are very rare and are called "linchpins"

They have many years of perfecting their trade

But the real key to them is their enormous PASSION for what they do

They don't go for the income which is important

And they wind up earning the higher wages

The employers fear losing them

They are the motor of the business that is growing

They are great leaders who help others perform much better

They accept full responsibility for any mistakes

Due to their work ethic, there are minimal mistakes or accidents

They know that it is so much better to do the job right the first time

Or waste time fixing the poor job that was rushed

Listen to me all of you, financial fools, looking for a job

You better get EXPERIENCE in what you do

And the key to your success is to find what is your PASSION

May God bless you so that you acquire the necessary EXPERIENCE

And to be truly happy with the PASSION to live the life you are meant to live!

Financial Education

by José Luis Vizcarra

"Father, why are you so stingy with your money?" Little Johnny asks
"Oh, my dear son, you have so much to learn!" Father responds
In this world, we have only two positions when it comes to money
Don't let the liberals fool you
And you thought there were three like the teachers lied to all of you
Most foolish people think there is the middle class
But sadly, most don't realize there are the rich and the poor
But why you may ask they don't teach me this in schools?
All the schools do is create financial ignorant slaves
    and abundant consumers
As you can see with so many cashiers having trouble giving you change
Most slaves work hard for the dollar
While rich have those dollars work for them
But that is not fair, you might say
You are the result of a great slave factory that screwed your life
Real education teaches to own and never to be owned
Rich people love the ignorance of employees and consumers
They have learned to use people to get ahead
They only buy assets that increase their wealth
They know the difference between an asset and a liability
They work very hard to build a transfer of wealth
Poor people couldn't care less what is left behind
Rich people begin with their spiritual life
For sure they don't love material liabilities and money

La Chancla (The Sandal)

BY JOSÉ LUIS VIZCARRA

I am a poor chancla that people step on
Those fools ignore me only until they can't find me
Time after time I carry all their weight
Sometimes more if they carry things
When I am lucky, they clean me well
And I thank them for being caring
Year after year I serve them well
I stay where they leave me every night
Only to be of service as soon as the sun is up
I come in different colors and sizes if it is brown and large
That way I will fit everyone
I love to walk on grass because it gives me support
At times I am not lucky because my idiot owner steps on dog shit
He blames me for being so careless
The fool now must clean me well before stepping inside the house
The more he wears me the more comfortable I become
So don't go ignoring me because I carry you everywhere
Because if you ignore me,
you will be the one stepping on the dog shit!
Once I serve my time, I retire at the trash can
to Rest in Peace no longer on that shit!

Oh Lord Why Did You Make Me Poor?

BY JOSÉ LUIS VIZCARRA

Oh Lord why did you make me poor?
  Oh man, how ignorant you are!
Oh Lord why did you make me poor?
  Why are you asking me that foolish question?
Oh Lord why did you make me poor?
  I don't choose your wealth, I gave you the greatest treasure,
  the five senses, that you ignore!
Oh Lord why did you make me poor?
  What did you do with the biggest asset
  that I granted you, your time? You wasted it!
Oh Lord why did you make me poor?
  Everyone is born with the same wealth,
  but a few take advantage and most destroy their lives.
Oh Lord why did you make me poor?
  You did not put yourself in the horrible public schools,
  but you put yourself in college debt.
Oh Lord why did you make me poor?
  You were foolish enough to beg for a job
  and the smart ones became business owners and investors
Oh Lord why did you make me poor?
  How many credit cards did you use to acquire
  useless depreciating trash with high interest rate?
Oh Lord why did you make me poor?
  Did you search for information in the right places
  and invested your time learning?
Oh Lord why did you make me poor?

Why did you buy brand name purchases
and advertise those companies without pay?
Oh Lord why did you make me poor?
Why would you accept such meager wages
and then earn one dollar and spend five or more?
Oh Lord why did you make me poor?
If you had studied only a small fraction of the time
wasted watching crap on TV, you would not be poor now
Oh Lord why did you make me poor?
When I created you, I knew you were faulty, then
I created woman, the one you needed to fix your problems
Oh Lord why did you make me poor?
If you understood that having a job would keep you poor
and yet you were financially insane to stay there
and waste your time and health
Oh Lord why did you make me poor?
Oh man! Despite your ignorance,
I love you and that is why the Bible has all the answers
to your poverty and a total wasted life

The Difference Between a Transaction and a Transformation

BY JOSÉ LUIS VIZCARRA

A transaction earns you a check

A transformation changes your future and that of others

A transaction helps a family

A transformation changes future generations

A transaction is immediate compensation

A transformation is a lifetime journey

A transaction requires one individual

A transformation is based on a team and a mentor

A transaction requires only two hands

A transformation has many hands in the process

A transaction is a very lonely activity

A transformation involves a "whole village"

A transaction has the fear of failure

A transformation welcomes failure to learn

A transaction is insignificant in the process of life

A transformation at a time changed the history of every nation

A transaction is financial

A transformation is spiritual

A transaction has a final date

A transformation is never complete

A transaction is about receiving

A transformation is about giving

A transaction is about learning to close a sale

A transformation is about an experience to change individuals' futures

A transaction is recorded in books and servers

A transformation is written in history for eternity

A transaction can be measured with numbers

A transformation is evaluated in the history books

A transaction is finite

A transformation is infinite

A transaction is about chasing a sale

A transformation is about pursuing greatness

A transaction may be corrupted by greed

A transformation is guided by unselfishness

A transaction is an obligation with consequences

A transformation is a crusade to improve yourself

A transaction has an expiration date

A transformation has no expiration date

A transaction has been done by many

A transformation has been done by a select few

Contributor Bios

Janet Lako Alexander is a poet, writer, and bilingual educator. A UC Riverside graduate, she was born in Blythe and raised in Rubidoux. While a teacher, she facilitated the Ontario-Montclair School District's annual Poetry Day celebration for several years. Now she looks forward to focusing on her own writing.

Don Bennett has worn many hats during his life: Deputy DA, private practice lawyer, food bank director, consultant, trainer, husband, father, grandpa, and heart transplant recipient. He found out about the Redlands Joslyn Joy Writers after reading a newspaper article about them, and joined their Zoom group in the summer of 2020.

Mary Briggs is a 1st generation, Mexican American, born in 1939, to a family of migrant workers, raised in East Los Angeles, has resided in Riverside since 1991.

Artist **Georgette Geppert Buckley,** BA and her husband celebrated their 40th anniversary driving to Santa Cruz. She values the knowledge and comradery she gained from CelenaDiana Bumpus' classes until the fateful winter of 2021. She has enjoyed Tim Hatch's spring zoom, summer and fall in Rose Monge's, and Wil Clarke's during her third year in Inlandia.

Alben Chamberlain is a retired teacher and retirement counselor. He Attended San Bernardino Community College, Brigham Young University-Hawaii Campus, and received an MBA from the American Graduate School of International Management in Glendale, Arizona. He began attending writing workshops in 2015 after leaving Nationwide Retirement Solutions.

Natalie Champion participated in the Chronologyland workshop. She is a poet and teacher who lives in San Francisco with her husband Rick and two cats, Princess Tabitha and Milo Morris.

Rick Champion has been a participant in the Inlandia Chronologyland workshop led by Carlos Cortes. He is a staff writer of

Natalie's Zine, which is self-published online. He is a polymath in exile and also contributes graphics art to the Zine. He is an expert in computational photography.

José Chávez is a retired bilingual teacher and dedicates his life to writing. He's had poetry published in the *Multilingual Educator Journal, Acentos Review, Inlandia Anthology* and has written two award-winning bilingual poetry books for children. He lives in Riverside, CA, is married, and has three grown children.

Deenaz P. Coachbuilder, Ph.D. is an educator, artist, writer, and environmental advocate. Her poetry, commentaries and essays have been published internationally. Her books of poems, *Metal Horse And Shadows: A Soul's Journey*, and *Imperfect Fragments*, have been received with critical acclaim. Deenaz is an active member of the Inland Empire's literary and cultural community.

A lover of story and word, **Sylvia Clarke** often writes memoir or poetry in response to suggestions she hears in Inlandia Workshops with Carlos Cortés, Rose Monge, or Wil Clarke. She and her husband, Wil, have called the Inland Empire home for over 35 years.

Wil Clarke tolerates writing, but loves having written. He was born and spent 27 years of his life in Africa. He misses the guidance and wisdom of CelenaDiana Bumpus and is attempting to keep her legacy alive in her former students through Celena's Scribes.

James Coats is a poet, performer, and educator born in Los Angeles and raised in the Inland Empire. You can take a poetry workshop with him through his organization Lift Our Voices Education which hosts an award winning workshop monthly called Be The Change. He is the author of four poetry collections; his most recent is *Midnight & Mad Dreams*.

Elinor Cohen likes to eat and write. She has a degree in Pre- and Early-Modern Literature that she currently does nothing with. Elinor resides with her family in the desolate desert after decades as an Angeleno, and is obsessed with her rescue dogs Beans and Floof.

Carlos Cruz is a PhD student in History at UC Riverside where he is Vice President of Underground Scholars Initiative which focuses on helping formerly incarcerated students succeed in higher education, and is President of the Native American Honor Society. He believes that education is the most important factor to achieving future success. Carlos Cruz participates in the Tesoros de Cuentos Workshop in Casa Blanca facilitated by Frances J. Vásquez.

Brian DeCoud lives in Los Angeles with his bride of 34 years. His New Year's Resolution is to spin the globe and visit a restaurant from wherever his wife's finger lands on the globe. He says, "If you can't travel there, maybe you can still experience their food."

Chuck Doolittle has dwelled in the Redlands area for nearly 30 years. He recently retired from teaching elementary and middle school. Throughout his career, writing was a focus and a passion. He's fortunate to have found the Joslyn Joy Writers to further that interest.

Edna Heled is an artist, art therapist, counselor and travel journalist. Her writing includes short stories, poetry, travel writing and non-fiction.

Jerry Ellingson lives in Redlands, California. Her goal is to record family stories so her genealogy work will not only have photos and statistics, but stories that should be told. She is a retired teacher with a Bachelor's degree in Dance and English. Her Master's degree is in education. The greatest joys in her life have been teaching Graphic Design and Computer to adults and her role as a mother and grandmother.

Ellen Estilai lives in Riverside, California. A two-time Pushcart Prize nominee, her work has appeared in *Phantom Seed; Broad!; Snapdragon; New California Writing 2011; Ink & Letters; Heron Tree; (In)Visible Memoirs, Vol. 2.; Fiolet & Wing;* and *Shark Reef,* among others. She is a founding board member of the Inlandia Institute.

Bryan Franco is a gay, Jewish poet from Brunswick, Maine. He has been published in the US, Australia, England, Ireland, India, and Scotland and has featured for poetry events in the US, England, Ireland, and Scotland. He hosts Café Generalissimo Open Mic, is a member of the Beardo Bards of the Bardo poetry troupe, painter, sculptor, gardener, and culinary genius. His book *Everything I Think Is All in My Mind* was published in 2021.

Nan Friedley is a retired special education teacher and graduate of Ball State University, Muncie, IN. Her writings have been published in a poetry chapbook, *Short Bus Ride*, by Bad Knee Press, Indiana Voice Journal, Inlandia Anthologies and *Three*, a nonfiction anthology collection by PushPenPress. Nan has participated in various workshops sponsored by Inlandia.

Camille Gaon is a seasoned, spicy Senior citizen who has been fortunate enough to have experienced all types of exotic cuisines in their countries of origin during extensive world travels. An opportune moment of setting a kitchen ceiling on fire served as a springboard to become a self-taught chef.

Richard Gonzalez is a native of San Bernardino. He served in the Navy as a Sonarman First Class. He graduated from Fresno State college with a degree in Economics. He served as a Building Official of several cities. He was active in various non-profit organizations in the IE.

Mark Grinyer has published poems in *The Literary Review, The Spoon River Quarterly, The Pacific Review, Perigee, Cordite, Crosswinds Poetry Journal* and elsewhere. A chapbook, *Approaching Poetry*, was published in 2017 by Finishing Line Press. He went to college at the University of California, Riverside, where he began writing and publishing poetry, and received a PhD in English and American Literature. He is currently living and writing on the edge of the Cleveland National Forest in Southern California.

Milan Hamilton, resident of Redlands, California since 1979, has been writing for many years. As a pastor and college teacher, he wrote scholarly papers and lectures, as well as sermons. As a non-profit executive, he wrote fundraising letters. As a retired person he began writing memoirs and joined a writing class at the turn of the century. He published a blog for several years and has since concentrated on poetry.

Doralba "Dora" Harmon cree que lo que define su personalidad es fe, positivismo y FORTALEZA. Ha vivido grandes tragedias en su vida, pero aprendió a hacer limonadas de los limones que le da la vida. Ella escribió un libro, *El Insondable mando del poder de tu mente,* y facilita dos clubs de lectura en Riverside. Dora participates in Tesoros de Cuentos creative writing workshop in Casa Blanca.

Nikki (Andrea) Harlin resides in the Inland Empire region of Southern California. She earned a Master of Fine Arts in Creative Writing – Concentration in Poetry from California State University, San Bernardino. She works as a congressional staffer in her hometown, San Bernardino. In her free time, she enjoys learning to dance salsa and playing survival horror video games. She participated in Inlandia Institute's Winter, 2021 Ontario Creative Writing Workshop facilitated by poet, Tim Hatch.

Richard "Rich" Hess is a retired physician. He practiced Obstetrics/Gynecology in Fairbanks, Alaska for 41 years. He is now living in Springdale, Arkansas with his wife, Marie. He enjoys writing about his medical and other life experiences.

Connie Jameson is a retired teacher, and enjoys reading, travel, nature, writing, and theater. She is a 40+ year member of Toastmasters International. Connie is pleased to have recently published her first book, *Dating 'n' Mating: Wit and Wisdom on Love and Marriage.*

Marlene Jones has lived in Riverside for the past 26 years. She was born in Jamestown, New York and is of Italian ancestry. She's married to Robert Jones and has three children. The retired couple owned Jones Backhoe Service, Inc. of which Marlene was the President.

Jessica Lea's poetry and photos have appeared in Spectrum Magazine, Inlandia, and Writer's on the Block zine. She was part of Riverside Art Museum's 52 Project 2019 and 2021 Exhibitions, authored *Diamonds and Yoga Pants* (2020), and collaborated for a visual Psalter (2022 Elyssar Press).

Merrill Lyew is a retired Geographer. After his postgraduation, he stayed in the academic world for a good decade. Thereafter he worked at a private company for about three decades. His job functions required frequent business travel to the metropolitan areas of Latin America, including sporadic visits to the provinces. These trips were always engaging, exciting, eventful, and charged with multitudes of stories, most of which went unperceived, enough remained unforgettable, and might be subject in some of his storytelling. Besides photography he likes to sketch short stories.

Jacqueline Mantz was born in Great Falls, Montana but immigrated to the Inland Empire as a young child growing up in Ontario, California. She resides in the Coachella Valley and works as a high school English and World History teacher for Riverside County Office of Education supporting new Special Education Teachers. Jacqueline volunteers for the Prison Education Project (PEP). She wrote a book with a woman currently incarcerated titled *Embracing Dawn* under her pen name Marie Rodriguez. She is currently assisting another fellow soul who is incarcerated in publishing their memoir. Jacqueline is currently working on a book about her experiences teaching. Jacqueline has a B.A. in English, two Master's degrees, and an Educational Doctorate. Jacqueline's loves are her husband, her boston terriers, and writing to improve the world one kind word at a time.

Mae Wagner Marinello has been a part of Inlandia since a 2008 writing workshop with Ruth Nolan. In 2014, she began facilitating a weekly writing workshop called Joslyn Joy Writers, at the Joslyn Senior Center in Redlands. During the pandemic lockdown, the weekly workshop continued on Zoom; it is now a hybrid class averaging between 10-20 combined participants on Zoom and in-person.

Ruthie Marlenée is a Mexican-American novelist, poet and screenwriter residing in the Coachella Valley with her husband. Marlenée earned a Writers' Certificate in Fiction from UCLA and is the author of *Isabela's Island, Curse of the Ninth*, nominated for a James Kirkwood Literary Prize and *Agave Blues* Honorably Mentioned by the International Latino Book Awards for the Isabel Allende Most Inspirational Fiction Book Award. An excerpt from the novel is also nominated for the Pushcart Prize. Marlenée is currently working on a sequel *And Still Her Voice*. Her poetry and short stories can be found in various publications.

Terry Lee Marzell lives in Chino Hills, California. Before retiring, she invested 36 years of her career as an educator. She earned her BA in English and her teaching credential from CSUF, and her MA in Interdisciplinary Studies from CSUSB. Terry earned an additional credential in Library Science from CSULB.

Mary McLoughlin lives in Redlands and writes with The Joslyn Joy Writers, facilitated by Mae Wagner Marinella, since 2015. Originally from Levittown, NY and lived in Ireland before coming to Redlands. Recently, she joined a poetry class with Romaine Washington.

KaShawna McKay, 40, of Riverside, California is a full-time student at Crafton Hills Community College. After encouragement from her professors and attending Inlandia's Even Butterflies Can Hollar workshop with Lydia Theon Ware i, she was inspired to publish her writing. Find her on the web at www.thestressaddress.webs.com.

Carmen Melendez-Gutierrez was born in Comerio, Puerto Rico on July 25, 1954. She currently resides in Riverside, California. Graduated from San Diego State University. She worked for the United States Postal Service. She is also a Life Coach. Her major achievements are the House of Puerto Rico cottage in Balboa Park, San Diego and the publishing of her book titled *Yuya's Adventures*, part of the series *The Beautiful Mermaids*.

Barbara Meyer has been married to Marvin Meyer for 63 years. They were blessed with three children and lost the first one, a son, at age 39. God brought them together and has kept them together for all these years. She is the reason that they are in this class.

Marvin Meyer was born and spent his first twenty years in Western Oklahoma. He then grabbed an opportunity to move to Southern California where he met and married Barbara Porter. They had a son and two daughters. The son died of cancer at age 39.

Rose Y. Monge has facilitated memoir classes at the Goeske Center since 2009. She encourages everyone to leave a written legacy for future generations. As an immigrant from Mexico, her memoir honors her parents' legacy of life lessons. Her activism since retirement has been advocating social justice, diversity and inclusion.

Barbara Mortensen is a California resident born and educated in New York, currently living in Rancho Mirage. A retired international consultant she spent most of her adult life working, dining and entertaining in Europe and South America. She is a foodie and never met a meal she wouldn't eat or try to duplicate. Barbara attended the 2021 Inlandia Food Writers Course and loved participating in this diverse and vibrant course and looks forward to attending future Inlandia Programs.

Cindi Neisinger believes curiosity will lead you to your passions. She is writing a memoir called, *My Life Between a Tortilla and White Bread*. Her children's book, *Mouse Wedding at the Inn*, is sold exclusively at the Mission Inn Museum in Riverside, CA. She serves on the Inlandia Institute Advisory Council. She participated in the Tesoros de Cuentos Creative Writing Workshop facilitated by Frances J. Vásquez.

S.J. Perry's work has recently appeared in Cholla Needles, MUSE, Last Leaves, and elsewhere. He studied at Emporia State University and the University of Kansas. A retired high school English teacher, he has lived in Southern California since 1985.

Christine Petzar lives in Riverside and has participated in Inlandia writers' workshops since 2019. Her career in educational administration involved professional writing and teacher education related to English Learners. In retirement, she is branching out to more personal writing — memoir and creative non-fiction. She participates in Adventures in Chronology with Dr. Carlos Cortés, Creative Writing Non-fiction Workshop with Jo Scott-Coe.

Janine Pourroy published her first article (on Back to the Future and The Goonies) in 1985 and still carries the thrill of seeing her name in print for the first time. She has since authored/co-authored five books, and is currently at work on a new one.

Writing, along with the fellowship of writers in the Inlandia workshops, have been heart openers for **Cindi Pringle** during the pandemic. She is glad to be back in the gym and socializing animals at the Mary S. Roberts Pet Adoption Center, as well as making distributions from Feed America.

Edgar Rider has been published in journals such as *Copperfield Review* as well as *Birmingham Art Journal*. He has written and published three books *Go Bare Maximum, 5990* and *Transcending In The Fictional Burnout*.

Robin Woodruff-Longfield has been participating in Inlandia Writers Workshop since 2017, mostly in Jo Scott-Coe's nonfiction workshop at the Riverside Public Library, and Stephanie Barbe-Hammer's Poety-TRY workshops. During 2021, she participated in Poet-TRY 10, Dr. Carlos Cortes' "Chronologyland", and the Tim Hatch/Victoria Waddell workshop at the Ontario Public Library. In the Fall of 2021, she also attended Jo Scott-Coe's Non-Fiction workshop, which resumed after a hiatus. Her piece "Another Yellow Brick Road" had many midwives. It began as part of a longer piece written during the "Chronologyland" workshop, and underwent extensive editing and revising in Jo Scott-Coe's workshop and further revising in the Ontario Library workshop. Both of the poems were generated in Poet-TRY 10.

Marilyn Sequoia lives in Riverside, CA. Marilyn studied with UCR's gifted creative writing professors. Ms. Sequoia's published poetry can be found in ten anthologies, such as *Raising the Roof,*

The Best of Kindness 2017, Nature's Healing Spirit, These Trees, Discovering the Spirit of Place... plus in her own chapbook *New Wilderness*.

Kristine Ann Shell lives in Redlands, California. Kristine is a retired school administrator and teacher. She holds a Bachelor of Arts degree in English and Secondary Education. She also holds Master of Education degrees in Elementary Reading and School Administration. Kristine has been a member of the Inlandia Institute since October, 2016 and Mae Marinello Wagner's Joslyn Joy Writers workshop.

Ben Simmons is from Ireland. He writes poetry, short-fiction and has been published regularly in Ireland and the UK. In 2016 he was selected for Poetry Ireland's Introductions Series and in 2019 was supported by the Arts Council to attend Can Serrat International Artist Residency. He lives in Riverside, California.

All her life, **Lynne Stewart** has expressed and reflected her world by writing journals, poetry, essays, while simultaneously, developing skills in the visual arts. She views writing and painting as tools for personal expression, in humble service of love and hope. Stewart views both as artforms and as such, she puts her mind, heart and soul into her work.

Scharlett Stowers Vai is a life-long resident — 70 years — of the Barrio de Casa Blanca in Riverside, CA. She is bilingual and bicultural. She taught preschool in Casa Blanca for 10 years and is proud to give back to her beautiful Barrio, and is active in the Casa Blanca CAG.

Scharlett participates in Tesoros de Cuentos creative writing workshops facilitated by Frances J. Vásquez.

Heather Takenaga is a daydreamer who yearns for global longevity, food for all, cat cuddles, and 36-hour days — in any order. She writes because life is colorful, and so are words. She attended the San Bernardino Creative Writing Workshop, the Poetry Workshop with James Ducat, and the Inlandia Ontario Workshop.

Elizabeth Uter is a double award-winning short story writer winning Home - Croydon City Of Stories Competition in 2022 and Brent City of Stories in 2017. She is also an award-winning poet winning the 2018 Poem for Slough Competition in two categories. She facilitated a Shakti Women's creative writing workshop and Farrago Poetry workshops; performed at the prestigious Queen's Park Literary Festival, London. Published works include: 2019 - *Reach/Sarasvati Magazines, Bollocks To Brexit Anthology, 2020 Writing from Inlandia; 2021, This Is Our Place Anthology, 2022, Nature, Framed - An Anthology of Nature Writing*.

Gudelia Vaden (Delia), is a poet, writer and artist. Born in Zacatecas, Mexico, but raised in Planada near Merced — Gateway to Yosemite. She enjoys illustrating and contributing to *Natalie's Zine,* an online magazine. Her stories can be found in *A Short Guide to Finding Your First Home in the United States: Inlandia Institute Anthology on the Immigrant Experience* and in *Writing from Inlandia* publications.

Frances J. Vásquez is native to the Inland region and graduated Riverside schools: Poly, RCC and UCR, where she attained AA, BS and MBA Degrees. She is Director Emerita of Inlandia Institute. An aficionada of arts and letters, she is passionate about Chicana/o history, *Celebrating Cultura* and *Tesoros de Cuentos*. Frances facilitates Tesoros de Cuentos Creative Writing Workshops in Casa Blanca

Irma Gabriella Vazquez-Garfield taught kindergarten for 31 years and moved to Redlands from Fillmore, California, shortly after she retired in 2018. She is an active friend, baker and volunteer who has always enjoyed writing and hit the jackpot when her neighbor, Mae Wagner Marinello, noticed her enthusiasm and kindly invited her to join the Joslyn Joy Writers in 2021.

Jose Vizcarra is a veteran, educator and naturalized citizen who published *Kiss from an Angel,* Inlandia anthology 2018,2019,2020 and *Natural Inspirations.* He became involved with Inlandia through CelenaDiana Bumpus's class. Jose continues to participate in two classes to improve his writing skills with Rose Monge and Wil Clarke.

About Inlandia Institute

Inlandia Institute is a regional literary non-profit and publishing house. We seek to bring focus to the richness of the literary enterprise that has existed in this region for ages. The mission of the Inlandia Institute is to recognize, support, and expand literary activity in all of its forms in Inland Southern California by publishing books and sponsoring programs that deepen people's awareness, understanding, and appreciation of this unique, complex and creatively vibrant region.

The Institute publishes books, presents free public literary and cultural programming, provides in-school and after school enrichment programs for children and youth, holds free creative writing workshops for teens and adults, and boot camp intensives. In addition, every two years, the Inlandia Institute appoints a distinguished jury panel from outside of the region to name an Inlandia Literary Laureate who serves as an ambassador for the Inlandia Institute, promoting literature, creative literacy, and community. Laureates to date include Susan Straight (2010-2012), Gayle Brandeis (2012-2014), Juan Delgado (2014-2016), Nikia Chaney (2016-2018), and Rachelle Cruz (2018-2020).

To learn more about the Inlandia Institute, please visit our website at www.InlandiaInstitute.org.

Inlandia Books

Pretend Plumber by Stephanie Barbé Hammer

Ladybug by Nikia Chaney

Vital: The Future of Healthcare, edited by RM Ambrose

Güero-Güero: The White Mexican and Other Published and Unpublished Stories by Dr. Eliud Martínez

A Short Guide to Finding Your First Home in the United States: An Inlandia anthology on the immigrant experience

Care: Stories by Christopher Records

San Bernardino, Singing, edited by Nikia Chaney

Facing Fire: Art, Wildfire, and the End of Nature in the New West by Douglas McCulloh

Writing from Inlandia, an annual anthology (2011–)

In the Sunshine of Neglect: Defining Photographs and Radical Experiments in Inland Southern California, 1950 to the Present by Douglas McCulloh

Henry L. A. Jekel: Architect of Eastern Skyscrapers and the California Style by Dr. Vincent Moses and Catherine Whitmore

Orangelandia: The Literature of Inland Citrus edited by Gayle Brandeis

While We're Here We Should Sing by The Why Nots

Go to the Living by Micah Chatterton

No Easy Way: Integrating Riverside Schools - A Victory for Community by Arthur L. Littleworth

Hillary Gravendyk Prize
poetry series

among the enemies by Michael Samra
 Winner of the 2020 National Hillary Gravendyk Prize

This Side of the Fire by Jonathan Maule
 Winner of the 2020 Regional Hillary Gravendyk Prize

The Silk the Moths Ignore by Bronwen Tate
 Winner of the 2019 National Hillary Gravendyk Prize

Remyth: A Postmodernist Ritual by Adam Martinez
 Winner of the 2019 Regional Hillary Gravendyk Prize

Former Possessions of the Spanish Empire by Michelle Peñaloza
 Winner of the 2018 National Hillary Gravendyk Prize

All the Emergency-Type Structures by Elizabeth Cantwell
 Winner of the 2018 Regional Hillary Gravendyk Prize

Our Bruises Kept Singing Purple by Malcolm Friend
 Winner of the 2017 National Hillary Gravendyk Prize

Traces of a Fifth Column by Marco Maisto
 Winner of the 2016 National Hillary Gravendyk Prize

God's Will for Monsters by Rachelle Cruz
 Winner of the 2016 Regional Hillary Gravendyk Prize
 Winner of the 2018 American Book Award

Map of an Onion by Kenji C. Liu
 Winner of the 2015 National Hillary Gravendyk Prize

All Things Lose Thousands of Times by Angela Peñaredondo
 Winner of the 2015 Regional Hillary Gravendyk Prize

CPSIA information can be obtained
at www.ICGtesting.com
Printed in the USA
JSHW082130021122
32522JS00002B/7